Beyond Despair

Copyright

Title book: Beyond Despair
Author book: Shirley Hoisington

© 2019, Shirley Hoisington/Forrest Lane Publishers
Self-publishing
First Edition

ISBN: 978-1-7334113-0-1

To my husband, Richard, who passed away in 2006. To my husband Robert, for his unfailing support and encouragement. To my three daughters, Barbara, Rachel, and Amanda whom I love dearly. −S.H.

Preface

I started on this journey in 2001 with a laptop my husband, Richard, brought home from work. Over the years, I went back to college to take an English course because I realized I needed to relearn grammar and punctuation. I joined a couple of writing workshops and took creative writing classes. Due to the loss of my husband and taking care of my mother who was in her 90's I just let things slide.

After remarrying, I wanted to go back to working on my book, Beyond Despair; because it was very close to my heart, but life seemed to get in the way. After the death of my mom, I made a decision that I was going to publish my book but wasn't sure where to start. I needed an editor, so I placed an ad on our local Craigslist and lo and behold, I hit the jackpot.

Without Lane, my editor, I may have published Beyond Despair, but it wouldn't be the book it is today. I told him upfront I did not want my story changed. I found with much of my experience in workshops and classes, everyone wanted to change what I had written. I wanted help with grammar and punctuation, but Lane challenged me. He made me change my writing from telling to showing, and I started to understand how the reader would be affected by my characters. He not only told me when he was impressed by something I had written, but he made me laugh. I will be ever grateful for his wholehearted support.

My husband, Robert, read my romance book, liked it, and encouraged me every step of the way. I will always be grateful for his support. I would also like to thank my daughter, Rachel. She

1

was always in my corner and kept encouraging me to finish and publish my book. I also want to thank my friends for their loving support.

Proglogue

Miranda's hands trembled as she smoothed back the hair from her ashen face. She sank onto the bench in the small alcove where she went to gather her strength. Resting her head against the back of the bench, she confronted what drove her here. Anguish and despair was all she felt. Roger was now married to Cindy! Miranda knew she didn't have a choice but to flee to this small alcove to gather her courage to face the rest of the afternoon.

Miranda couldn't tear her eyes away as Roger pulled Cindy into his arms, kissing her with unrestrained passion, as if unaware of anyone else...it was all too much to bear, and she needed to escape for a few moments.

Miranda knew she must return to the wedding reception soon, but she just wasn't ready. Her eyes sought out Cindy. Catching her breath in a faint sigh, Miranda gazed at the lovely vision of Cindy standing at her groom's side as they greeted the wedding guests. Cindy was dressed in a long, flowing gown of chiffon and satin. The bodice was fitted with a high-choker neckline while the top of the bodice was ivory and matched the ivory ribbon at the waist, yet the rest of the dress was all in white. A sheer floral ruffle was draped over her shoulders and her lace skirt shimmered with her movements.

Miranda watched enviously as Roger glanced down at his new wife; while waiting to respond to someone in the reception line. Cindy proudly looked up at him, joy and happiness shining in her eyes. Miranda noted the way Cindy tucked her arm trustingly

3

into Roger's as she turned to greet a close friend, who waited to congratulate them.

Miranda's eyes glittered with unshed tears as she watched the interplay between the loving couple. She wanted to look away but felt mesmerized by the silent messages passing between them; the loving touch, the secret smile, and the searing glance; filled with passion. . .holding promises of the future.

Miranda brought her hands to her lips as a broken sob escaped. With tears threatening to overflow at any moment, Miranda watched in silent agony. Roger gazed after his lovely new bride as she moved gracefully across the room to speak to the musicians.   Later, as if unable to bear being away from her, he chuckled at something a friend said, and quickly made his way over to where Cindy was now surrounded by her friends. He tucked a strand of hair behind her ear, and leaning in, whispered something to her. They exchanged an intimate smile, and she snuggled up to him while making a laughing rejoinder to her friend's comment.

One moment they were with friends and the next they were slipping away together. In an open doorway, Roger gathered Cindy into his arms. She gazed into his face, love shinning from her eyes, and returned his kisses with hunger. They seemed oblivious to the laughter, music, and sounds of the people around them.

"No," moaned Miranda. "No more! I can't bear anymore! Please help me!" she whispered as her body started to tremble violently. Despite herself, Miranda couldn't look away. She watched, transfixed, as the man she longed to be with cradled Cindy's face in his hands and tenderly kissed her.

Deep inside, Miranda could feel his kiss, her heart throbbing in ecstasy as it remembered. Her whole being yearned for something she knew she would never again experience. Her heart ached for what she lost. She pressed a hand to her mouth to stifle the sob which tore from her throat. She could feel her heart pounding, and for a moment, she thought it might leap right out of her chest. Another low whimper came from her lips as she started to shake uncontrollably. Leaning her head against the wall, despair filled her soul.

How would she survive this? She clasped her hands over her mouth, desperate to quell the nausea rising to her throat. Her head sank to her chest as silent tears trailed slowly down her cheeks. As she felt the tremors in her body threaten to take control, she took a deep breath to steady herself, and then slowly exhaled. She sat there, seeking serenity, breathing deeply for a moment. Eventually, feeling a little calmer, she rose to her feet.

As she stood, she felt the tremors in her body threaten to take control again, assuring her she still needed to calm down. Otherwise, her friends would know immediately something was wrong. She knew she had stayed away too long already, so she closed her eyes for a moment until a quiet peace soothed her. She must go back out and join her sister soon, or Cindy and Roger might come to look for her.

Miranda and Cindy were identical twins, and growing up as close as two sisters could, they shared the same feelings, hopes, and dreams.

Miranda felt as if her life was shattered into a million pieces; as if she were standing alone while she watched her beloved sister live the dream she thought would be hers. Even though it had been a short time since she met and fell deeply in love with Roger; she was unable to reconcile the fact Cindy was now married to the man she loved with all her body, mind, and soul.

The battle which raged inside her for most of the day——keeping the knowledge of her love from both Cindy and Roger——was the reason she retreated from the reception. In the alcove she hoped to find the strength and fortitude to make it through the rest of the day without giving herself away.

She was struggling with such a mixture of feelings it was hard to resolve everything in her mind. First and foremost, her love and loyalty was to Cindy, but it was all mixed up with the agony she felt over the loss of Roger. Her grief over losing the man she loved with her whole being was more than she could bear. However, Miranda knew she must find some way to lock her love and emotions away into the deepest part of her soul for the sake of her sister's happiness.

Chapter One

One cold, rainy October evening, typical for Oregon, Miranda was alone at home with Cindy. The girls being fifteen, their parents, John and Trina, knew the girls would be OK on their own. John was receiving an award for his work over the last two years. It wasn't very often Miranda and Cindy were left alone at night, but their parents knew they were both responsible and wouldn't have any problems for a few hours. Both girls finished their homework, took their baths, and were getting ready for bed when the doorbell rang.

Being cautioned never to open the door without knowing who was there, Cindy looked through the window. Her shocked face turned to Miranda. "It's the police! What are they doing here?"

"I don't know, but why don't you answer the door and find out?" Miranda answered, her heart pounding.

Deep in her gut, Miranda knew something was badly wrong when she saw the policewoman's face. It was grave, and she asked quietly if they could come inside. Both girls listened in shock while they were told that their parents were in the hospital after a bad car accident.

Gripping Cindy's hand, Miranda asked, "How badly are they hurt?"

"I'm not sure," Officer Owens answered quietly. "Do you have someone you can call to take you to the hospital?"

"Our Aunt Patricia. She lives about a mile away." Cindy said as she dashed to the phone.

Aunt Patricia immediately left to pick them up and raced to the hospital.

Miranda walked into the hospital on leaden feet, clinging to Cindy's hand. She felt like she was underwater, unable to comprehend clearly what was happening. Her parents were what kept her grounded, gave her the confidence to be who she wanted to be, and always supported her and Cindy no matter what. They were open-minded, but taught their girls how to think through their decisions, and about the consequences if they made the wrong ones. They taught them to be hardworking, telling them how hard work always paid off in the end. They didn't hesitate to talk to them about drugs and the lives drugs destroyed. They spoke earnestly about people they knew whose lives had been devastated by drugs. A couple of their oldest friends lost children to its addiction. One, a daughter, ended up on the streets as a prostitute and no matter what the parents tried to do to save her, nothing worked; and she died a horrible death at thirty-five. Another child turned to crime to support his drug addiction and was later shot by police while robbing a convenience store.

Their mother was very straightforward when she talked to them about boys and sex. She spoke gravely about the consequences of casual sex and what could happen by being careless with your body and heart. She taught them about true love and what a wonderful miracle it was to find the right person to spend your life with.

Miranda's parents were quietly religious. From the time the girls were young, they attended a small, non-denominational church near their home. John firmly believed anyone who thought they were better than others, just because they attended church, was not a Christian. "Treat others better than yourself," was always his motto. He often encouraged them to be kind to their friends, neighbors, and co-workers. He mentioned how he sometimes returned hatefulness with a kind action. He said it didn't always change the actions of the person involved, but sometimes it worked; and they began to treat others more kindly. Any lies or cheating would not have been tolerated by either of their parents and the girls would have suffered the consequences.

They grew up with a man who lived by these principles always. He was a kind man, tender and forgiving. Yet, he sometimes became negative and frustrated after watching the news and realizing there was nothing he could do to make things better.

And now here she was walking into the unknown. Were her parents OK? Were they badly hurt or were they dead?! She must quit thinking this way!

Their parents were clinging to life as the girls entered the hospital. Heroic efforts were made to save their lives. A drunk driver hit them head-on and plunged their car down an incline. Cindy and Miranda were both able to say a heartbreaking goodbye to their mother. She weakly held their hands, telling them over and over she loved them more than life, and she would be watching over them always.

Their father opened his eyes for a moment but couldn't speak. Then they were both gone! Just like that, the two most important people in their lives were just gone! How were two young girls supposed to comprehend what was happening to their lives?

Numbly, they returned home with Aunt Patricia. Aunt Patricia knew it would be better for them to stay in their home so she grabbed a few things and came to stay with them until after the funeral. Hundreds of people came to the funeral, but neither Miranda nor Cindy were able to grasp what was happening. They functioned on automatic, too stunned to understand, much less comprehend their lives were changing irrevocably. Afterward, they went to live with Aunt Patricia and Uncle Mark.

Cindy was unable to cope with the loss of their parents. She became almost catatonic, not speaking, eating or sleeping. Finally, she was admitted to a care facility where she stayed for over six months. Even after she came home, it was more than a year before they heard her laughter again. Slowly, she mended, but Miranda now took on the role of caretaker and always looked out for her. Miranda kept Cindy close, making friends with the same girls so they would be together most of the time.

Miranda coped with the loss of her parents differently. She walked around in a state of shock for several weeks, unable to comprehend that her parents were really gone. She would never again hear their voices, touch them, laugh with them; or hear her mother singing sweetly while she prepared dinner. They wouldn't be there for her and Cindy's graduation—something they were always talking about; knowing both girls would graduate high in their class. Her dad would not get to walk her down the aisle for her wedding. She wouldn't have her mother around to teach her how to be a good mother, and she wouldn't get to watch them spoil their grandchildren.

Miranda was unable to cry. Her pain was so deep inside and the hurt so intense she was afraid to cry. She knew if she started, she would never stop.

Aunt Patricia was so devastated over the loss of her brother, John, it took her a few weeks to realize both girls were not coping. She hugged them and took care of their needs and tried to talk to them, but both girls were shut off.

After Aunt Patricia realized Cindy needed help and got her to the hospital where they could treat her, she began to realize she hadn't been paying enough attention to the girls.

"Miranda, can you come and sit with me?" she requested after returning home. Putting her arms around Miranda, she held her silently for a long time. Finally, easing her away, she stroked her hair, tears sliding down her cheeks. "I'm so sorry, honey. I've been so caught up in my own grief, I failed to realize how much you two were suffering. Cindy is getting help now, but tell me what I can do to help you. It's so hard to accept what has happened, but eventually, we have to; so we can make some sense of our lives now without them."

Tears slowly gathered in Miranda's eyes and silently trailed down her cheeks. "I just want them back! I want what we used to have. I need mom's arms around me right now. I just miss them so much."

"I know, love, I do too," Patricia said as she pulled Miranda back into her arms. "It's going to be hard to learn to live without them."

"I miss Daddy and Mommy so much!"

Sobs escaped, and for a long time, Miranda cried for what they all lost. Afterward, she felt drained and cold. Aunt Patricia helped her to her bedroom, covered her up, and sat by her bedside until she fell asleep. Miranda slept for fourteen hours before waking. Afterward, she slowly started to heal, taking care of Cindy and getting back to school.

Going to school became a chore. Miranda loved school, but now she didn't care if she went or not, and her grades suffered. She became a very angry and bitter person. She blamed God for the loss of her parents. She could not understand why He allowed them to die so young. She was angry because they were not at the breakfast table in the morning. Her mother didn't lightly tap on her door at night and then come in to kiss her goodnight and talk for a few minutes. She was angry and unforgiving of the young man who drove drunk and destroyed their lives. Even when he was arrested and charged with her parents' deaths, she didn't feel any sense of closure.

Over time, Miranda's anger lessened, but her faith was severely shaken, and she no longer attended church. Through it all, she became Cindy's protector, shielding her from every hurt. While Cindy was in the Good Samaritan Mental Health Facility, Miranda went every day to see her, and spent time trying to help her cope with the loss. She tried to be cheerful and positive, but for a long while, she couldn't get Cindy to respond. Gradually, over time, Cindy started to notice things around her; and eventually they cried together, letting their tears heal some of the hurt and pain.

She tried to never let Cindy see her own anger and helplessness. She must be the strong sister. Because of the lost months when Cindy wasn't able to cope, Miranda worked tirelessly through the spring and summer to help her catch up with her grades. Because of her help, Cindy didn't have to repeat her sophomore year.

After Cindy returned home, Miranda poured herself into her schoolwork, graduating with honors; but never letting Cindy know just how abandoned she felt, how unable she was to make things better. Miranda tried to be positive and encouraged Cindy in her chosen career, helping Cindy apply for colleges, while Miranda put aside her own needs.

Cindy's love of the fashion industry, and her beautiful dress designs were what finally pulled her out of herself. From the time she was young she had been drawing and fashioning beautiful clothes. So now she threw herself into her career, happily traveling around the world, especially New York and Paris; finding unique fabrics for her new designs, as well as keeping abreast of what celebrities were wearing at any given time.

The global fashion industry is always dependent on ever-changing trends to keep customers buying; who are driven by the need to wear the latest clothing. The newest trends have a short shelf life; so designers, such as Cindy, were always trying to meet tight production schedules and deadlines. Cindy thrived on all of it. She loved watching the models "strut their stuff" as they showed off the newest styles. A couple of times, Miranda accompanied Cindy to New York and was proud of how talented Cindy had become, and to see the respect she earned from professionals in the industry.

Miranda was able to concentrate on her own career after seeing Cindy was going to be alright, even though Miranda missed her more than she thought possible. It was hard to see Cindy head off to college and only see her during the holidays, but they always found summer jobs in Eugene so they could be together. Life was not easy for either one without their parents, but they were slowly healing and making a new life for themselves. It was a mutual decision when they decided to make Eugene their permanent home after college.

Chapter Two

Now, because of her earlier decisions, Miranda had no choice but to hide her emotions. She made the decision to stay silent. She chose to let Roger and Cindy develop a relationship, secretly hoping it would eventually fall apart and Roger would realize he loved her instead of Cindy. It was too late to make a different decision because she would not do anything to hurt Cindy.

As Miranda watched like an unseen ghost, she knew if Roger had fallen in love with anyone else, she would have fought with her last breath to win his love. But, because it was her sister he fell in love with, she didn't know where to turn. She was willing to sacrifice her own happiness for the sister she loved more than life.

Miranda shuddered as she thought about what a nightmare the wedding itself had been. With all the excitement of getting ready, her sister, thankfully, did not notice she was barely keeping it together. There were times when Miranda left the room for a few minutes to get control over her emotions, otherwise, she would give herself away.

Miranda couldn't remember a time when she and Cindy weren't best friends, sharing their toys, clothes, hopes, and dreams. Miranda would rather die than rip the heart out of her beloved sister. Miranda couldn't let Cindy know that she was married to the man Miranda loved more than anything else in the world...except her sister Cindy.

To heal and make a new life for herself, Miranda knew she must acknowledge the resentment and disappointment she could no longer hide from herself. She hated being angry at Cindy, but sometimes, she felt betrayed by her best friend.

Their mother told them they created their own language when they were small. She said they would chatter incessantly but no one else could understand them. Miranda was born first and took on the leadership role from the beginning. She was bossy and controlling and always told Cindy what to do, getting them both into trouble because she was so curious about everything. Their parents made sure they were separated in school so Cindy could develop her own personality aside from Miranda. They were best buddies, and didn't think they needed anyone else. More often than not, they chose to play together rather than making other friends.

Cindy was bubbly and more of a peacemaker. She chose to follow along with whatever Miranda chose to do when she was young. As they grew older and started making friends, they often chose the same friends. Going to dances and concerts with friends, they always chose to go together. Even though they were absolutely identical in looks, most of their acquaintances and friends were able to tell them apart because of their personalities. For a long time, they chose to wear the same hairstyle, but as they grew older things changed.

Miranda took her studies very seriously while Cindy preferred to read and dance. Cindy started dance classes with Miranda when they were six years old. Cindy immediately loved it. Miranda liked to dance but didn't enjoy the discipline it took to become a good dancer. Trina left Miranda in class for a couple of years, but then accepted it wasn't something she enjoyed, so she let her quit. She was much happier reading a good book. Cindy went on to excel in both ballet and jazz. Later, in eighth grade, Miranda joined debate and science club and loved them both.

After the tragic death of their parents, things changed in a lot of ways. For a long time, Miranda became more like Cindy's parent than her sister. Cindy trusted her completely so when Miranda made the decision to cover up the truth about her relationship with Roger, Cindy believed her.

Many times, over the last few months, Miranda let her thoughts go back over the years and their relationship. She dearly wished Cindy was able to sense her answer was false, but for some reason, she wasn't able to pick up on Miranda's reactions.

"*Yet,*" Miranda admitted to herself, "*I was the one at fault. I should have told the truth about how important Roger is to me, but I didn't, and now I am paying the price for my dishonesty. Dad always taught me to tell the truth. Why-oh-why didn't I listen to his advice?!*"

Miranda remembered a discussion she once had with her dad about reasons for always being truthful, no matter what. Miranda recalled asking him about keeping the truth from someone if it was going to hurt or harm them or someone else.

She clearly recalled his answer.

"To deliberately lie to someone in order to protect yourself because of something you've done, is wrong. Or, if you lie or distort the truth for your own agenda, you are not only hurting yourself, but others as well. Some people lie so that people will perceive them in a certain way. There are so many ways of lying and most of them are harmful. However, if you need to keep from telling someone the truth because it will hurt or harm them, then, in my mind, you are doing the right thing."

In making her decisions about what to say to Cindy and Roger, Miranda thought long and hard about her father's advice.

Miranda's decisions were made whether they were good or not. As a result, she now needed to hide how she was feeling from everyone. She couldn't let Roger or Cindy know she was hurting. She didn't want Roger to know she loved him, ever. What would it accomplish? She could have told him how she felt, but she chose not to do so. Pride, maybe? Or, she could have told Cindy from the beginning how she felt about Roger. She knew without a doubt, Cindy would have immediately walked away. But once again, Miranda made the choice not to confide in Cindy about Roger. And, the biggest reason of all, Roger didn't love her. He had never loved her. He loved Cindy.

Because of the choices she made, Miranda hoped with all her heart that Roger would never know he broke her heart. She knew innately all of her choices were made because of the loss of their parents at such a young age. She needed to make sure Cindy was always happy. Deep down inside, she knew it wasn't her responsibility, and she could have chosen differently, but protecting Cindy became ingrained in her from an early age.

She felt she must keep her feelings from both Roger and Cindy in order to insure their happiness together. She would keep her secret, no matter the cost to herself, knowing she would always love Roger. He had stolen her heart and she was sure no man could ever replace him.

The closeness she and Cindy always shared; a true twin connection, kept her terrified that Cindy would know intrinsically something was very wrong with her...and start to ask questions. The bond which drew them together whenever they were hurt or upset could never be broken. For the last few months Miranda felt as if she was walking around in a horrible nightmare, and, oh, how she wished it could be someone else's nightmare. She felt she didn't have anyone to turn to because Cindy was her closest confidant; the one who knew her secrets, her longings, and her dreams. Putting on a smile and acting as if she was thrilled for her sister was almost beyond her ability.

Somehow, reaching down deep for reserves she didn't know existed; Miranda suffered in silence, not willing to let her pain intrude on Cindy's happiness. Having the knowledge that Cindy would sacrifice her love for Roger in a second if she knew Miranda's true feelings, was no comfort. That would be unbearable, because, despite the feeling of betrayal she recognized in herself, she would have died rather than cause Cindy a moment's grief. The months of watching her suffering, unable to function after the death of their parents, was always uppermost in Miranda's thoughts. She could never watch Cindy withdraw into herself again, blocking out the world.

Miranda thought back to all the lighthearted conversations between her and Cindy about what they would wear, and how they would look in each other's weddings. The idea of standing beside Cindy while she married the man of her dreams was something Miranda always envisioned and looked forward to, knowing the joy it would bring both of them. Now, all Miranda felt was pure dread. She knew in her heart that when Roger slipped the ring onto Cindy's finger, her heart would break...and it did. Hearing the words; "You may kiss the bride," came close to bringing her to her knees. Only by slipping away in the excitement, was she able to keep from sobbing out her heartbreak in front of everyone.

Chapter Three

Over the last couple of months, Miranda sensed Cindy was beginning to notice something wasn't quite right with her. A time or two she looked up to find Cindy watching her with a concerned look on her face. Making a valiant effort to cover up the turmoil she was feeling, Miranda tried to appear normal while laughing and chatting with the friends and acquaintances who always seemed to be around. Miranda thought she was succeeding when Cindy didn't ask her any questions.

Not long after, Miranda found out she was mistaken about her sister. One evening Cindy showed up at her door, and despite everything, Miranda was really happy to see her.

"Hi Cindy, I wasn't expecting anyone, especially this late," Miranda said, as she gave her a warm hug. "I assumed you would be out with Roger."

Wrapping her arm around Miranda's waist as they walked into the living room, Cindy asked, "Miranda, what's wrong? Don't tell me 'nothing,' because I'm not going to believe you."

With a quick smile, Miranda turned away from Cindy and said seriously, "Just some things at work I've been dealing with, but nothing for you to worry about."

Concerned, Cindy pulled her around to face her. "What kind of problems?"

"Oh, just the usual I guess, when you work in an office. One of my co-workers has been taking credit for my work. I'm not sure what I'm going to do about it yet, but it's getting old."

"I can imagine. But how is this happening? I thought you were in charge? How long has this been going on and why haven't you said anything if it's bothering you this much?"

"You've been so happy and busy with your wedding plans, so I didn't want to bother you with my problems."

"What nonsense!" Cindy said heatedly. "You know better than that. What concerns you, concerns me, and you should know not to try and keep something from me. You know I'm going to find out sooner or later, so you might as well tell me sooner," she grinned.

Returning her grin and giving her a light punch on the shoulder, Miranda said, "I know, and ditto for me."

"Back to the subject," Cindy said. "How long has this been going on?"

"For a while now," Miranda said. "I haven't done anything yet, but I'm considering looking for another position. Yes, I'm in charge, which doesn't keep others from trying to undermine me and that's what's been happening."

"Are you thinking about changing companies? What do you have in mind?"

"Oh, I'll probably try for another position in my company, but if that doesn't work, I'll have to look elsewhere."

"This must be more serious than you're letting on," Cindy said with concern. "I can't help but notice you're losing weight. In fact, your clothes are starting to hang on you, and you've been looking very pale. Is something else going on you're not telling me about? I know your career is very important to you, but I get the impression something else is upsetting you."

Hastening to reassure her before she really started noticing other things, Miranda said quickly; "Well it is my career, and Kelsey is starting to really tick me off. The problem is, Franklin likes both of us, so I'm not sure how to approach this without hurting my own career."

"Have you documented your work?"

"Yes, of course," Miranda said.

There was a slight edge to Miranda's voice. She didn't like being untruthful with Cindy, but she was laying the groundwork for the move she would have to make after Cindy was married. It was better to prepare her now, so she wouldn't be completely blindsided later.

"I'm sorry," Cindy said. "I can tell this is upsetting you so I'll quit asking questions. Just make me one promise..."

"What's that?"

"Make sure you find a job around here. I couldn't bear it if you moved somewhere else. It would break my heart if I couldn't see you whenever I wanted. You know you're my best friend!" Cindy leaned over and kissed her cheek, tears glinting behind her smile.

Surprised at Cindy's emotions, and yet not surprised, because Cindy was voicing her own feelings, Miranda said, "I know hon. I feel the same way. No promises though, because I love my work, and it's not much fun dreading to go into work."

For a moment Miranda closed her eyes, remembering her dad's words, and she knew she was doing the right thing.

"I'll focus on finding something that works, but since you travel so much, a little distance won't hurt. You can always fly in to see me if I have to move." Miranda smiled at her sister as she picked up her purse. "Let's forget about all of this and go get some coffee."

"Sounds good to me."

* * *

Chapter Four

Renting an apartment in town more than a year ago proved to be the best decision Miranda ever made. Since college, she and Cindy shared a small house until Miranda decided she wanted her own place. Now Miranda's apartment became her refuge. Every time she saw or spoke to Roger, she wanted to run into his arms, feel his touch and taste his lips. If she was still living with Cindy, with no place to retreat, she would have broken. She wasn't strong enough to withstand seeing him every day.

The weather didn't make it any better. This time of year, in Eugene, it constantly rained and the dark, dreary days didn't help. Some sunshine would be such a blessing...

One day at work, as Miranda walked down the hall lost in thought, she heard her name called. Turning, she saw a friend she badly neglected hurrying towards her. "Hold up for a minute, Miranda, I'd like to talk to you."

"Hi Shawn," she said absently; her mind still on thoughts of the upcoming wedding. "What can I do for you?"

"Let's go get a cup of coffee."

"Sure. I could use one about now," Miranda smiled. "I need the caffeine. It's been a long day."

Miranda liked Shawn from the first time she met him. His eyes held an intensity, an honesty; which spoke to Miranda. He wasn't handsome in the traditional sense, and he was freckled with the fair skin of a redhead. He was about six feet with a muscular build. He was fun to be with and soon became like the big brother Miranda always wanted. He was also super smart, and his specialty was cancer research. He was one of the top chemists in the company, and she knew he was responsible for the progress they were making with several drugs.

Shawn took her arm as they crossed the street to the nearby family-owned coffee shop, Wake Me Up. It was small, crowded, and catered to the young, busy, office crowd.

"O-oh, this feels good," Miranda commented as they found a seat in the sunshine. Miranda didn't realize she was cold until the sunlight touched her skin. She was so happy the sun was finally breaking through the clouds; and her spirits lifted a little.

Sipping her coffee, Miranda found her thoughts drifting again and she missed what Shawn said. "Sorry Shawn, I'm afraid I have a lot on my mind these days. What did you say?"

"I just said, I heard Cindy was getting married. When is the wedding?"

"A couple of months."

"Wow, I bet you do have a lot on your plate. How are the plans coming?"

"Everything's about ready...You had a question?" Miranda asked listlessly. She was so tired it was hard to concentrate on her companion.

Shawn eyed her closely, concern in his eyes, as he asked, "I was wondering if you would like to go horseback riding? It's been a long time and I've noticed you've been putting in a lot of long hours. Kimberly mentioned the other day that you've also been working a lot of Saturdays. In the meeting this morning, I couldn't help but notice you were not your usual, sunny self, and you looked more subdued than usual. Everyone is used to your challenging and useful input at our meetings. A couple of people noticed and asked me if you were feeling OK."

"I'm OK. Just a little tired and distracted I'm afraid. Sorry about that. A horseback ride sounds absolutely wonderful! I've missed you and should have called and suggested something before now."

Sudden animation lit her eyes as they made plans to meet at seven o'clock Saturday morning. Shawn's attention was just what she needed. A change of scenery and someone to talk to about other things. She was so tired of hearing about wedding plans. Miranda and Shawn were in the habit of getting together to ride horses, hike, or swim at least once a month before Roger became a part of her life. She was really looking forward to Saturday.

"I'm sorry we haven't done anything for a while. I guess I haven't been a very good friend, have I?" Miranda asked.

"Well, it goes both ways," Shawn smiled. "I could have called you. In fact, I thought about it several times, but something always came up. I have missed our times together, but I'm sure you've been too busy to think of anything but the wedding. See you Saturday," he said as they parted on the stairs. He headed up to his office.

Saturday morning dawned bright and cloudless. The air was crisp with a slight chill early in the morning, but it would soon dissipate, and she felt her heart lift with anticipation.

"Hey Shawn, did you listen to the weather report? There's no chance of rain is there?"

"I don't think so. There's not even a breath of wind, so I doubt there'll be any problems."

After they picked up horses at Green Mountain Stables, they headed up a well-traveled trail. Miranda leaned over to pat Lucy, the beautiful palomino horse she was riding. "Lucy. That's a good name for you. I think it's going to be a beautiful day, don't you?" She turned her face toward the warm sun, and for the first time in months, she felt a peace come over her.

As she rode along, her mind wandered back to her childhood. She remembered the many times her parents rented two horses and a couple of ponies for her and Cindy and headed out for the day. She and Cindy loved their ponies and were unhappy when they got too big to ride them. After which, their dad allowed them to ride together on a horse they called "Black Paint." He was a big, gentle Friesian horse with such a soft gait that the girls never feared him.

While riding Black Paint, their dad explained that during the Middle Ages, it was believed the ancestors of Friesian horses were in great demand as warhorses throughout Europe. It was thought the breed became nearly extinct on more than one occasion. Dad explained how the modern-day Friesian horse grew in numbers and popularity over the years, and now they were used both in harness and under saddle.

Both girls listened avidly as Dad described the horse they were riding. "Friesians have long, arched necks and well-chiseled, short-eared, 'Spanish-type' heads. Their sloping shoulders are quite powerful. They have compact, muscular bodies with strong sloping hindquarters and a low-set tail."

Dad said it was because their limbs were comparatively short and strong; allowing "Black Paint" to carry them both up the hills easily.

For a moment, Miranda could almost hear his voice and she felt a longing to go back in time to a more tranquil place. She missed her parents every day, but at times, she especially missed her dad, and this was certainly one of those times.

She and Shawn traveled about an hour and were now climbing, so Miranda needed to concentrate to make sure Lucy didn't stumble. The trail became rough and there were a lot of rocks underneath. After riding her for a while, Miranda knew Lucy was very sure-footed, so she wasn't too worried about the horse tripping. Shawn was up ahead, and she knew they were getting close to the top.

They traveled for a while through a forest of tall, western white pines with long, slender cones glinting in the sunshine. She could see the small male cones clustered at the very ends of the branches. The difference between them and the female cones had always interested her. Some cones were very small, yellow, and densely clustered at the very ends of the branches. But, the female cones were much longer, greenish-pink, and could be found toward the front of the branches. As a teenager, Miranda looked up information on these magnificent pines. She found out they could live as long as 400 years and could grow as tall as 154 feet. She wished she could see them in their natural environment. "Maybe I will travel to see them someday," Miranda murmured as she stopped for a moment to admire them. The trees were tall and slender but as they climbed nearer the summit, they became shorter.

Breaking free of the trees, Miranda caught her breath at the beauty surrounding her. The sun was glistening and bright, but as she dismounted and led Lucy to the edge of the cliff, she stared in admiration at the stunning lake below; shrouded in early morning mist. It was mystical and enchanting and Miranda smiled at Shawn as she stated, "I'll never get used to seeing this no matter how many times I come up here."

"I know what you mean," Shawn said as he took the reins from her and tied the horses to a cluster of short pinions. The horses would be left to graze while Miranda and Shawn enjoyed their morning. Miranda pulled out a thermos of coffee she brought, and after giving Shawn a cup, wandered around looking at the splendor surrounding her. She and Shawn chatted idly about work and the friends they had in common. Miranda felt at peace for the first time in a very long time. They left the horses and took an overgrown trail which led down to the lake. Even though the water was icy cold, they couldn't resist taking their shoes off and trailing their feet in the water as they drank in the tranquility and peace of the mountains.

"I'm thinking of looking for another job," Miranda murmured as she gazed off into the distance.

"Why on earth would you do that? I thought you liked your job?"

"I do, but I think I need more of a challenge. I've been doing the same thing for a couple of years, and I'd like a change."

"I assume you mean a job with another company in Eugene? I'm sure you wouldn't want to be separated from Cindy."

"Actually, I'm thinking of looking statewide. There's been no good jobs posted in Eugene for awhile, especially executive positions, which is what I'm looking for. Besides, Cindy will be married so she won't miss me as much if I move somewhere else," Miranda said. She wished she could confide in him the reason why she really wanted to move. It would be so good to talk to someone, but the hurt was too deep. She knew talking about Roger and Cindy would be so painful, and she wasn't ready to handle the pain that talking about it would bring.

Shawn stared at her for a moment but didn't say anything else. He knew there was something else going on but didn't want to intrude. Rumors circulated about her seeing Roger before he and Cindy started dating, but he didn't want to ask her about it in case it was a painful subject.

"I guess we'd better start back up because I'm getting hungry," Miranda said. "It'll be about one before we get back."

As they made their way back up the hill, Miranda noticed some dark clouds which suddenly appeared.

"Shawn," she called worriedly, "Look at the sky! We might be in for a bad storm. We'd better hurry or we'll get drenched."

"I know," he called back. "The wind kicked up since we arrived. I'm sure it'll be OK, but maybe we should make tracks in case it does decide to rain. I'd hate to get caught out in a storm."

"Me too," Miranda laughed. "I wouldn't want to ride home all wet."

Neither were too worried, but they set out at a brisk pace as they started back down the trail. Sheltered by the trees for a while, they were stunned as they rode out into a clearing to see the sky dark and lowering with a feel of rain in the air.

"Wow," Shawn turned around to look at Miranda, concern in his eyes. "I can't believe it's changed this much in such a short time. I guess we'd better hurry. It looks like we're going to get wet anyway."

"Looks like," Miranda yelled as she set off at a fast pace. She only rode a short distance when the heavens opened, and torrents of rain pounded her unmercifully. Suddenly, the sky was lit up with brilliant flashes of lightning which zigzagged across the sky.

"Shawn, that's too close," Miranda shouted, but she wasn't sure Shawn could hear her. The lightning seemed too close for comfort. Frightened, she also heard a loud clap of thunder which startled Lucy and made her shy and sidestep.

Shawn raced back and stopped beside her, concern written all over his face. "I know it's not safe to seek shelter under trees, but I don't see that we have much choice. It's raining too hard to keep going," He sounded very worried as he said, "Maybe it won't last too long, but the lightning is too close for comfort."

Dismounting, Miranda took Lucy's reigns and started to lead her toward a clump of pines, but more streaks of lightning crossed the sky just in front of them. Thunder crashed just over their heads, causing Miranda to scream. Terrified, eyes flashing, Lucy suddenly reared, her hooves beating the air, her frightened whinny echoing through the woods.

Shawn leapt up, grabbed Lucy's reigns, and yelled at Miranda to hurry. In between the lightning flashes and the claps of thunder, they got the horses tied under the trees. Sodden, they stared at each other wondering how long they would be there. Miranda shivered violently, unable to control the tremors which swept over her. Shawn moved over and put his arm around her, tucking her up against him.

"I'm sorry I don't have anything to wrap around you," he said as he rubbed her arms trying to stop her shivering.

A smile crossed Miranda's face, as she huddled up to him. "I guess we'll just have to keep each other from freezing until this blows over, huh?"

"Sure," Shawn grinned at her. "What's a little rain when you're having fun?" they both chuckled as they huddled together.

Thankfully, it wasn't so cold that they would get hypothermia, but it was uncomfortable. After about an hour, the storm moved on and out of the area and they were then able to mount up and make their way back to the stables.

"Well, aren't you two a sight?!" Marvin chortled as they rode in and dismounted.

Marvin was the owner of the stables and had been renting horses to them for awhile. Miranda took to him the first time she rented a horse from him. He was a bow-legged cowboy with bright red hair. He moved to Oregon from Texas when he was thirty and started the stables. He loved the area even though it rained a lot. He told Miranda he often wanted to high-tail it back to Texas, just to see the sun...but reckoned he'd just stay put.

"It's not that funny," Shawn grumbled good-naturedly.

"No, it most certainly isn't," Miranda protested. "I don't know if I'll ever get warm again," she shivered as she spoke.

"Well, come on in the house and get some hot coffee, and we'll throw your clothes in the dryer," Marvin said.

"We'll take the coffee," Shawn said; "But it will take too long to dry our clothes. Besides, they'll have to dry from the skin out because we are both soaked. We'll get in the car and turn the heater up high. It's not very far, and Miranda should really get out of these wet things as soon as possible. I don't want her getting sick. I can't believe the weather changed so quickly!"

"It happens up here more often than you think," Marvin said shaking his head. "I wasn't expecting it today, though."

Shivering, they downed some hot coffee, thanked Marvin, and dashed to the car. Shawn started the car and let it run for a few minutes until the heater warmed up. Then he turned it up full blast.

"Getting any warmer?" he asked.

"Slightly," she shivered. "I've been in the rain lots of times but this beats all! But it was fun, wasn't it? Despite the rain? A little exciting too."

"You bet. Let's do this again tomorrow, huh?"

"Yeah, you wish, you nut!" Miranda laughed. Then she turned sober for a moment. "Shawn, today was wonderful and I can't tell you how much I appreciate it."

Patting her hand, Shawn said, "I think of you as my sister so if you ever need to talk, you know where I am."

She took his hand and held it for a moment. "I do know that, Shawn."

When Shawn stopped the car at Miranda's house, he turned to her. "Miranda, have you looked at yourself in the mirror lately?"

"Why, what are you trying to say?"

"I can't help but notice you are losing weight, and you look sad all the time. I'm not sure, exactly. You always have a smile which brightens up any room, but lately, I don't know, you just haven't been yourself." Shawn reached over and touched her shoulder. "Call me if you change your mind and want to talk to someone about what's going on?"

"I will, Shawn, and I really appreciate your wanting to help." Miranda turned to look at him for a moment before opening the door. "I just can't talk about it right now, but thanks for being my friend. Today was wonderful and I will see you tomorrow."

"You take care of yourself, and I will see you at work. Bye now."

Chapter Five

Several hours later, Miranda was hot and cozy after a hot shower; but she wasn't feeling too well as she climbed into bed. She hoped after some rest she would feel better, but she awoke the next morning with a raging headache and a bad cough.

A few days later, Miranda was back at work, tired and lethargic, but the excursion with Shawn brightened her life for a brief time and made her realize she must find other distractions or the stress would really make her ill.

Her long working hours was a good excuse for not getting together with Cindy and Roger. She always kept very busy at work. Miranda was the office manager of a very prestigious company called Barnes and Cummings, a well-known local pharmaceutical company. Her firm handled new medications being tested for market. Miranda's job was to oversee and evaluate the testing. She worked alongside the pharmaceutical chemists who designed and synthesized the new drugs for the pharmaceutical industry. She was also involved in evaluating drugs already on the market.

Miranda first earned a Bachelor of Science Degree in Chemistry and then went on to get her master's degree. It took two years to find a job she liked in her field. After working for a couple of smaller firms, she was elated when she landed the job with Barnes and Cummings.

Using her job as an excuse the last few weeks before the wedding, she worked ten to twelve hours a day. Too many long hours, the stress of the job, and her unhappiness forced her to realize just how exhausted she was becoming. She knew she must change something, but she just didn't know how.

After getting home late at night, trying to eat, and taking a bath, Miranda really wanted to sleep. She tried watching television, listening to soft music, and even counting sheep, but most of the time, nothing worked. She was too apprehensive of closing her eyes for fear of the dreams she knew she would have; but there were other nights she cried herself to sleep and would awaken almost too tired to drag herself out of bed and get to work. If Cindy's wedding was later in the year, Miranda knew her resolve and energy would not be enough to get her to the wedding day. Miranda was fast becoming too tired and exhausted to function well at the office.

Miranda knew, even though she was putting in long hours at work, her usual quality of work was missing. She often found herself sitting, almost in a daze, just staring out the window. A few days after getting back to work, Kimberly brought back something Miranda submitted the day before.

"Miranda, this data doesn't seem right. Could you please go over it and see what's wrong? If what you have here is correct, we're going to have to retest Tramedal. Your data shows it's a long way from being ready and I thought it was almost ready to market."

Blanching, Miranda reached for the paperwork. "I'll look at it right away. Thanks, Kim."

"No problem. I just hope your data isn't right. This gives us a lot more work if it is. Are you doing OK?" Kim asked as she was leaving.

"Sure, why do you ask?"

"You just haven't been yourself for a while. You seem distracted and it looks like you've lost weight," Kim explained.

"I'm OK, just some family issues I'm trying to sort out. Thanks for your concern. I'll pay more attention and get this sorted out, OK?"

"OK, thanks," Kimberly said before shutting the door.

The next day, there was a note on her desk from her boss, Franklin, asking her to come to his office.

"What now?" Miranda muttered as she looked at the note. She sat at her desk for a minute wondering what he wanted. She loved her boss. He was wonderful to work for, but he could be pretty tough at times if your work wasn't up to par. Thankfully, she had never been in a position to be admonished by him, but she witnessed it a couple of times with others.

Trembling slightly, she walked into her boss's office. Everyone who worked for Franklin liked him. He was honest and straightforward. You always knew where you stood with him. If you were doing a good job, you got praised. If not, he would sit you down and explain what he expected from you. He was tough and to the point, but Miranda saw him give an employee more than one chance before letting them go. He was a serious man, but with a ready smile. He dressed in a business suit every day and expected his employees to follow his example. A few times during office parties, Miranda was able to see how warm he was. His wife was a beautiful woman and he obviously loved his two sons.

Miranda always felt he liked her, and he often praised her work by giving her a pat on the shoulder. Every once in a while, she worked personally with him on a tough project and was impressed by how his mind worked. He could spot a possible problem during a drug test and would work tirelessly to correct it.

Seeing her, Franklin got right to the point. "Miranda, would you sit down for a moment?"

"Sure, what's going on?"

"Well...for one thing, I've noticed you're losing weight, and I'm wondering what's causing it! I'm not sure if you realize you bring joy to all those around you with your positive attitude. You may not even be aware of it, but you often hum when you work. Your presence just seems to make people happy, but the Miranda we've come to know and appreciate has been missing for a while. Aside from all that, the real reason I called you in today is to let you know you made a mistake on the draft I gave you for Pittman's yesterday."

Alarmed, Miranda jumped up and started to pace. "Oh no! I'm so sorry! Did it cause any problems, or do I have time to redo it?"

"Of course. Sit back down. Kimberly fixed the problem and it's been sent to them. Is there anything you need to talk about? What's going on with you? Where's the Miranda I'm used to working with?" Franklin smiled kindly at her; coming around the desk and handing her a cup of coffee.

With a sigh, Miranda sipped her coffee and then leaned back and closed her eyes for a moment. "Just some personal issues I'm dealing with. I'm truly sorry they are affecting my work, and I'll start paying more attention." Even though she was dealing with personal issues, her comment made her realize she kept repeating the same excuse for herself, but she didn't know what else to say to people.

"I'm not too worried," Franklin said thoughtfully, "but if you need to take a few days off, just tell me. You know you are irreplaceable around here and I, personally, would like to see the 'old' Miranda back."

Getting to her feet, Miranda said, "Thanks, Franklin. I may take you up on your offer to take a few days off. I'll let you know. I'm going to start taking better care of myself, I promise."

* * *

Chapter Six

Franklin's advice kept running through her mind. She couldn't jeopardize her job just because she was unhappy. She had worked too long and too hard to get to where she was, and she had to stop letting her personal issues affect her job.

After Cindy and Roger became engaged, Miranda started using her job as an excuse to work on Saturdays. Being busy at the office kept her mind from dwelling on her anxiety about the wedding, but she needed to find a way to get her mind back on the job. She couldn't continue to use working every weekend as an excuse to avoid seeing her sister, and consequently Roger.

In the past, whenever Cindy was in town, Saturday was their day to be together; so even though Cindy spent a lot of her time now with Roger, she was not going to give up her time with Miranda. She still expected to see as much of Miranda as possible and would immediately suspect something was wrong if Miranda made excuse after excuse to not get together.

Even so, Miranda found herself becoming very inventive. She surprised even herself at times by the excuses she was able to come up with so she didn't have to go to Cindy's place; and hopefully avoid running into Roger. Of course, she never knew when Cindy might drop in on her. As a result, she started staying away from home as much as possible, but she became very worried Cindy would sooner or later realize the explanation she gave about her job problems was just a cover.

To keep this from happening, she substituted phone calls instead of visits, just to keep Cindy from wondering why, suddenly, she was so busy at work. Miranda would pick up the phone several times a week and call Cindy in whatever city she was in, and chat for a few moments; finding out what exciting things were happening in the fashion world. Although, she soon began to realize Cindy was not doing a lot of traveling before the wedding.

Miranda was able to keep her emotions under control a lot better by talking on the phone as opposed to seeing Cindy and Roger in person. Because Cindy was so caught up with wedding plans and the demands of her job, so far, she accepted Miranda's excuses; but if the wedding had been scheduled any later in the year, she wouldn't have escaped without an explanation.

Miranda knew her sister so well. She knew how single-minded and obsessed Cindy became when she was working on a big project. Cindy was always driven when it came to her career and Miranda was used to her being fully-focused on a specific project. Miranda also knew the loving sister who always wanted to know everything that was going on in her life. Cindy's job and getting ready for the wedding was the one blessing Miranda was thankful for. They kept Cindy so busy, she just didn't have time to focus on Miranda, or realize something was very wrong. Sooner or later, Cindy would notice and start asking questions if Miranda couldn't continue to keep up a good front.

As well as worrying about Cindy, Miranda started worrying about Roger. When would he start asking questions about why she was never around? Would he think she was avoiding him? He would certainly be right! Miranda was simply afraid she was not strong enough to see him without giving away the fact that she loved him.

As things were, it was just too late to change anything. Miranda knew she would not change her mind. Whenever she talked to Cindy there was no doubt about how much Cindy loved Roger. She was happy and bubbly, her life a whirlwind of plans for the future. There was no way Miranda would do anything to disrupt Cindy's life.

Roger begged Cindy to marry him soon because he loved her so much and didn't see any reason to wait. Miranda was in shock and immediately realized she would have to find another job; somewhere away from them.

Alone in her apartment, and unable to process the news, Miranda's heartbreak was too deep for tears. Unable to go to work, she called in sick for a couple of days. Soon, they would be married and she could run away and hide, and try to accept the loss of her dreams. Miranda could not have endured several months with a despair tearing her into little pieces every time she was with them.

Ever since Miranda heard they were getting married, she tried to act as normal as possible around them. As a result, the grief of Miranda's loss and the anguish she lived with minute by minute began to take its toll on her health. Miranda struggled constantly to keep up a façade the few times she was with them.

As the wedding day drew closer, it became impossible for her to stay away from them. Miranda didn't have a choice but to become actively involved in the wedding preparations. It was excruciating to watch Cindy and Roger together. They were so in love and it showed every time they touched each other. Even across a room, she could see the love radiating from their faces. It was even harder to watch as they kissed passionately, their breath mingling, their lips clinging. Their laughter often rang out, and Miranda ached to be able to share it, to be happy for them; instead, she turned away, lonely and sick at heart.

Almost against her will she would find herself standing and watching, unable to turn away and wishing with all her heart Roger was holding her in his arms, loving her and giving her hope for a beautiful future. Miranda longed to be the one to share his laughter. She thought about his heart-stopping smile, his kindness and tenderness with her while they dated. Fighting back tears, she would hurry away to cry quietly alone. Later, she would come back with a forced smile on her face. Of course, she could only do this after putting on makeup to hide her tears.

Miranda realized, under different circumstances, without a whirlwind romance and wedding, Cindy would have never overlooked what was happening to their relationship. In fact, when Miranda thought about it, she was shocked. The only way she could fathom what was happening with her and Cindy, was to remember how she felt when she was with Roger herself, just months ago. She couldn't forget the euphoria, joy, excitement, and ecstasy just thinking about seeing Roger. She couldn't blame Cindy for overlooking what was going on with her.

If anyone took the time to really pay attention to Miranda and notice how sad her eyes looked, they would know just how unhappy she had become. Miranda was grateful everyone was much too busy to realize how she was feeling. Many nights she went home to weep bitterly; wishing none of this ever happened, that she had not been the one to meet Roger first and fall deeply, madly in love with him. And, sometimes she found herself wishing they never met!

As well as feeling unhappy, she was not getting very much sleep and her appetite was non-existent. Consequently, she became very tired and depressed, and as the days went by, it was getting harder and harder to paste a smile on her face.

One morning, after stepping out of the shower, Miranda started to put on her makeup. Moving a little closer to the mirror, she stared at herself. When had she changed so much? Astonished, she noticed the dark shadows under her eyes and realized her cheeks looked hollow. Her shimmering, flaxen hair was losing its shine and looked dull. The eyes, which stared back at her, looked almost haunted.

She had to do something because if she kept going this way, she was going to become ill. Yesterday, when she put on her skirt for work, she used a pin to tighten the waist or it would have fallen off; and the jacket, which used to fit her beautifully, was getting too loose. She decided, at that moment, even though food was tasteless, she was going to try and eat three meals a day; and sunshine was a must. She was determined to start getting out of the office to find a place in the park to eat lunch and just relax.

A couple of weeks before the wedding, she went into the bridal shop alone. She hadn't made much effort to get to know the staff, but Katherine, the owner, was a nice lady. She was not a small lady, but she had beautiful auburn hair which fell to her shoulders, and appeared to have a cheerful personality. Seeing Miranda, she walked over and offered her hand with a warm smile.

"Miranda, it's nice to see you. What's going on? I thought everything was ready for the wedding? Cindy is going to pick up the dresses next week."

"I know," Miranda said. "There's something I need to have you do."

"What's that?" asked Katherine.

"I've lost a little weight since the dresses were made, so I need to try mine on and see if you can take it in a little. I'm glad it's a loose fit so it shouldn't be hard for you to alter, I hope."

"Just a moment, let me get my pins while you try the dress on. Shanna, would you please bring the dress for Miranda? I think you know which one it is," reminded Kathrine.

Miranda's gown was a flowing one-shoulder gown in green silk georgette, highlighted with a lush petal corsage at the shoulder with a sweetheart neckline. What Miranda really loved about the dress was how it was shirred at the bust with crossover detail. It was the empire waist with decorative edges of pleated fabric at the waist seam which would make it possible for her to hide her unusually slender body. She liked how it floated around her; making her feel like a princess. Any other time she would have celebrated the beauty of the dress.

Miranda waited patiently while Kathrine worked.

"I thought you said you lost a little weight," Kathrine looked up at her from where she knelt on the floor. "Girl, you've lost a whole dress size! What's going on, because I know you're not dieting? I'll even have to take in the bust because it just hangs on you now!"

Miranda held back a sob as she said, "I was afraid of that. I'm just dealing with some emotional problems and haven't been eating right." Miranda sighed as she said, "I know I have to gain back what I've lost but it won't happen in two weeks, so just do what you can. Please don't say anything to Cindy, I don't want her worrying."

46

"Of course not, honey, your secret's safe with me, but please try taking care of yourself."

"I will," Miranda said. "Thanks so much. You'll never know how much I appreciate this." Miranda waved as she left the store, relieved it was possible to alter her dress without ruining it in the process.

Even with her precautions she was desperately hoping Cindy would be too busy to notice the difference in her size. It was a miracle no one noticed the extra layer of make-up she put on to cover up her pallor. At least, no one commented, so she assumed they were too busy to notice. She would give anything to feel differently. She just kept hoping and praying she could be able to get through all of this and say goodbye to Cindy and Roger without letting anyone know how she felt. She knew that for her own sanity, she should have confided in someone, but she just couldn't.

She made the decision some time ago that as soon as Cindy and Roger were married, she would try to transfer to a branch office of her company, Barnes and Cummings, located in Medford. She knew she couldn't stay in Eugene where she would be forced to see them all the time. With some distance between them, she would be able to get some perspective on her life, rather than vicariously live a dream which wasn't hers to dream. She was afraid being near them might destroy her, or loving Cindy as she did, it might really hurt their future relationship.

Chapter Seven

Miranda met Roger first. One day, in a big hurry to get home, she grabbed her groceries out of the cart and dashed from the store. She stumbled as she collided with someone who was unable to avoid her headlong rush.

Of course, all her groceries spilled everywhere. As she hurriedly grabbed things before they rolled away, she heard someone laugh softly and apologize for bumping into her. Out of the corner of her eye, she noticed that whoever it was started to help pick up her scattered groceries. Glancing up to say quickly; "Oh no, it was my fault! I shouldn't have been in such a hurry..." she felt her breath catch in her throat. He was gorgeous. Laughing blue eyes, framed by unbelievably long lashes, seemed to smile down at her. He reached up to push back a strand of blond hair out of his eyes; his locks turned almost white by the radiance of the sun.

Miranda, herself was lovely. Her charming face was framed by blond hair which floated in a golden halo almost to her waist. Surrounded by beautiful eyelashes, her eyes were a striking hazel color, changing from a blue, to green, to warm brown, depending on her mood. Like a changeling, her eyes would mirror whatever color she was wearing. Her nose was small and upturned, cute and kissable, and her mouth was full and generous. Her lovely full-busted figure had a tiny waist which a man could almost span with his hands. Her eyes always seemed to be full of laughter. They stared at each other for a moment, neither speaking before he said a quiet, "Hi..."

In a moment, she regained her composure and said, "Hi, sorry I was so clumsy."

"No problem," he said. Handing her the rest of her groceries, he grinned and casually waved his hand as he turned to leave.

Without conscious thought, Miranda turned and watched him walk away. "Wow," she breathed. He was handsome! Beautiful blond hair glinted in the sunlight; he was over six feet, with broad shoulders and slim hips, which hinted at a lean and powerful body.

Miranda discovered her thoughts returning to their intriguing meeting, and she wondered if she would ever see him again. She certainly hoped their unexpected encounter, though brief, would not be their last. Fate intervened, and she did meet him again a few days later when her friend Gail called to ask if she would like to attend a small party she was giving.

She and Gail were friends from middle school. In fact, she was the one friend she and Cindy did not have in common. She was vivacious, with curly brown hair worn to her shoulders. Gail wasn't beautiful, but was so outgoing and interesting that people just seemed to gravitate to her. She was currently dating a nice man whom she met at a party a few months before. After college she moved into a nice, two-bedroom condo with a large open kitchen and living room which held enough room for entertaining.

Miranda arrived a little late, and after Gail welcomed her, she introduced Miranda to some of her friends. The room was rather dark and noisy, and the music was so loud you needed to yell to be heard. Miranda chatted with a couple of guys for a few moments and then went to a nearby table loaded with food. While trying to decide what to eat, she sensed someone was watching her.

Turning, her eyes searched the room trying to decide if it was just her overactive imagination or if someone was, in fact, scrutinizing her...and that was when she saw him. He was across the room with a group of people, but he didn't seem to be paying any attention to them because his eyes were on her.

Time seemed to stand still. The noisy room faded away until they seemed to be the only two people there. Her heart started to race, and even though she wanted to look away, she couldn't. It seemed an eternity while they stared across the room at each other, and then she turned away quickly trying to catch her breath.

As she was staring blindly at the food, someone touched her arm. Turning, slowly, she found him standing at her side. "Hello, bumped into anyone else lately?" he asked.

She laughed quietly and said, "No, not since you."

"Don't you think it's about time we became acquainted?" he asked. "I'm Roger."

"It's really nice to meet you. I'm Miranda," she said holding out her hand. He took it in his and clasped it warmly.

"I'm very pleased to meet you, Miranda."

"This is such a surprise. I didn't think I would ever see you again. How do you know Gail?"

"Actually, I don't. I am a friend of Pete's."

"Pete?" Miranda felt slightly breathless as she glanced up at him. "Oh, Pete...Gail's friend!"

Taking her arm to steer her around a group standing near the table, Roger asked; "Would you like to get some food, and find a quiet place to talk?"

"Quiet?" Miranda giggled.

"Well, sure. I bet we can find a place in the backyard. Gail has chairs set up out there and it shouldn't be as noisy."

"Wanna bet?" Miranda giggled again.

Miranda hardly noticed what she put on her plate while standing so close to this fascinating man. She glanced at him, noticing how his grey shirt seemed to fit his broad shoulders. He carried himself like a man who knew who he was, and she loved the way he looked directly at her when he talked to her.

They were able to find a couple of chairs on the lawn but it was still very noisy. "We're not exactly being good guests are we?" Roger asked with a smile as he bit into an appetizer. "This is good. I didn't realize how hungry I was."

They sat and ate while chatting quietly for a few minutes before Gail came to drag her over to meet some more of her friends.

Miranda looked back at Roger as she got up. In the few minutes together, she knew she wanted to see more of him. She assumed he didn't have a girlfriend since he seemed interested in her, but there was no way to be sure without asking.

Roger caught her arm as Gail was leading her away. "Miranda, could I get your phone number?" He handed her a small piece of paper and a pen, and Miranda's hand trembled slightly as she wrote the number down.

As he said, "Goodbye, for now..." and walked away, Miranda watched him, eyes glowing, a feeling of excitement coursing through her. She just might see him again!

Chapter Eight

Miranda's phone didn't ring! Every night she stared at the phone, willing it to ring. A week later, she gave up. She assumed he was just intrigued by a new girl for the moment, and lost interest. She was so disappointed because he interested her more than any other man she ever met.

It was after nine on Friday night, and the sound of the phone ringing startled her as she got ready for bed. Heart racing, she grabbed the phone and said a breathless, "Hello?"

"Miranda, it's me," laughed Cindy. "Why do you sound out of breath?"

Depressed, Miranda sank onto the bed. He wasn't going to call. Normally she would have told Cindy about him and they would have laughed together over her waiting for a phone call, but for some reason she didn't. She really wanted to see him again and the disappointment kept her quiet.

After hanging up, Miranda grabbed a book to help her sleep but she couldn't seem to concentrate. What was it about Roger that was keeping her awake? She felt a strong emotional attraction for him, and he made her heart sing, which she didn't understand. Suddenly, the phone rang again. Startled, she sat up and reached for it, thinking Cindy must have forgotten to tell her something.

"Hello?" she said.

"Miranda?" At his question she sat up, excitement surging through her. It was Roger. She would know his voice anywhere. "It's Roger. I hope it's not too late to call."

"Of course not," she said breathlessly.

"Sorry about not calling sooner, but I got called out of town on an emergency for work. I've been almost too busy to sleep."

"That's OK. I'm just glad you called."

"I really enjoyed meeting you at Gail's the other night, and wondered if you would you be interested in going out to dinner?"

Elated, she responded; "I would love to! What do you have in mind?"

"Have you heard of The Lighthouse? It's a nice nightclub with live music and dancing. Would you be interested in going?"

"Absolutely! Dancing is one of my favorite things to do. I love all kinds of music," Miranda replied.

"It's a date then! Pick you up at five tomorrow. I'll need your address, of course."

After giving him her address she asked, "How should I dress?"

"I usually wear a dress shirt and slacks. It's dress casual so I'm sure whatever you choose will be perfect. See you tomorrow night, Miranda."

Trying to keep her excitement in check, Miranda left work early to get ready. She chose a pair of black silk pants with a green silk top with long flowing sleeves. She stepped into a pair of black four-inch heels, and chose to wear her hair up with soft tendrils framing her face. When the doorbell rang, she opened the door eagerly, a big smile on her face.

"Hi, ready to go?" Roger asked. As she closed and locked the door he said causally, "By the way, you look very nice."

"Thanks," Miranda glanced up at him and said, "So do you."

The Lighthouse was dimly lit with soft music playing in the background, creating a soft, romantic atmosphere. The sounds of light laughter, clinking of silverware, and conversation made the ambiance warm and welcoming.

"This is a lovely place," Miranda said glancing around. "I love the way the smaller tables are set apart from the others. It makes it more intimate for couples who want to be alone."

"I agree," Roger said. "I hate it when I go to a restaurant and have to strain to hear someone. Most large groups get very loud and it's hard to concentrate on your companion."

"That's happened to me more than once." Miranda agreed.

"Would you like a glass of wine?" Roger asked, changing the subject.

"Sure," Miranda nodded.

Roger discretely motioned for their server. When he arrived Roger asked for the wine list. "What kind of wine do you like?" he asked Miranda.

"I'm not too fussy. A chardonnay or merlot? What sounds good to you?" Miranda asked.

Roger asked the waiter to bring them a sample of both and they chose the house chardonnay.

Miranda ordered the halibut dinner and Roger chose a New York steak. Curious about him, she asked," "What kind of work do you do?"

"I'm a graphic designer for an advertising firm."

"That must be interesting, but it also tells me you are artistic and smart. I've never met anyone who does that kind of work, but I see examples of it all the time. What are your specific skills?" Miranda asked.

"Mostly graphic design, creating layouts and web pages. Our company works for large businesses all over the country. I can be sent almost anywhere to solve a problem at a moment's notice which is what happened last week. What about you? What kind of work do you do?"

They talked easily over their meal. They learned small details about each other's lives, including likes and dislikes in music and sports. Miranda was captivated, listening to him, and they never seemed to run out of things to talk about.

She was enjoying every minute, and when Roger reached for her hand to lead her to the dance floor where several couples were dancing, she went gladly. While they were eating, a local band set up their instruments and began to play a medley of songs. They played music from the '50s, '60s and '70s, and were very good. Their lead singer was a strong tenor with a backup soprano.

As she stepped into his arms and felt them close around her, Miranda experienced a feeling of coming home. A warm glow slowly stole over her as she moved to the rhythm of the music. She glanced up and found his eyes studying her as they danced. "This is wonderful," she said as she smiled up at him.

"You said it! I don't know when I've enjoyed dinner so much." Miranda felt his arms tighten as he twirled her into a quick step, laughing as he did so. "By the way, you're a very good dancer!"

"Ditto," she murmured as the music changed to a slow waltz, and she snuggled closer to him, her heart beating a little faster.

Later as they sat, having coffee before going home, Miranda told him about her dance lessons as a child. "It was fun but it was such hard work trying to learn all the steps."

"So then, how did you become such a good dancer?" Roger asked, intrigued.

"I took a dance class at college just to have fun and de-stress from all the studying. It was such fun, I took a couple of other classes the next term. West Coast Swing was really fun."

"Well, it really paid off. You are good!" Roger teased, as he held the door for her.

At her apartment, Roger asked if he could see her again. Excitement coursed through her as she said; "Yes," before going inside. Over the next few weeks they went to movies, saw an opera, and even went bowling!

One date, which really stood out above the rest, was the wonderful late afternoon and evening spent sitting in the bow of a boat, while he slowly rowed around a lake. The air was crisp and breezy, and the day was unusually warm for March. Miranda and Roger wore light jackets which kept them warm enough. They stopped and shared a bottle of wine in the middle of the lake along with a scrumptious picnic basket filled with mouthwatering food. As it began to grow dark enough that they needed to head home, their path was lit by a brilliant moon and stars which were just starting to glow in the night sky. Their soft, warm laughter floated across the water.

Conversation flowed so easily between them. She found herself telling him things about herself she never told anyone, not even her beloved sister.

She was surprised one day when Roger mentioned he played a guitar. "When did you start playing?" she asked.

"I helped create a band when I turned sixteen."

"Really?" Miranda asked. "What kind of music?"

"I was crazy about the Beatles, but also loved Elvis along with Elton John and others. So, I guess, we played a little bit of everything," he laughed.

"How many were in the band, and how long did you last?" asked Miranda, amused.

"Four of us. Actually, we still play once in a while when all of us are in town together. It doesn't happen often, but it's fun when it does."

"I bet," said Miranda. "I hope I get to hear you guys sometime."

"Maybe you will," Roger grinned. "I guess I still dream about being a big star someday, but realize it's probably just a pipedream. Still, it's fun to dream. Do you have anything you would really like to do but haven't been able to?"

"Not so far. My career is very important to me and I plan on working hard to move up in my company. Someday, I would love to have an executive position, which allows me to travel and see the world. I want to continue building my career."

"You haven't mentioned family. I know you have a twin sister, but would you like to have your own family?" Roger asked.

"I suppose everyone dreams of having a family. Since you know about the death of my parents, I will say having my own family is something I've tried not to think too much about. It was such a painful time, I have been afraid to think about a husband and children. It's really hard to explain."

"I'm not sure I totally understand, but it makes sense. If you have your own family and something happens to them or you, you wouldn't want to relive what happened to you and Cindy."

Roger reached for her hand, comforting her. A warmth stole into her heart and she leaned her head against his shoulder. He made her feel so safe and secure and she felt her heart changing. She was no longer afraid to dream of a future and children.

Ever since the death of her parents, and without her mother's guidance, Miranda was afraid to dream of a future. Even after Cindy found her true profession and was beginning to make a name for herself in the fashion industry, Miranda still felt isolated; and unattached in some ways.

Her career was going very well, but she knew she was floundering in her personal life. Her parents' deaths shocked and angered her so much that she found herself putting an emotional distance between herself, friends, co-workers, and any man she chose to date. The worse part about her detachment from others was she found herself also putting some emotional distance between herself and Cindy. Maybe, somewhere deep inside, she was trying to find a niche for herself apart from Cindy. She and Shawn had developed a comfortable friendship but she even kept him at arm's length when it came to anything personal.

Miranda often found herself weeping for the old days. The carefree life with Cindy with nothing to worry about but school and running around with her friends. She longed for her life before their whole world changed; an alien world where everything was upside down. She knew she could never get those days back again, but she could support Cindy with her career and whatever choices she made in her personal life.

Now, suddenly things were changing for her. Roger made her feel like she could have a future, a life apart from her job. Ever since meeting him, her dreams changed. She found herself fantasizing about being his wife. She hadn't known him very long, but it just seemed right. She knew she was growing to love this man who had burst into her life so unexpectedly...

* * *

Chapter Nine

Miranda missed Cindy and couldn't wait to tell her about Roger. Cindy worked for a high fashion clothing company, and they often sent her out of town on extended visits to other parts of the country. Over the past few years, after college, she was sought after for her unique and one-of-a-kind dress designs and her work was highly praised by top designers in the field. This trip, she was out of town for several months to attend a designer workshop, plus she was scheduled to go on to Paris before returning home. It was one of the longest periods Miranda remembered Cindy being away from Eugene. The ever-changing fashion industry made it hard to keep up, especially as each season brought new styles, and retail stores were always competing to be the first to market them.

Cindy's company wanted her to incorporate the latest trends into their newest clothing line; and they wanted her to take advantage of the fact that a fashion designer from Paris was going to be at the workshop. He would host a fashion show highlighting some of the latest styles, and the company was very excited about what she would bring back to show them. They wanted Cindy to go on to Paris to attend other fashion shows which occur around the same time of year, and to also visit some of the fashion houses.

Now, after meeting Roger, Miranda became anxious for Cindy to get back because she wanted to see Roger's reaction to her twin. She wanted Roger to like Cindy. She didn't want to tell Cindy anything about Roger on the phone, so she didn't say anything to her, wanting to tell her in person. She needed and wanted Cindy's blessing. It was vital to her that Cindy approve of her choice of the man she wanted to marry. More than anything, Miranda wanted to curl up on the couch with a cup of hot chocolate and tell Cindy everything about Roger, how much she loved him, and how she longed to become his wife someday.

Miranda and Roger dated for a few months before she felt comfortable enough to ask him over to her apartment to test her skill at cooking. She knew she was falling in love with him, but on the surface, she was calm and serene. Because of something which happened earlier, she wanted to let their relationship grow, to form a bond which couldn't be broken. She was willing to wait, but her love for him showed in her laughing eyes and glowing face when she looked at him.

He gave her a casual goodnight kiss a time or two but overall, they were good friends. This was alright with Miranda, because more than anything, she wanted to be friends with the man she loved. She wanted someone she could laugh with, cry with; someone who was real. Miranda wanted to get to know him and find out what made him happy. Besides his guitar playing, Miranda also wanted to find out what kinds of things he liked to do. She was perfectly happy to let their friendship grow slowly and steadily.

There was one exception to their comfortable relationship, and because of that, Miranda had no doubts about what it would be like to be loved by Roger. One night, after a very romantic dinner, they decided to drive high above the city where they could park and look out over the river. Roger put the top down on his Mustang and they leaned back against the seat as soft, romantic music played on the radio. Roger's Mustang didn't have bucket seats and she loved to be able to scoot across and sit next to him.

After putting the top down, Roger reached out and casually drew her to his side. Snuggling against him, she sat quietly and enjoyed the lights from the boats which traveled along the river at night and the myriad of lights which could be seen on the far shore. It was lovely, peaceful, and enchanting. The stars were vibrant in the sky above them, and the moon a full golden globe just sitting on the horizon.

She watched, fascinated, as Roger pointed out the various constellations and stars. The Big Dipper seemed so close she felt like she could reach out and touch it. She listened in awe as Roger told her the myths and facts about the constellation Orion. "Perhaps second only to the Big Dipper in Ursa Major, the constellation of Orion is one of the most recognizable patterns of stars in the northern sky."

He moved away slightly as he showed her Orion, the Hunter, and she struggled to see the pattern he was pointing out. "Orion stands by the river *Eridanus* and is accompanied by his faithful dogs, *Canis Major* and *Canis Minor*. Together they hunt various celestial animals."

"Can you see *Lepus*, the rabbit, and *Taurus*, the bull?" he asked, as his finger traced the patterns in the sky above their heads. Her eyes eagerly followed as he pointed out the different configurations in the sky. "According to Greek mythology, Orion was in love with Merope, one of the Seven Sisters who form the *Pleiades*, but Merope would have nothing to do with him. Orion's tragic life ended when he stepped on *Scorpius*, the scorpion. The gods felt sorry for him, so they put him and his dogs in the sky as constellations. They also put all the animals he hunted up there near him. Scorpius, however, was placed on the opposite side of the sky so Orion would never be hurt by it again."

"Wow!" Miranda sighed as he stopped speaking. "Where on earth did you learn so much information?"

"Oh, I took a science class on the constellations, planets, and stars when I was in college. It is really fascinating, isn't it?"

"I love it. Maybe we can visit a planetarium soon. You've made it come alive and now I'm eager to learn more."

"Sure, we'll just have to go together one of these days," Roger smiled warmly at her, as he slipped his arm back around her shoulder. She snuggled up close to him again, her heart beating a little faster as she thought about the future.

She slowly became aware that his hand was gently moving up and down on her arm. She felt her heart flood with warmth and a flush started to bathe her skin. Soon a sensation she had never experienced before made her more than aware of what he was doing. His hand moved from her arm to slide underneath her hair as he gently ran his fingers through it. He didn't seem to be consciously aware of what he was doing, but she certainly was! Her breath became shallow and rapid.

Trying desperately to control her reactions, she sat perfectly still, her heart racing. She succeeded, temporarily, until his hand moved up to cup her chin.

Sensing what was happening to her, he gently turned her face until their lips were touching. His were soft and tender, but by now, Miranda wanted more. Her mouth opened urgently under his, her hands clutching at his shoulders as he kissed her with a hungry, mounting passion. Her senses were heightened by his touch, and she became consumed by feelings she had never known before.

Of its own volition, her body moved, pressing against his. She trembled as his lips released hers, seeking out the curve of her throat. Sighing, she let her head fall back, giving him access to her breasts. His hands moved urgently on her body, touching her breasts, her shoulders, her face, his kisses burning wherever they touched.

Cupping his face with her hands, she brought his lips back to hers, begging him for she knew not what. She felt alive all the way to her toes. Every part of her body seemed to burn with sensation. Fighting for control, Roger's breathing sounded as ragged as hers.

Suddenly, he shocked her by pulling away abruptly. When her confused eyes met his and her hands reached out for him, he shook his head as if trying to clear it and reached out and shook her urgently.

"Miranda, we have to stop, or soon we'll be unable to."

"No," she whimpered, rubbing her face against his hand. It felt so good.

"Yes, we have to stop now!" Shoving open the door, he stumbled out of the car, almost falling to his knees. Regaining his balance, he turned and walked out of her sight. Making a movement to follow him, Miranda fell back against the seat, breathing harshly. Taking a few deep breaths, she tried desperately to calm herself and slow her heartbeats down. After a couple of minutes, she slid out of the car and drank in the cool night air. There was no sign of Roger. Where on earth was he?

Returning about ten minutes later, he got into the car and turned gravely towards her. "Miranda, I'm sorry I let this get out of hand. It should never have happened. In a few more minutes I would have made love to you and you wouldn't have stopped me."

"But…"

"Shhhh…Let me finish. We haven't known each other long enough to make this kind of commitment, and if…or until we are ready to…this must never happen again. Do you understand? I don't believe in casual sex and I don't think you do either. Am I right? You've told me about your parents and many of the things they taught you growing up. From what you've told me, you want a family like you had growing up."

"My mother was very open with me about sex and relationships," Roger continued. "When I was fifteen, I learned she became pregnant and gave birth to a child before she met my father. She gave her up for adoption, and my mother never got over the loss. Because of her example, I will not disrespect a woman by having casual sex. Neither will I treat sex like it is a recreational activity as so many young people do today. I made a decision about this a long time ago."

Nodding her head numbly she remained silent, too stricken to say anything. *"What have I done? Have I ruined everything?"* kept repeating over and over in her head.

Silently, he drove her back to her apartment. After walking to the door with her he started to leave without saying anything but she put her hand on his arm, stopping him.

"Roger, nothing like this has ever happened to me before, and I didn't know how to handle it. Thanks for being strong for both of us, I'll never forget it."

"I'm just glad I was able to stop when I did. Let's try to forget this happened and go back to being good friends for a while, OK?"

Gathering her into his arms, he hugged her tightly. Sighing, he pulled slightly away from her and gazed into her eyes for a moment before leaning down and kissing her tenderly on the lips. Then he turned and walked away.

Leaning dazedly against the wall, she pressed her fingers against her lips, and watched as he got into his car and drove away, knowing she would never forget what happened. Ever! Lying in bed that night she relived every moment of their magical evening. Even if it was a mistake because they did not know each other well enough to have a more intimate relationship, she was still glad it happened. The whole evening was surreal and she felt like dancing around the room.

"I love you, Roger," she whispered.

She hugged her pillow to her, remembering every touch, every kiss. His arms around her felt so right and she would always treasure those moments with him.

"I hope there will be other times. I want to lie in your arms and make love to you." Miranda murmured as a tenderness crept over her. Realizing she was talking to herself, Miranda giggled.

Even though their relationship couldn't help but change after that night, they continued to see each other, and, after a certain amount of awkwardness, gradually got back on almost the same footing as before. For the first time since her parents died, what

Miranda was experiencing was amazing, and it was hard to wait until she could see Roger again. On every date she learned more about him and she wanted so much to spend the rest of her life getting to know everything about him.

They took off one Saturday to spend the day in Portland. It was fun walking through all the different displays, and trying the hands-on experiments at the OMSI museum. Miranda was familiar with the museum because she went there on school trips and with friends over the years. She especially liked it when they featured special exhibits such as moonrocks from the first landing on the moon. The Body Worlds exhibit blew her mind when she went with some friends to see it while the exhibit was on tour. Being there with Roger though, made everything much more special. They watched a wonderful airshow in the OMNIMAX Theater. She almost shrieked when she felt like she was upside down in one of the trick planes performing on the screen. It was so interesting, they went to watch a second show featuring great white sharks. She grabbed Roger's hand and held on tightly because it seemed like the sharks were actually coming right at her.

"Wow," Miranda shivered slightly as they left the theater. "That really scared me more than once. I felt sure a monster shark was going to swallow me!" she giggled.

Laughing, Roger agreed. "I actually thought you were going to jump out of your skin more than once. It's weird how the IMAX theaters make you feel like you're in the middle of the action, actually travelling with them. The other theaters seem tame after watching something here."

Later in the afternoon, Roger ushered her into the planetarium to watch a show on the constellations. Emotionally it took her back to the night they almost made love, and she leaned against his shoulder as she gazed up at the stars glittering overhead in the theater. She could feel her heartbeat quicken as he reached for her hand.

One unbelievable weekend, they threw their winter coats, hats, and gloves into Roger's truck and spent the day at Salt Creek Sno-Park. The day was cold and crisp with a few snowflakes drifting through the air. They rented inner tubes, spending an hour or more trudging up the tubing hill and flying back down, racing and trying to be the first to reach the bottom. It was exhilarating but their hands were soon cold, their cheeks ruddy from the wind, and fast becoming too tired to struggle back up the long hill.

On the last run, Roger's tube veered off to the left where it hit a snow pile, flipping him into the snow. Chagrinned, he was making an attempt to get to his feet, his laughter echoing up the slope, when a snowball hit him full in the face. It burst open on impact showering snow down his neck. Trying to brush the snow out of his eyes, he heard Miranda giggling and looked up to see her dance away, gathering up more snow.

"Now you've done it!" he growled as he gained his feet, grabbed a handful of snow and took chase.

"Come and get me," Miranda giggled as she sneaked behind a bush and danced out the other side, hitting him again. Two snowballs hit her as she fled, and glancing back, she was hit full in the face with two more. Whirling, ready to hit him again, her boots sank down into the snow throwing her to the ground. She was laughing so hard she tried to get back up with little success at first. Finally, she managed to gain her feet, but Roger immediately tackled her to the ground where they lay trying to catch their breath. Thinking the fight was over, she relaxed until Roger teasingly tossed snow into her face.

"Got you now," he laughed. The cold air made his breath visible in the cold morning air.

"I give," Miranda protested, clearly out of breath.

Roger was laying crosswise of her body and as she gazed into his eyes, he slowly lowered his head, his lips cold and rousing as he kissed her. She slid her arms around him, eagerly returning his kiss. Thrilled, she was disappointed when he broke the kiss and got to his feet.

"Had enough?" he asked casually reaching for her hands to pull her to her feet.

"Not near enough," Miranda thought still feeling his lips on hers, but instead she said; "I think so. I don't know if your hands are as cold as mine, but I'm ready to take a break." She reached up and put her cold hands on his face before chuckling, and heading for the lodge.

Back at the lodge they spotted a table near the fireplace and placed an order for lunch, including hot chocolate. While waiting for lunch they discussed what to do next.

Picking up a brochure, Miranda asked, "What about going to Salt Creek Falls? The brochure says it has a 'main drop', whatever that means, of 286 feet and it's the third highest plunge falls in Oregon. I guess Multnomah Falls is the highest."

"How do you propose we get there?"

"We could drive, but that wouldn't be much fun. Bye the way, do you happen to know how to cross country ski?" Miranda asked.

"I used to. It's been a while since I've skied, why?"

"We can rent cross country skis and there's a good path to the falls. It sounds like fun if you're game."

"Sounds like fun. Let's do it." Roger said as the waitress set their lunch down.

The temperature was in the mid-forties, but the sun was glistening on the snow, the wind stirring slightly through the pines. It had snowed the night before and the trees were beautiful, their branches blanketed with snow.

It took a while for them to get used to the skis, but after a few mishaps, they set off. The sound of the falls reached their ears a while before they were able to see it. Rounding a corner, they both stopped in awe to listen to the roar of the falls and watch as it cascaded over a ledge high on the cliff. It came crashing down into the gorge after washing over the huge boulders at its crest. It was such a breathtaking vision they stayed for a while just watching the flow of the water after it hit the rocks and flowed on down the river.

Both were exhausted when they arrived back at the lodge and were quiet on the drive home. Saying goodnight to Roger, she closed the door, her heart singing. *"I never dreamed my life could be this perfect,"* she thought as she got into bed.

The weeks following were like a dream come true. She noticed how he interacted with people; she went with him to serve meals for the homeless, and watched as he played touch football with random kids in the park. His laughter touched a place in her heart she thought would never heal, and made her hope for a bright and shinning future that never seemed possible before.

Chapter Ten

Sometimes Miranda felt like she was living a fairytale, but it all came crashing down around her one night when she asked Roger over to her apartment for a special dinner. It was the night everything started to go terribly wrong for Miranda. Her relationship with Cindy was so close that they often dropped in on each other without calling. She knew Cindy would be home from her trip soon and Miranda was anxious for her to meet Roger. Miranda and Roger were having a drink prior to eating when the doorbell rang. Laughing at something Roger said she opened the door to find Cindy standing there. Surprised and thrilled when she saw who was standing there, she gave Cindy a warm hug and said, "Come in sis, because there is someone I've been wanting you to meet."

When she introduced Cindy to Roger, she sensed something was different about his reaction. He couldn't seem to take his eyes off Cindy, and he didn't let go of her hand immediately.

"OK, Roger, you can let go of Cindy's hand," Miranda laughed. "I told you she was my identical twin. Now maybe you believe me, huh?"

Roger chuckled and released Cindy's hand. "Sorry, I didn't mean to stare."

Turning to Miranda he said, "She looks like you, yes, but I see subtle differences." Sweeping his hand towards Cindy, he said, "The hair... the clothes... are all different. It's fascinating."

As they talked and laughed, Roger and Cindy seemed to have an instant rapport. Feeling left out and slightly jealous, Miranda didn't know what to do.

"This can't be happening," she thought, "*I met him first! He's supposed to be mine!*"

This just wasn't like her — to be jealous of her own sister! To try to make amends for her mean thoughts, she said, "Hey Cindy, how about staying for dinner? There's plenty."

"Are you sure? I really don't want to intrude. I just came over to visit for a little while. I didn't know you had company."

"Yes, join us," Roger coaxed, not noticing the slight frown on Miranda's face.

She changed it to a smile, saying "Please do, I'd like you and Roger to get to know each other."

"Well sure, if you both say it's OK, I'll be happy too. Thanks." Cindy said. Smiling at her sister, Cindy crossed the room to sit down on the couch. Miranda hated feeling hurt when Roger went over and sat down beside her.

"Can I get you anything to drink?" she asked almost sharply.

Glancing at her sister quizzically, Cindy said, "What you're drinking's fine." Belatedly Cindy asked, "Can I help with anything?"

"No, it's fine, sis. Everything's ready. I'll just be a minute." Feeling vulnerable, but not knowing why, Miranda knew she needed a moment alone or she might start to cry. Cindy had never given her any reason in the past to feel jealous, so she couldn't understand why her feelings were so raw.

Miranda didn't want to upset Cindy and make Roger feel uncomfortable, so she made a determined effort to enjoy dinner.

Laughing and talking with them, Miranda was actually surprised to find herself enjoying the evening; that is, until she glanced up, realizing Roger was totally focused on Cindy. It was as if she wasn't in the room.

"Maybe I'm just imagining things because I love him so much, and don't want him looking at any other woman. Even my sister! After all, he looked at me the same way at Gail's party. Maybe he's just intrigued by meeting two sisters who are identical in looks but with subtle differences." These thoughts ran through Miranda's mind as she tried to understand what was happening to her.

"Why am I so insecure? I really don't understand myself, and I need to get it together." Miranda shrugged her shoulders, trying to get rid of the stress which was eating away at her.

Even though she and Cindy were identical twins, it was very easy to tell them apart. While Miranda wore her hair long, Cindy chose to have hers cut short. Soft curls framed Cindy's face, giving her a slightly pixie look. When it came to clothes, Cindy's clothes were the height of fashion, while Miranda tended to dress more moderately because of her job.

Way before their college years there was a distinct difference between the two girls. As they headed for college and the four years they were separated; except for holidays and summers, the differences became evident. Cindy was attending a college in California, training to be a dress designer, and wanted to break into the fashion industry. Miranda was studying Business Administration along with taking science courses at the University of Oregon. Miranda's goal was to become a business executive. She was considering several career choices, but she liked the idea of something in the medical industry.

Shaking herself mentally, Miranda laughed and offered to get some more coffee. She didn't know why she was having such negative thoughts tonight. After all, Cindy and Roger only just met each other.

"I just have to believe what Roger and I have is real," Miranda murmured to herself as she said goodnight to Cindy. After she left with a cheerful wave, Roger lingered for a few moments.

"Miranda, thank you so much for a wonderful and unexpected evening. Your sister was a big surprise! I'm intrigued by how different the two of you are. You said you had a twin sister but I guess I was expecting her to be more like you."

"A lot of people think the same way until they get to know us. We are very different."

"Well, I sure like her," Roger smiled. "I bet you two have a lot of fun together."

"We do. Roger, I'm so glad you came tonight. Will I see you tomorrow?"

"Not sure. I have a lot of work at the office, but I'll call. Thank you for a wonderful dinner. It's been lovely, especially meeting Cindy. She sure is different from what I expected," he chuckled. "I guess I was expecting someone exactly like you. You are calm, peaceful, and warm. Your smile is contagious, and I watch people respond to you when you smile at them. Cindy reminds me a little of a whirlwind, constantly changing and moving. I know, I've only seen her this once, but I find the differences very charming. See you soon," Roger smiled as he kissed her softly.

"Bye, Roger," Miranda said quietly as she closed the door.

After closing the door, Miranda walked over to the couch and sat down. A dull feeling of loneliness crept over her. She couldn't understand why. Cindy was home, and she was dating a wonderful man.

Roger always held Miranda's hand, their fingers intertwined, when they walked together. He would often put his arm around her when they sat together, but he always held back when it came to kissing her. Most of the time, he would kiss her lightly on the cheek or lips when saying goodbye, but there didn't seem to be much passion, except for one unforgettable moment which she could not get out of her mind.

She needed to feel his arms around her. She wanted to experience the same passion and ecstasy she had felt once before, but she sensed he was holding back and she didn't know why. She was physically and emotionally attracted to him, but she didn't know if he felt the same way. She wanted so badly to tell him she loved him, but her instinct always kept her from speaking. Maybe the fact that she was unsure about how he felt, and was afraid of getting hurt, was what kept her from saying anything.

A few times she had thought about initiating a more intimate moment, but for some reason, she always held back. He seemed to really enjoy being with her and they talked and discussed so many things; sometimes having a friendly argument when they disagreed about something. Where was the chemistry, the fire? She remembered his warm kiss at the falls, but again, he pulled away. She loved and wanted him with all her heart; and yearned for Roger to let her know he felt the same way.

She was so afraid. She didn't want to admit it even to herself, but after watching Cindy and Roger together, she acknowledged there was something between them.

She got slowly to her feet as her mind formed the words; *"I'm too scared and tired to think about it tonight, I'll face whatever comes tomorrow."*

Chapter Eleven

Even though Roger called Miranda a couple of times, and they went out to dinner and to the movies, it was not the same. Something was missing from their relationship, and Roger seemed preoccupied while asking a lot of questions about Cindy.

A few weeks later, Miranda was home alone and feeling very sorry for herself. She and a few of her friends went out to dinner at a blues nightclub a couple of times, but her heart just wasn't in it. She wanted so badly to see Roger. She called and talked to him several times, but they made no plans to do anything. Miranda didn't want to believe she was losing Roger, but what else could she think? She talked to Cindy several times a week, but nothing was mentioned about Roger; so Miranda began to think she was just imaging things until one night, her doorbell rang.

Shock whitened her face when she saw Roger standing on her doorstep. Heart pounding, she said, "Roger, this is a surprise. I haven't seen you for a while."

"I know," Roger said quietly. "Can we talk?"

"Of course," Miranda said, dread settling into her stomach. Not for one moment did she think he was there to say he loved her. Why, she didn't know, but she just felt this was not going to be something she wanted to hear.

Roger sat without speaking for a moment before turning to her. "Miranda, I know we've been seeing each other for a while and I know you like me and enjoy being with me. I really enjoy doing things with you, too."

Miranda sat without responding. Roger paused for words, then he went on; "I'm not sure how I'm going to explain myself to you. I'm so afraid of hurting you, but there's something I want to ask."

Bravely, Miranda looked up at him. "Roger, you have become very important to me and we are friends, so you can say anything you need to and I'll try to understand."

"I don't really know how to explain this. From the moment I met Cindy, I can't get her out of my mind. I've wrestled with this all these weeks, and have been unable to sleep. I know it's not right. You and I have been dating, so it's wrong for me to think about going out with your sister." He got to his feet, pacing around the living room while Miranda hid her shaking hands.

So this was it. She was not wrong about what was happening. Tears threatened as she watched Roger struggling for words. She drew a deep breath and asked, "Roger, does Cindy know about this? About how you feel?"

"No! Absolutely not! This is my struggle. I would never speak to her without your blessing." He came back and sat down, taking her hands. "Miranda, I don't want to hurt you, and if you have any objections at all, I won't say a word to her. I promise!"

Steeling herself in order to answer, Miranda said; "Roger, you are very important to me. We are friends, but I will never stand in the way of your happiness." She loved him enough to let him go. Even though she wanted so badly to wrap her arms around him, and tell him she loved him, her pride wouldn't let her. He was thinking about Cindy, not her, so she would give him her blessing.

Maybe he would realize it was just a phase with Cindy and come back to her. If not, then he didn't love her anyway.

"I know this isn't right, Miranda. I should never have asked you, and you have every right to kick me out of your life and tell me what a selfish bastard I am. I'm going to go and we will forget this conversation ever took place. Please forgive me, Miranda." Roger said as he opened the door to leave.

Miranda touched his arm before he could shut the door. "It's OK, Roger. I'll be here if you realize Cindy is not the one you want."

Roger reached for her, but she stepped back slightly. "Just go, Roger. We'll talk again."

Too numb to cry, Miranda crawled into bed. Lying there for hours, she resolved to face whatever the future held, the way she was able to when her parents died. Just as then, anger would not change anything.

Miranda immersed herself in work, trying to block out what was happening in her personal life. She ran into a friend at work and asked if he would like to go hiking one Saturday. Shawn was very happy to hear from her because they hadn't seen each other for a while. The day turned out very nice and she tried to have a good time. Being outdoors always cheered her up, but it fell short this time. After she got home, she called Cindy to see how she was doing. Cindy was not her usual, chatty self and Miranda asked her what was going on.

"I called you earlier to see if I could come over, but you didn't answer. There's something I need to discuss with you, OK?" Cindy asked.

Miranda clutched the phone and sank into a chair as she answered. "I went hiking with Shawn and I'm a little tired, but if it's important, come on over."

"OK, if you're sure. I'll be over soon."

Miranda's heart sank because she knew what Cindy wanted to talk to her about. Tears filled her eyes and slowly trailed down her cheeks. She let herself indulge in pity for a couple of minutes before washing her face and adding a light makeup.

When Cindy rang the doorbell, Miranda was composed and smiling, through sheer willpower. She was going to see what Cindy wanted to tell her and then decide what to do.

"Hi Cindy," Miranda said giving her a hug. "Haven't seen you for a few days and you are looking good."

"Thanks sis. I'm good. Just doing a lot of research for a trip I want to take next month. You know me, always looking ahead. I've also been working hard on a line of clothes for a fashion show I hope to participate in soon. How are you doing? Work going good?"

"Sure. We're always busy and will probably be getting a little busier soon, as we have a couple of very promising trials starting in the next few weeks. Would you like something to drink?" Miranda asked.

"A glass of wine would be nice. You having anything?"

Miranda nodded, and walked into the kitchen to pour them each a glass of red wine. Returning, she handed one to Cindy and said, "You said you wanted to discuss something with me. It must be important to come over this late."

Sipping her wine, Cindy seemed at a loss for words for a moment. "This is a little difficult for me to explain so I wanted to discuss it with you and see how you feel. Roger called me out of the blue the other night and we talked for a long time. Needless to say, I was surprised. I haven't seen him since we met at your house. I'm sorry I've been so busy, I haven't really asked you about your relationship with him. I assume you are dating him?"

"We...we were," Miranda said with a catch in her voice. "Actually, we've been seeing each other for several months, but we haven't seen much of each other lately. Why did he call you?"

"It's a little hard to explain. He told me you two dated for a while, and that you are good friends. I have to admit, he intrigues me. Actually, he reminds me a lot of Dad. Have you noticed it?"

Miranda scowled. "No."

"He does. I spotted it right away. He has the same crooked smile and sense of humor; two things I always recall about Dad. Remember when Dad was younger, his hair was blond, but changed to a lighter brown as he got older?"

Ignoring Cindy's comment, Miranda said a little stiffly; "So, Roger called. What did he want?"

"I thought it was a little strange, but he said he talked to you about asking me out and you assured him it was OK. Is that true? I could tell he didn't feel good about the whole situation, but he also told me he's been thinking about me a lot, and wanted to find out if his feelings were real."

"I think he's nice, but since I thought you two were dating, I wouldn't dream of doing anything to upset you. Is there anything special between the two of you? Would it bother you if I went out with him?" Cindy asked.

For a moment or two Miranda couldn't have answered if she wanted to; then, "No Cindy, Roger and I are just good friends, so you go ahead and go out with him."

"Are you sure, sis? You would tell me if there was anything I should know, wouldn't you? After meeting Roger at your apartment, I assumed you two were together. Even though I really liked him and felt drawn to him in some way, I wasn't about to do anything about it. You haven't really told me much about your relationship, which surprises me. We've always talked about things which are important to us, which made me think Roger must not be too important to you, or you would have talked to me before now."

Miranda's thoughts were in a whirl. If only she had confided in Cindy when she came home, things might be so different. Now it was too late unless she was willing to keep Roger and Cindy from pursuing their feelings. Since Roger had already called Cindy and indicated to her how he was feeling, Miranda knew she would feel foolish if she said anything different now. It was simply too late.

As Miranda struggled to keep the tears at bay until Cindy left, she said; "I'm not upset with you. You should know I would tell you if there was anything wrong. We've always tried to be honest with each other. Roger and I enjoy each other's company, but if he's asked you to go out with him, that means he's not really interested in me except as a friend."

Cindy stood up to leave and turned to Miranda, giving her a gentle hug. "You're sure, sis? You know I love you to death, and if you tell me different, I won't have anything to do with Roger."

"I'm sure." Using her last ounce of self-control, she hugged Cindy back and said goodnight as she watched Cindy walk to her car.

Tears streaming down her face, Miranda thought about her decision to let Roger go; to at least let him explore his feelings for Cindy. There was still hope it wouldn't work out and Roger would call and tell her he made a mistake. Even her pride wouldn't let her tell him she didn't want him in her life anymore. Her love was all consuming, and right now, she couldn't bear to think about her empty future without him.

Cindy was the most important person in the world to her, and even as Miranda knew she loved Roger more than she would ever love another man, Cindy must be her priority. She could not put her own happiness first. When she remembered Cindy, fragile and broken at fifteen; unable to face a world without their parents, she knew she was making the right decision. She needed to let Cindy explore a relationship with Roger to find out if there was anything between them. She could give Cindy a chance at a wonderful life even if Miranda had to give up her own dreams to make it happen. It would be worth the sacrifice to see Cindy happy.

Chapter Twelve

Feeling like her dreams of a life with Roger were crushed, Miranda was devastated. She couldn't explain, even to herself, why she fell so deeply in love with Roger. From the moment she looked into those eyes, sparkling with a warm smile which resembled a deep blue sky, Miranda felt lost. He was her first thought when she awoke each morning and, the touch of his hand was her last thought before snuggling down to sleep at night. He was in her thoughts every waking moment, and she could hardly wait to be with him.

He was smart, funny, sweet, and incredibly handsome; with a smile which took her breath away. His kindness became apparent when he went out of his way to aid an elderly woman who was struggling to load groceries, or to assist a young boy in a wheelchair; or to quickly grab a door for a mother struggling with her children. He talked about his mother who lived with the pain and disability of MS, and his father who was so gentle and caring of her. In passing, Roger mentioned how he often gave his father a break from caregiving in order for his father to spend some time with his friends.

Miranda simply loved him. She loved the man he was, his strength, gentleness, and most of all, she could not forget the passion she experienced in his arms. She loved Cindy with her whole heart but she wasn't yet ready to accept the two of them together.

For the first time in her life Miranda felt anger toward Cindy. *"Cindy, why couldn't you see how I felt about Roger?"* she asked herself bitterly. Crying, she pounded her fist on the back of the couch. *"You should have known,"* she said angrily. *"I would have!"*

Sobbing wildly, she flung herself down on the bed. Wracking pain tore at her body; making her feel helpless. Numbly, she lay there long after she couldn't cry anymore. As the long night turned into morning, she came to terms with the choices she had made. Roger might never be hers, and she would have to deal with seeing Roger and Cindy together. There was a chance they might get married someday, and that was something she would just have to accept if it did, indeed, happen.

Several weeks passed. Even though she spoke to Cindy often, Cindy didn't say much about her personal life. She did tell Miranda she and Roger were seeing each other, but Miranda felt she was trying to spare her feelings by not elaborating. From what Cindy did say, she knew they were spending a lot of time together. Cindy said she was putting off a trip to New York because she and Roger were going to a Shakespeare Festival in Ashland for the weekend.

It finally started to sink in that Cindy was getting serious about Roger. Cindy was so focused on her career, she never let anything get in the way of her travel and making connections for her future. Now, she was willing to put off an important trip to be with him. Miranda felt like she was in freefall. The life she wished and longed for was becoming out of her reach. Her only choice now was to try and pick up the pieces and create a different life from the one she wanted.

Miranda's heart finally broke the night her life changed completely. It was late when the ringing of the doorbell startled her so much she almost spilled the glass of wine she was taking to the bedroom. Work was tough lately, especially as she was feeling out of sorts; still trying to keep up the pretense that everything was OK. "*A glass of wine just might help me get to sleep*," she thought as she got ready for bed. Her apartment felt so lonely most of the time. She could almost remember a time when she used to love coming home to her quiet, peaceful home, but not anymore. There were too many ghosts.

"Who on earth could that be," she muttered. She had been feeling sorry for herself all day and missing Roger so much. She certainly didn't want to see anyone. Ignoring the bell, she continued toward the bedroom.

The ringing persisted, so finally she went to open the door. "Better be something important..." Her heart sank as she saw Cindy and Roger standing there, his arm around her, and smiles on their faces.

"Hi sis, OK if we come in?"

"Of course," Miranda said opening the door wide. "What brings you two out this late? It must be important?"

Smiling, Cindy said, "We have some news and I couldn't go to bed without sharing it."

She pulled Miranda into a hug, laughing softly. As she stepped back, she reached for Roger and faced Miranda again before holding out her left hand.

"Congratulate us!"

Miranda's eyes dropped to the stunning diamond ring on Cindy's hand. She felt the deep thud of her heartbeat, and felt her hands start to shake as she looked up at Cindy.

A trembling smile crossed her face and she pulled Cindy into a hug. "I'm happy for you." She whispered into Cindy's hair before she pulled away. "You too, Roger. I'm really happy for both of you."

"I hope we have your blessing," Roger said softly. Concern touched his face as he reached for Miranda's hand. "Are you OK with this?"

Miranda quickly pulled her hands away on the pretense of offering them some wine. As she stepped away to get the bottle, she said over her shoulder; "I'm just great and really happy for both of you." Instead of picking up the wine bottle, she turned back for a moment, her eyes searching theirs.

"You love each other?"

"More than you can imagine," Cindy said.

"I love your sister more than I ever thought it possible to love anyone," Roger said.

"Then I love you both and wish you nothing but happiness," Miranda said.

Her mind was a fog and she felt like this wasn't really happening, but deep down she knew her dreams were over. Cindy was going to marry Roger, her beloved, her heart.

Her heart breaking, Miranda watched them leave. Her dreams were shattered. She might have been able to have a different future if she had made different decisions from the beginning, but now it was too late. Way too late.

* * *

Chapter Thirteen

Now the day she dreaded, and hoped would never come was here, and she wasn't sure if she would survive. As she stood watching her sister, she thought about what a nightmare she was going through, and what she still had left to face.

When the wedding march started, she forced her feet to start moving down the aisle; *"One foot after the other, one step at a time."* Somehow, some way, she would get through this. *"Just don't look at Roger, look anywhere but at him,"* she told herself.

Who was his best man? Miranda hadn't met him before because he made the drive up just before the ceremony. To avoid looking at Roger, she found herself gazing at a very striking man. He seemed about as tall as Roger, but his hair was such a sharp contrast to Roger's she caught herself staring at him for a moment. It was jet-black and worn slightly long, curling into his collar. Even in a tuxedo, she could tell he was very well built. *"Keep your eyes on him, think about what he looks like, and just don't look at Roger,"* she thought.

With all these thoughts churning through her mind, she arrived at her place in the front of the church... Turning, she watched her sister come up the aisle. At least she didn't have to look at Roger. She had made it this far! Her sister was so beautiful, and as she came closer, Miranda could see the glow on her face, her eyes full of love as she gazed at Roger. Miranda felt tenderness well up in her chest. She wanted so badly to be completely happy for her sister and not feel this jealousy which seemed to consume her a lot of the time. *"Why couldn't Roger have been hers? Why did Cindy have to fall in love with him?"* But why think about what might have been? It was too late now.

As the ceremony started, in an effort to keep from crying, she glanced over at Roger's best man only to find him watching her. She managed to give him a brief smile and hoped he would think the tears shimmering in her eyes were from happiness.

The eyes she regarded were steel gray and seemed to see into her very soul. He couldn't be called truly handsome, as his features were hard and rugged, but he was a very good-looking man. He had the type of face which would cause women to turn and stare. Embarrassed, she turned quickly away, but in doing so, she found herself looking at Cindy and Roger.

That was almost her undoing. She flinched and pressing a hand against her stomach fought down the sudden panic she was feeling. Lightheaded, she felt for a moment as if she might pass out. Closing her eyes for a second until the faintness passed, she took a deep breath. Finally, with her feelings partially under control, she opened her eyes and looked straight into those same steel gray eyes, her cheeks growing warm as he stared at her.

She could feel an antagonism as well as sympathy coming from him. It was hard to put a name to what she was sensing. It was almost as if he felt her pain but despised her for it. Why? He didn't know her. He didn't know about the sacrifice she had made and would go on making for the rest of her life.

Her relationship with her sister would never be the same again. No matter how hard she fought it, she might always be jealous of Cindy's life. Something like this couldn't help but erode their friendship over time. Miranda decried a fate which brought so much anguish into her life.

Even though serene on the outside, she wept inside because of the loss of her childhood closeness to Cindy. She was afraid they might never again be as close as they once were. Worst of all, to survive herself, she would have to be separated by distance from the sister she loved with her whole being.

She only hoped with time, the pain would lessen and start to go away. Maybe someday, someone else would come along and help her forget, and then she could start a new life. Only at this moment in time, she didn't think anything would ever be right again...

The minister's "You may kiss the bride," startled Miranda back to reality. She heard very little of the ceremony. Moving out of Roger's embrace, Cindy turned and gave Miranda a fierce hug, and the joy on Cindy's face made it all worth it. As Miranda watched, slowing dying inside, Cindy turned a beaming face up for another kiss; before hugging Roger close to her side as they walked slowly down the aisle amidst congratulations from everyone.

Feeling more pain than she could ever imagine possible, Miranda suppressed a sob as she too started back down the aisle. Feeling someone gently take her arm, she glanced up into steel gray, questioning eyes. Knowing he couldn't help but feel the trembling in her arms, she looked away and walked as swiftly as possible toward the back of the church. It took a few moments to get through the throngs of people, but as soon as she could, she excused herself, almost running toward the bathroom. There, she checked her face and took a deep, calming breath. Sitting quietly for a few moments, she tried to compose herself enough to go back outside. As soon as she felt strong enough, and with a resolution she didn't know she possessed, Miranda put a wane smile on her face and went back out to the reception line. No matter what she must suffer, she could not ruin her sister's wedding day. Cindy's face was radiant with happiness as she gave Miranda an exuberant hug.

"I'm so happy, Miranda," she whispered.

Miranda gave her a fierce hug in return and then said, "That's wonderful, darling. Stay happy for me, OK? I have some news for you before you leave for your honeymoon, so be sure and talk to me before leaving."

She chose not to tell Cindy about her job situation earlier, because she knew Cindy would try to get her to change her mind. Miranda put off telling her until the last possible moment. This way, she hoped, Cindy would be so excited about her honeymoon, that she wouldn't make it so hard for Miranda to leave. Hopefully, by the time they got back, Cindy would accept Miranda's decision.

Miranda knew she wouldn't be able to take a lot of questions without breaking down in front of Cindy. She had been through so much the last few months in an effort to keep Cindy in the dark about her true feelings for Roger; so now she just needed to keep up the act for a while longer. The consequences of Cindy finding out now were too horrible to contemplate. She would just have to stay strong for just a little while longer...

Chapter Fourteen

Now, standing alone in the atrium, Miranda faced the fact that even though her personal life was in tatters around her, she must go and say goodbye to Cindy and Roger. She had already been away too long, and it surprised her when Cindy didn't send someone to look for her. The last hour took every ounce of energy she possessed; and it was hard to smile and laugh through one photograph after another. She was afraid when they got the pictures back, that her smile would look unnatural.

Cindy's request a few days earlier for Miranda to give a toast left Miranda wondering how she would be able to do so. As everyone lifted their glasses, Miranda found an inner strength she didn't know she possessed as she got to her feet. Despite her heart breaking, she was able to stand and honor the sister she loved. She loved Roger, but Cindy was a part of her; her other half, and she would always put her first.

"Everything changes, and yet, everything stays the same. I love you Cindy, for your strength, your kindness, and your sparkling, captivating personality which draws people to you. I love you so much sis, and that will never change. We are a part of each other. I wish with all my heart, Mom and Dad could have been here to watch you marry the man you love." She paused for a moment, eyes sparkling with tears.

"You, my dear sister, deserve every hope and dream you've ever had." Miranda's voice was strong as she spoke. "Roger, I...I love you as a friend and as my brother-in-law. I'm trusting you to always take care of Cindy and make her happy. Cheers!" Smiling sweetly, Miranda lifted her glass to her lips before slowly sinking into her chair.

She watched silently as the cake was cut and laughter surrounded her. It was over. Cindy and Roger were truly husband and wife and her dream of a life with Roger was gone. Even though she was truly happy for them, Miranda hated herself for the jealousy she felt as she watched achingly from the sidelines.

Steeling her resolve, Miranda walked quickly across the room toward where her sister was standing, surrounded by friends. Sensing someone was watching her, she glanced up and found herself staring at the man who helped get her through the wedding ceremony; unbeknownst to him. Realizing she should go and meet him, she walked over to where he stood.

"Hello, I just realized you and I still haven't been introduced. I'm Miranda."

Instead of answering immediately, she looked up to find him quietly studying her. He had a questioning look in his eyes as if trying to understand what was going on with her.

"Yes, I know," he grinned and continued, "Even a fool could see you are Cindy's twin, but I still didn't know your name, until I asked Roger a few minutes ago. It's nice to meet you. I'm Brian."

Miranda wasn't surprised by his firm grip when she put her hand into his. What did surprise her was the sudden tingling which ran along her arm. Shivering slightly, she pulled her hand out of his and rubbed it against her arm to get rid of the strange sensation. When she looked up at him again, she found him once again studying her face, a puzzled look in his eyes.

94

"It was a beautiful wedding," he stated.

"Yes, it was lovely, and Cindy was breathtaking, wasn't she?" Miranda asked.

"Absolutely stunning, but I haven't met your parents. Now that I think about it, they weren't in any of the wedding pictures. I also recall, you mentioned wishing they were here. Were they unable to make it?"

A sadness came into Miranda's eyes before she said, "No, they're not here. They died when Cindy and I were young. A drunk driver ran through the barrier on the freeway and hit them head-on. They both died shortly after."

"I'm sorry. I didn't mean to bring up such a painful subject," Brian murmured.

"There's no way you could have known." Miranda said. "I just wish they could have been here for Cindy's wedding. I miss them so much. They would have been so happy for her."

"Of course they would have. It must have been sad for Cindy not having them here. Roger's a terrific guy and will make her a wonderful husband."

"Have you known him very long?" Miranda asked curiously.

"Sure, we've been friends for several years and went to college together."

At that moment, Cindy announced she was ready to throw the bouquet, so Miranda joined the others as they excitedly tried to be the one to catch it. *"Just a few more minutes,"* she prayed, *"and it will all be over!"* Then Miranda could go home and cry her heart out. Because she wasn't paying attention, she didn't notice the bouquet Cindy deliberately tossed to her. The bouquet almost hit Miranda before she flinched and caught it, just in time before it landed on the floor.

Shocked surprise showed on Brian's face as a few minutes later, the casually tossed garter landed in his unsuspecting hands, amidst a lot of mirth. Miranda glanced over at Cindy to find her eyes twinkling as she gave Miranda a thumbs up, before she and Roger ran out of the room. Surprised, she turned and looked at Brian. He was staring down at the garter in his hand. Sensing her attention, his eyes slowly lifted. Hazel eyes clashed with eyes the color of the sky just before dark. Unable to look away for a moment, Miranda studied his face before turning and walking away.

Now, it was time to go up and help Cindy change. Miranda hated to tell Cindy about her move to Medford, but it was something she could no longer put off. Miranda was very unhappy about leaving Cindy and moving away. Making new friends would not be easy, either. Miranda was hoping that maybe, in the isolation of a strange town, she would learn to live with the pain of knowing Cindy and Roger were now married.

Thinking of them in each other's arms tonight was almost unbearable; Miranda knew she must somehow get through the next few minutes, without giving herself away. She had made it this far, surely, she could let Cindy go away on her honeymoon without knowing anything was wrong. Tomorrow, Miranda would start packing, and in a few days, she would have something else to concentrate on. Maybe not being around Roger all the time would lessen the pain? She hoped time and distance would help her start to put her life back together again.

Walking quickly upstairs, she helped Cindy out of her wedding gown and into her beautiful maroon two-piece suit.

Slipping into the skirt, Cindy looked at her and asked, "Where did you go? I was so busy with everyone it took me a while to realize you were not around."

"I got a little tired and slipped away for a few minutes. I guess all the music and organized chaos got to me and I needed a break," said Miranda. "By the way, I know you asked me not to throw you a party last night because you were so exhausted, but, I still feel guilty about not doing anything. I should have organized a family dinner."

"I thought a lot about it and Roger and I discussed what we should do," Cindy said. "We agreed we were both exhausted and just wanted a quiet night. We went over to see Roger's parents for a little while. They are really nice, but his mom is not doing too well right now. Did you get a chance to meet them?"

Not wanting to admit she was deliberately avoiding Roger's parents because she knew meeting them would be painful, she just said, "No, not yet. I'll meet them sometime later. I noticed they left shortly after the ceremony."

"Roger said she was in a lot of pain, so his dad took her home. I'm just glad they were able to make it."

"Now, let me look at you for a minute," Cindy said. "I've been so busy and caught up with everything I've forgotten to ask how you are doing. I'm sure all this chaos with the wedding has been a trial." Wrapping her arms around Miranda, Cindy hugged her tight. "I'm going to miss you, you know."

"I know," Miranda sighed hugging her back. "Life will be different for both of us, but that's what's supposed to happen. We're

97

expected to, and want to build our own lives, separate from each other. I'm so happy you've found your happiness. Roger is one of a kind and will make you happy. By the way, you look so lovely," she murmured.

"Thanks, and now what was it you wanted to talk to me about?" Cindy asked.

"I hate to tell you this, but you're married now, and have Roger to take care of you. So what I have to tell you might not be so hard for you to hear. I answered a posting for a very good executive position with the company. It would be a really big promotion, but the only problem with it is, I'll have to move to Medford."

"Oh, no!" cried Cindy, "You can't be serious!"

"I'm sorry, but it was just too good to pass up. I am to be the president's right hand which will give me a lot more responsibility. It's a wonderful step up for me. Be happy for me, please Cindy. I need a change in my life right now."

"Well why couldn't you have found something in Eugene?"

"Don't be silly! Do you know how hard it is for a woman to get the kind of position I've just been offered? It's a once in a lifetime chance, and I just couldn't afford to pass it up." Trying to act casual Miranda joked, "I could become vice president, or maybe even president someday, you know."

Trying desperately to get Cindy to accept her decision without a lot of struggle, she quipped, "Women have come a long way, you know." She was quickly running out of reserves and knew she would not be able to hold it together much longer. She was so tired and unhappy all she wanted to do was lay down somewhere, and go to sleep for a very long time.

"No, I mustn't think this way. This is self-destructive, and I am made of stronger stuff." Miranda acknowledged to herself.

"Don't be silly, Miranda, I know you could become anything you want to, but I'm going to miss you so much. What will I do without you?" Cindy asked, unable to stop the tears which rolled down her cheeks.

"I know, darling. I'll miss you too, but I promise I'll keep in touch, and we'll see each other often," Miranda said, feeling the tears hanging on her lashes. Swiping at the tears, she pulled Cindy into her arms, hugging her tightly.

Muffled against her shoulder Miranda heard; "Promise?"

"Yes, I promise. We probably won't see each other as much as we would like, but I'll call you every week and try to get up to see you as soon as I can. Of course, you can always come to see me." Keeping their arms around each other they clung together for a moment.

After kissing Cindy tenderly, Miranda said, "Let's go find that husband of yours. He's sure to be getting anxious by now."

"I'm sure he is too," Cindy said, laughing tearfully.

After quickly repairing their makeup, they hurried downstairs.

"I know you'll have a wonderful honeymoon, sis. Have you decided where you are going to live?"

"Probably Roger's house for a little while. We've talked about finding another place but with our work schedules, it may take a while."

"Just let me know when you guys get back and get settled," Miranda said.

"We will, and you send us your new address and phone number as soon as you have it."

"I'll call and leave it on your answering machine, so you can call me when you get back." Shoving her teasingly, Miranda said, "Now go and find Roger. I'm sure he is missing you already. He's waited long enough."

Roger was eagerly watching for them and slipped his arm around his wife. "I missed you," he said. "What took you so long?"

"I'll tell you about it later, darling. Let's get out of here."

"I thought you'd never be ready to leave. Let's go before something else delays us, shall we?"

Laughing, Cindy threw a teasing look back at him as she said, "I know somebody who can't wait to get on with their honeymoon."

Miranda heard him murmur; "Just wait until I get you alone, lady!" Cindy gave Miranda a final hug, turned, and left to go outside. Most of the guests were chatting and waiting to toss rose petals in the air as Roger and Cindy waved goodbye.

Now Miranda knew she must force herself to go and say goodbye to Roger. He held out his arms and she slowly moved into them. As he bent to give her a goodbye kiss, she turned her face so his lips touched hers. She couldn't help it; she needed to feel his lips on hers just one more time. Her heart was thundering in her chest and she felt as if time stood still. She broke the kiss and slowly moved out of his arms.

Roger paled slightly as he looked down at her, a question in his eyes. *"Don't let him guess how I feel,"* she prayed. Before he could say anything, she smiled and touched his shoulder lightly. "Cindy's waiting. You'd better get going."

He put out his hand, gently touched her face, and said, "We'll see you when we get back." Numbly, she watched him leave, before turning away. Leaning her head against the wall, after watching him walk away, she struggled to hold back her tears. She felt weak and overwhelmed by everything. When she was finally able to look up, she found Brian observing her again. Before she could move, he was at her side.

"Miranda, you don't look well. Is there anything I can do?" Brian asked quietly.

Looking up at him, tears shimmering in her eyes, she said, "No, just leave me alone, I'm OK."

Before Brian could respond, Miranda turned on trembling legs and hurried out to her car. Sliding behind the wheel, she put her head down on the steering wheel, fighting her tears. She was afraid if she allowed herself to cry she would never be able to stop. It seemed like an eternity, although it was only a few moments, before she was able to sit up and get the car started. She managed to drive the short distance to her apartment. Once there, she couldn't seem to find the energy to move.

Miranda sat there, her mind churning; thoughts of how overwhelming her life was now compared to a year ago. She was unable to stop these thoughts from running around and around in her head. How on earth was she able to get through the last few months? Where had the strength come from to get her through the wedding today and say goodbye to Cindy and Roger without totally breaking down? Even though her faith was weak, Miranda believed God gave her the strength to keep going. She was so thankful Cindy and Roger were finally married, and the torment was over so she could start to build a new life for herself.

She thought about her weight loss and wondered how she managed to get through the last few weeks without Cindy noticing. It made no sense to Miranda, but that's what happened.

Since Miranda knew she lost a whole dress size, she must have been covering up extremely well. She knew her clothes were baggy, and her face held a slightly gaunt look. Before the wedding, she went to an exclusive shop to find a makeup which would cover up her pallor but wouldn't make her look artificial. Although she knew makeup could only do so much, she hoped for a miracle! It must have worked because several people told her how beautiful she looked. Kathrine was a miracle worker and the dress fit her perfectly without showing the weight she lost.

Today's ordeal weakened her so badly, she could barely move. She couldn't recall the last time she ate anything. She remembered nibbling at a piece of wedding cake, but it made her feel nauseated, so she put it down. She felt lethargic and weak, and her whole body seemed to be trembling.

Somehow, she managed to get from the car to the steps. Once there, she put her hands to her aching breasts, as she sank onto the steps with a whimper. She wanted Roger so much. She could almost feel his hands touching her, his lips kissing hers. The sound which came from deep inside her seemed to come from her very soul. It was a high keening sound, like that of an injured animal.

With a moan, she slumped back against the steps. Feeling faint, she just sat there for a few moments until she gained the strength to get to her feet. Weakly, she made her way to the door and tried to unlock it. Fumbling, she dropped the keys. When she leaned over to pick them up, she slumped forward into a welcome oblivion.

Chapter Fifteen

Miranda woke up disoriented. She lay on the couch in her living room with something wet and cold pressed to her forehead. She glanced out of the window and realized it was dark. The last thing she remembered was trying to get the door opened. Puzzled, she tried to remember getting into her apartment; but nothing came to her...it was all a blank.

An unfamiliar sound, like the rustle of paper, startled her as she looked up to find Brian sitting in a chair next to her with a newspaper in his hand. "What on earth?" she whispered.

Questions churned through her mind. *"How did I get inside? Did Brian help me? I don't remember opening the door. Did he follow me home from the wedding? And, if so, why?"*

"Brian," she murmured, "What are you doing here?"

"I'm glad to see you awake, finally. You didn't look very well when you left the reception; and I was worried about you," he said softly. "As it turned out, it's a good thing I followed you home."

"How long have I been asleep?" Miranda asked weakly.

"Several hours," Brian answered. "Do you have any brandy in the house?"

"I...I think...so. It's somewhere in the kitchen. Why?"

"I think it will be good for you," Brian answered. "It's obvious to me you've been under a lot of stress. Just lie still and I'll get you some," he said. A moment later he was back holding the glass up to her mouth. He managed to get her to take a sip or two before she pushed his arm away and lay back against the pillow on the couch.

A shudder passed through her and a small moan escaped. Trembling, she turned her face into the pillow and cried as if her heart would break. Alarmed by her vulnerability and unhappiness, Brian slid onto the couch and lifted her so she lay against his chest.

"Just let it all out, Miranda. You'll feel better."

"I'll never feel better, I just want to die!" Her slight frame shook as sobs wracked her body, and to Brian she sounded like a small, wounded animal. Not knowing what else to do, he held her while she wept. Brian hoped it was some small comfort to her knowing that someone was there. Soon, his shirt was soaked with her tears, but Brian wasn't about to move her. At last, too spent to cry anymore, she lay exhausted against him.

Sliding to the edge of the couch, Brian picked her up. He looked down at her as she lay in his arms, seeing the trace of tears on her pale cheeks. He was really scared for her, and from the way she trembled, he was afraid she was very weak. While carrying her into the bedroom, he bent and lightly kissed her cheek. "Poor Miranda," he murmured. "I wish I knew what happened to you and what I could do to make it better."

She didn't seem to be aware of anything; and felt like a ragdoll as he laid her carefully on the bed. He sat on the edge of the bed, and pondered what to do next.

"Miranda?" he said quietly.

She opened her eyes for a moment, looked at him, but couldn't seem to focus.

"Miranda!"

But she had already closed her eyes and didn't respond.

He stood and looked down at her; trying to decide what to do. She probably needed something to eat, but he didn't seem to be able to wake her up enough to find out. Deciding to let her sleep for a while, he walked over to a chair by the window and picked up a light blanket he saw laying there. Bringing it back to the bed, he started to cover her with it, and then stopped. She was still in the dress she wore to the wedding and he knew she couldn't be comfortable lying there. It was a beautiful dress, but it was long, with several layers, and could easily become twisted around her. He didn't know much about sleeping in a dress, but he knew how uncomfortable sleeping in clothes could get from twisting and turning. With no other solution, he sat her up, cautiously unzipped the dress, and eased her arms out of it. Then he slipped it over her hips, before carefully carrying it to the closet and hanging it up.

With a quiet tread he moved over to her dresser looking for a nightgown. He couldn't find anything but several silky, feminine gowns, so he chose a yellow one, hoping she wouldn't get cold.   Not wanting to intrude on her privacy any more than necessary, he eased her out of her slip, and then gently slipped the gown over her head. Miranda was a striking woman. She was not only beautiful, but there was a vulnerability about her which struck him more than once during the day. She obviously loved her sister very much, but at times he would have sworn she was unhappy; and now she was in so much pain. He couldn't help but wonder why. The only way he could think to help her was to stay until he saw that she was doing alright.

He pulled the covers up over her shoulders and started to move away. Miranda made a soft sound and reached for his hand, surprising him. "Don't go, please," she murmured, "Please don't leave me."

"I'm not going to leave you," he said tenderly as he reached for her hand. "I'll stay as long as you need me." Even though she clung to his hand, he was able to slip his out of hers for a moment so he could move to the other side of the bed. He removed his wet shirt and tossed it aside as he slid into bed with her. Trying not to scare her, he put his arm under her shoulders, pulling her close against him, and cuddled her head against his warm chest.

Feeling her soft, warm body against his, he knew it wasn't going to be easy to get through this night himself; but she seemed so weak and defenseless. He just couldn't go and leave her like this... She might do something to hurt herself, and he couldn't live with himself if some harm came to her because he left her alone and miserable. As he lay there, his thoughts returned to earlier that day. All day he found his eyes drawn to her and wondered why the others, especially Cindy, couldn't see the pain she was hiding. Even he could see the pallor under her makeup and her eyes held a haunted look. Maybe she was ill and was not willing to tell anyone, but he still couldn't understand how those closest to her didn't realize she was in trouble.

It was a very long night for Brian. He lay for hours listening to her soft breathing. Occasionally, she would thrash out restlessly mumbling words too low for him to catch, but he couldn't miss the pain in her voice.

"It's OK, Miranda. I'm here. Go back to sleep," he said softly. "Everything will look better tomorrow. Shhh..."

Even though he wasn't sure she knew who was with her, his voice seemed to calm her because she would settle back to sleep for a while.

Just as the dawn was breaking, Brian finally managed to fall into a troubled sleep. Awaking slowly, and slightly disoriented from lack of sleep, he felt a soft, warm body snuggled against him. With a tenderness which surprised him, he looked down at her; so softly nestled close to him. As he moved slightly, she lifted her hands and touched his chest and ran her hands over his shoulders. Sighing, she snuggled closer and lifted her face to his. Not fully awake and unable to resist, he softly kissed her cheek. Warm, moist lips covered his face with tender kisses until, incapable of resisting her any longer, his lips sought hers. A sigh whispered softly from her throat, and she seemed to come alive in his arms. As her lips parted, her hands burned as they stroked and caressed; tender fingers touched his nipples which hardened at her touch, lips pressing soft kisses to his burning skin, her mouth warm and alluring.

Aroused, Miranda slid her arms up his shoulders, moving closer to his hard, male body, entangling their legs. He gathered her to him, his hands sweeping down her spine, and molding her body to his. As he thrust his hands into her hair, her head fell back as his lips burned a trail down to her throat. His whole body ached for her, and when she took his hand and guided it to cover her aching breasts, he felt a groan move up from his throat.

"Roger, oh Roger," she whispered, "Please make love to me."

Roger! Instantly, his body turned to stone. Stunned, he lay there unable to move. Unsteady, he wrapped his arms around her tightly to still her body's movements because he needed to regain some control over his own body. "It's OK, Miranda. Just go back to sleep. It will be better tomorrow," he murmured, as he felt her slowly sink back into the oblivion of sleep. As soon as he felt her relax, he slowly levered himself out of bed.

Going over to the window, he pushed it open, and took a few deep breaths. He leaned his hands on the window sill struggling to straighten out his thoughts. He felt as if someone kicked him in the stomach. He couldn't ever remember experiencing such aching pain in his life; he wanted her so badly, and it took all his strength to resist crawling back into bed with her. It wouldn't be him she was making love to, and he certainly was not going to be a stand-in for his best friend. He was shocked by his immediate physical attraction to her. He remembered feeling it like a kick in the gut when she walked up the aisle, and he sensed his destiny was walking toward him. Brian didn't usually give in to fantasies, and this really confused him.

After the initial shock of hearing her utter Roger's name wore off, he turned slowly to look at Miranda. She seemed to be peacefully sleeping, and he felt for his own peace of mind, he should leave. Brian was ashamed of himself for letting things get out of control in the first place.

He wasn't sure what Miranda would remember when she awoke. She had spoken his name when she woke up earlier, but he still wasn't sure if she was completely aware of his presence. He also hoped she would think it was all a dream, and knew it would be best if he left before she woke up. She didn't have a fever and seemed to be able to function.

Brian thought about leaving a note, and under different circumstances, he would have done so. She was in love with her brother-in-law, and Roger was his best friend. Getting involved did not seem like a wise thing to do in this instance.

Brian made his way into the living room and sat for a few moments thinking about Miranda and what she was going through. He was still reeling from what happened with her, and he didn't want to drive while he was this distraught. Finally, he tiptoed back into the bedroom to check on her before he let himself out the front door and headed for his car. It was a long trip and he really wasn't looking forward to it. He was afraid it would be a long time before he got a certain beautiful blond out of his head. He knew Miranda was unique, and he would probably never meet anyone like her again.

Before starting the car, he sat for a moment, head bowed. It was going to be much harder to say goodbye than he thought, and was surprised when he felt tears on his face as he looked back at her apartment. This certainly wasn't like him.

He knew there was always the chance they would meet again, since he and Roger were such close friends; it wasn't unusual for them to get together a couple of times a year. Maybe he would meet Miranda again.

Brian wasn't sure if the prospect of seeing her again made him happy or not. This wedding was one of the hardest and most intriguing weddings he ever attended. *"Do I need this kind of drama in my life right now?"* he sighed as he started the car. All he knew was that she fascinated him, and under any other circumstances, he would have made sure to see her again. He hoped someday she would be able to put Roger behind her and go on to find someone who could make her happy.

Despite knowing part of the story behind Miranda's heartbreak, Brian was still captivated by the lovely woman he just left. He hoped someday to hear Roger's side of the story.

After first seeing her today, she intrigued him. It was almost immediately clear to him she was hurting, especially during the wedding. Her eyes looked haunted, and he couldn't help but see her eyes sparkling with unshed tears. She disappeared for awhile after the wedding and even though he tried to find her, no one seemed to know where she was. Later, her smile seemed unnatural as she moved among the guests, and he got the impression she was miserable; but doing a good job of hiding it from others.

Fascinated by the situation, he paid close attention to the relationship between the two sisters. They seemed very close, loving, and affectionate with one another. He wasn't even sure himself what he was sensing. Maybe it was just his imagination!

He was just getting ready to step outside with everyone else, when he noticed Miranda and Roger together. Intrigued, he watched her body language with Roger and was surprised when she kissed him. It wasn't a passionate kiss, but it still shocked him a little.

Now, after spending time with her for the last few hours, and knowing she was in love with Roger, it made a little sense, but it left questions in his mind about his best friend. He really hoped Roger had not been playing fast and loose with Cindy and Miranda.

Knowing Roger, he sincerely doubted that to be the case. Roger was one of the most honorable men he knew, and he would bet there was a reasonable explanation.

Brian found himself wishing there was more time to find out what was going on. Now he knew part of the story, but would love to learn more about Miranda and Roger's history. "Unfortunately," he sighed, "unless I ask Roger, I guess it will just have to remain a mystery, but I sure hope Roger and Cindy will be happy."

Now, turning his thoughts toward the dinner he missed the night before, he pulled out of the driveway and headed for the nearest restaurant.

* * *

Later in the morning, Miranda awoke slowly. Feeling bewildered and numb with pain, she felt a gnawing in her stomach. She sensed there was something she should remember about the previous evening, but she couldn't wrap her mind around anything concrete. There was the fleeting memory of someone holding her... was it her imagination or was someone with her during the night; calming her down and letting her sleep peacefully? Miranda wondered how it could be anything but a dream because she still felt totally alone.

She touched her lips and wondered why they felt bruised. As she shifted in bed, she realized she was in one of her nightgowns. "*How did I get undressed?*" she wondered aloud. "*I don't remember much beyond waking up here in bed.*" Bewildered, she continued to toss and turn with her thoughts. Miranda realized she wasn't sure of anything after she drove home from the wedding.

"Was Brian really in my house, or was he part of my fantasies as well?" Did he hold me in his arms while I cried, or am I going crazy?" As Miranda lay there in confusion, she vaguely remembered the fiery burn of alcohol in her throat. *"Why would Brian even be in her apartment? Since they didn't know each other, how could he have known where she lived?"* As Miranda tossed and turned, her mind completely muddled, she wasn't sure there would ever be any answers to her questions. Shivering slightly, she crawled back under the covers assuming it must have all been a dream, or her imagination working overtime. She knew she should really get up and get something to eat, but sleep would make her pain go away for a little while longer. No matter what, sooner or later she would have to face tomorrow.

Chapter Sixteen

It took so much courage for Miranda to stumble out of bed a few hours later and make herself something to eat; intrinsically she knew if she didn't start taking care of herself, she might just curl up and die. She believed she embodied too much fortitude, spirit, and strength of character to just give in and let life destroy her.

"I've proved over and over how strong I am," Miranda said staunchly. "I gave up my chance of a wonderful future and I would gladly do it again. My sister's happiness means more to me than my own life. I will not let depression rule me. I will make a new life! I will!"

It was like stumbling around in the dark. Miranda wondered if her life would ever be the same again. She remembered a time when she was happy and carefree — content with her life. Often these days, she found herself wishing she never met Roger. She loved her job and enjoyed having a lot of friends. She knew plenty of men who loved to take her out. In the past, a couple of her dates developed into more than casual relationships, but they never led to anything beyond a few kisses, and light fondling. Whenever her date found out she wasn't into casual sex, he would either leave her alone or ask her out again and treat her with respect.

Miranda dated a lot from the time she was a senior in high school and through her college years; typical for her age. She observed her friends fall in and out of love, sleep with various partners, and sympathized with two of her closest friends dealing with an unexpected pregnancy. Her friend, Marion, decided to have her baby and raise the child with the help of her parents. Her boyfriend wanted nothing to do with being a father so he broke up with her immediately after learning about the pregnancy. Thankfully, with the help of her parents, she was able to continue with her college education and got her degree as a biochemist.

Her other friend, Breanna, chose to have an abortion, and Miranda watched her suffer; her grief almost devastating her. She didn't have the support of her family or the boyfriend and her depression was overwhelming, causing her to quit college.

Miranda wanted to concentrate on her education, and simply wasn't interested in a serious relationship while in college. Some of the men she dated were simply into having sex, and not interested in an honest relationship anyway. She would never take sex lightly, because without a physical and emotional bond, sex was just sex. To Miranda, it would have been a physical act, just like playing a game of basketball, nothing else. One date was all she needed and they were history.

She had several male friends who were a lot of fun and she enjoyed going out with them. She loved having heated debates about politics, sports, and any other hot topic, and valued the camaraderie; but never became emotionally involved with any of them. She never forgot her mom's advice about her responsibility as a woman; but she often wondered why she wasn't experiencing the same yearnings and desires her friends were. She liked and enjoyed her male friends. They were fun to be with, but their kisses never left her breathless and longing for more.

Miranda knew the death of her parents at an early age caused her to shut down emotionally in many ways, but she wasn't completely innocent. It was just that no man had touched her heart, leaving her trembling, yearning for love; causing her to lose control over her emotions and actions. She never felt the excitement that seemed to be so prevalent in today's society. The few romance books she tried to read left her skipping over the steamy sex scenes because they embarrassed her and left her wondering if a lot of it came from the imagination of the writer.

Roger changed all of that. He was the first man to make her understand what it could be like between a man and a woman. Only Roger opened her eyes to a world of passion and love, and suddenly she understood what the novelists were writing about. Her heart opened and from the moment she met him, he was never far from her thoughts.

Miranda dreaded all the things she needed to do to get ready to move. Thankfully, the company was doing all the major packing and moving. It was just a matter of organizing everything, packing a few precious mementos; some of which she treasured and would never part with because Roger gave them to her. After working hard for a couple of hours, her strength ebbed. Miranda picked up her favorite stuffed cat and curled up on the couch. She loved it because it was a gift from Roger. Her mind wandered back to a day she and Roger spent together...

They walked hand in hand along a beautiful garden pathway, enjoying the fall flowers and trees which were now glorious in their rich autumn colors of red-gold, orange, russet and crimson. Later, they sat under a huge oak, enjoying a picnic lunch.

There was a local fair in town and as they wandered through the games, Roger stopped to play the "Ping-Pong Ball and Fishbowl" game. She laughed until tears ran down her cheeks as he tried over and over to get the ball to bounce into the small fishbowl. After seven tries, he triumphantly presented her with a soft, stuffed cat which almost appeared real.

Tears dried on her cheeks as she fell into a fitful sleep. Her dreams haunted her and she awoke feeling more alone than ever.

Cindy and Roger were taking two weeks for their honeymoon, and she wanted to be gone before they returned. She planned to get to Medford ahead of the moving van and would hopefully have somewhere for them to unload by the time her furniture arrived. She would have plenty of time to get moved and settled because her boss didn't expect her to start her new job for three weeks.

She knew she couldn't survive another meeting with Roger until she was able to get a little perspective in her life. She was hoping her new job would help by keeping her so busy that there was no time to think. She felt as if she was only half-alive for the last few days and was really frightened of the pain she would start to experience when this feeling of numbness finally disappeared.

The days were hectic and busy, but the nights were long and lonely. The weather didn't help either. The beautiful sunny days turned rainy and dark. It seemed to match her mood. The evening fog lay like a shroud along the river, making the nights appear darker than they were.

Eugene was home to Miranda and Cindy. They were born there and even the thought of leaving made her sad because it would always be home to Miranda. Eugene was a delightful, small town, and because of the hippie influence it was quite a bit different from other towns and cities. The University of Oregon was home to the Oregon Ducks, famous for football, basketball, and baseball. Lane Community College was home to the Titans, well known as well because of the varied sports played there; basketball, baseball, cross country, track and field, are all popular sports at the college. Eugene has a rich history in music and arts, much of which got its influence from the hippie population.

The Willamette River, which runs directly through Eugene, meanders from the mountains down through the Willamette Valley and on to Portland. Miranda and Cindy spent some happy, carefree times with their parents rafting, swimming, and learning to fish on the river. Some of the most beautiful nature trails can be found along the river; and Miranda remembered many hours of hiking along these paths and trails.

The steady months of rainfall, wind, and stormy weather was something Miranda never got used to, along with most of the population in the Northwest. However, there were so many times she could remember enjoying the rain. She smiled when she thought of how often, as young girls, she and Cindy would run outside into the rain to play until they were both soaking wet. The scolding from their mother never seemed to deter them the next time. Trina scolded them because she was terrified of them getting caught in a lightning storm.

Warm, beautiful weather right now might have helped lighten her spirit, but there didn't seem to be an end in sight. The rain continued a steady downpour for the next several days.

Chapter Seventeen

Miranda's job kept her preoccupied during the day since she wanted to finish out a few more days at the office. Saying goodbye to old friends wasn't easy, but it kept her mind from dwelling on what might have been. She knew she would be seeing them again from time to time, for the simple reason that she would be working for the same company. She assumed she would be making trips back to Eugene in the course of her employment, besides her trips back to visit Cindy. But, she knew life just kept changing and friends often grew away from each other when there was a distance between them.

She found it especially hard to say goodbye to Shawn. Before Roger entered her life, she thought that maybe she and Shawn would become more than just friends. He was a fun companion, a true friend, and she hated saying goodbye to him.

"I am really going to miss you, Miranda," Shawn said sadly. "I look forward to coming into work every day because I know you will be there. Promise me you will keep in touch. I'm really going to miss our outings with the horses."

"Me too," Miranda said. "I loved riding out into the country with you. I won't forget you, and yes, I will call. When I come back, which will probably be often since Cindy lives here, I'll get in touch and we can go riding. Deal?"

"Deal," Shawn said as he held her tightly for a long moment. "Promise you will take care of yourself. The next time we meet, I want to see the happy, carefree, Miranda I know and love,

OK?" Tears shimmered on his eyelashes and a tear trailed down his cheek as he held her hand tightly before releasing her.

"I'll try. I promise," Miranda said as she turned away before Shawn could see the tears in her eyes.

A few days before she left for Medford, Miranda asked Kelsey if she would like to come over for dinner. Miranda felt so guilty about making Kelsey a scapegoat when she made up the story about problems at work. For a while, Miranda was scared Cindy would seek Kelsey out at work and accuse her of hurting Miranda. After all, she, Cindy, and Kelsey knew each other from their years together at school. Cindy's first instinct was to protect Miranda, just as Miranda was protecting Cindy now. Miranda gave a sigh of relief when nothing happened.

She was so tired of her own company and the walls seemed to close in on her as the evening wore on. She hoped Kelsey would help her forget her misery for awhile. She and Kelsey had been good friends in high school and it was a wonderful surprise when they ended up working for the same company. She was so ashamed that she had grabbed on to a quick solution to her problems and used Kelsey as a scapegoat. Kelsey certainly didn't deserve to be treated that way even though she was unaware of what Miranda had done.

Kelsey arrived just as she was putting dinner on the table. They ate while talking quietly about the company and Miranda's move. Even though she tried, Miranda couldn't seem to concentrate on the conversation. Her mind kept slipping back in time.

Knowing her so well, Kelsey sensed the black mood Miranda seemed to be in, even though she tried to be cheerful.

"Miranda, what's wrong? I know your sister just got married to a fabulous guy, and you'll soon be starting out on a wonderful new career. I would have thought you would be excited, yet you seem so miserable."

Kelsey looked at her closely for a moment, letting her eyes brush over Miranda's body. Seriously, she said, "I know you've lost weight, and I can see how pale you've become. Your cheeks are almost gaunt, and you have dark circles under your eyes."

Sitting on the couch and taking both her hands Kelsey asked, "Are you sick and haven't told anyone? I've wanted to ask you for a while, but you've been so busy I didn't want to bother you. Maybe I should have." Pleading, she asked, "Please tell me what's wrong. Maybe I can do something to help."

Tears came into Miranda's eyes. She pressed her hands to her eyes as her shoulders started to tremble. Sympathy was not her friend at the moment.

Finally she blurted, "Oh Kelsey, I'm so unhappy!"

Tears silently trailed down her cheeks. Stunned, Kelsey pulled her into her arms, holding Miranda as she cried. Miranda was the most positive person she knew and always comforted others who were upset. This was new, and Kelsey whispered, "What has happened to upset you this way?"

"I love him so much it's tearing me apart," Miranda sobbed.

"Who...who are you talking about? You have someone special in your life? You've never mentioned anyone to me, even though I've asked."

"I couldn't tell anyone. I had to be so careful, so Cindy and Roger wouldn't guess, and it's been sheer hell!" Miranda said tearfully.

Kelsey was puzzled. "Cindy and Roger! What do they have to do with this?"

"I love Roger. A few days ago, I watched him marry my sister," she sobbed.

Appalled, Kelsey continued to hold Miranda until she stopped crying. "I'm so sorry, love. You should have told someone, because keeping something like this to yourself isn't good for anyone. It can eat you up inside."

"I know," Miranda murmured tiredly, "but I was so afraid if someone else knew, I wouldn't be strong enough to keep Cindy from finding out."

"So you've kept this secret for how long...months? How on earth did you pull it off? It's no wonder you look like the ghost of yourself!" Kelsey sat there stunned as she took it all in. *"Miranda loved her sister's husband! Wow!"*

As close as the two of them always were, it would have taken a miracle for Miranda to deceive Cindy this way.

Miranda spoke quietly, "I don't know. Just sheer willpower, I guess. But, I've got to get on with my life and stop dwelling on the past or I'll never heal. I'll tell you a little bit of the story. It will probably do me good to talk about it, now that they are married."

"Of course I want to hear, but only if it will help," Kelsey said.

Kelsey silently listened to Miranda's story. It now made sense to her why Miranda had changed from a vibrant, happy woman to the disillusioned, sad, and shattered woman she was now. Before Kelsey left, she made Miranda a hot cup of tea. Then, she sat and talked quietly with Miranda until Miranda fell into a troubled sleep. She was restless and kept muttering Roger's name.

Leaning over and giving Miranda a light kiss, she smoothed Miranda's hair from her hot cheeks. "Poor baby," she said gently, "you sure are having a rough time of it. I wish I knew what I could do to ease some of the pain you must be feeling." After putting some soothing music on the stereo, Kelsey left quietly, not really knowing what else to do.

Realizing it was good for Miranda to have someone to talk to, Kelsey stayed in touch with her until Miranda left for Medford. Miranda knew there was something she had to do but she dreaded it. She called Kelsey the day before she left for Medford.

"Kelsey, can I come see you for a few minutes? There's something I need to tell you, and it's important."

"Sure. I'm going to stop at the store on my way home from work but I should be home in forty-five minutes. Will that work?"

"Yes," Miranda said.

Slightly sick at her stomach from nerves, Miranda walked up to Kelsey's door and knocked.

"Hi, come on in. I didn't think I'd see you again since you're leaving tomorrow," Kelsey said, motioning her into the house.

"You wouldn't have, except there's something I have to tell you and I hope we will still be friends after I tell you," Miranda said as she walked into Kelsey's sitting room.

"What are you talking about? There's nothing you can tell me that will keep us from being friends," Kelsey said in a shocked voice.

"Just hear me out, please," Miranda said. She quietly explained to Kelsey how she had deceived Cindy by saying that Kelsey was undermining her and taking credit for her work at the office.

"I have no excuse for what I did, and I won't blame you if you hate me and want nothing else to do with me," Miranda said.

"I agree," Kelsey said a little sharply. "There is no excuse, and I'm shocked you would do something this wrong. Who else did you tell this to?"

"No one. I was at my wits end and just said it without thinking. I'm so sorry, Kelsey. I'll leave now and hope you will forgive me someday." Kelsey didn't say anything as Miranda left quietly.

Later that night, Kelsey called.

"I'm not mad at you Miranda, although I should be. We do unexpected things when we're under stress. You explained to me the other night what you've been going through for a long time, and I accept your apology. We'll talk in a few weeks and put all this behind us. Send me your new phone number."

Miranda was very thankful for Kelsey, and her forgiveness. It was such a relief to have someone to talk to about Roger.

Chapter Eighteen

It was very strange, but often, in those days while moving and getting settled, Miranda still felt this vague sense of disquiet. She asked herself many times, *"What happened to me after the wedding? I know there's something I should remember but it's mostly a blank...I just don't understand why I keep imagining Brian...and think I saw him at the house...I hardly know him!"*

She doubted she would ever find answers to the questions which now plagued her, because who could she ask? Brian? She didn't know where he lived, or his last name. She couldn't remember anyone mentioning it to her. It was very possible she heard it from Cindy or Roger, but because she went through most of the wedding day in a daze, she just didn't remember hearing it.

Arriving in Medford, she immediately went to a real estate office. Letting an agent find her a rental would be the best way to quickly find a nice place to live. They were very helpful and she soon found a lovely two-bedroom apartment situated quite close to her office.

The moving van wouldn't be there for a couple of days, so she checked into the Hilton until she could unpack and get settled into her apartment. With time on her hands, she spent the next few days getting acquainted with the Medford area. It wasn't an extremely large town, but the people she met were very friendly.

Miranda did some research to find out what the climate was like and how it differed from Eugene. She found out most of the rain associated with the Pacific Northwest, and Oregon in particular, skips Medford. Which meant it would be much drier and sunnier than what she was used to. From what she read, Medford's climate is considerably warmer, both in summer and winter than the Willamette Valley where she came from.

A few days after arriving in Medford, she went to check out Roxy Ann Peak. The information she looked up before going said it was a 30-million-year-old mountain. The summit was 3,576 feet above sea level. It was named for Roxy Ann Bowen, an early settler who lived in its foothills. The peak is enclosed in Medford's largest park, a 1,740-acre protected area which is called Prescott Park. From her research, she learned the land was set aside in the 1930s and named in honor of George J. Prescott. He was a police officer killed in the line of duty in 1933.

She spent part of the day walking the trail with a panoramic view of the Rogue Valley. The valley is the cultural and economic heart of Southern Oregon; near the California border. The largest communities are Medford, Grants Pass, and Ashland. Ashland is famous for its Shakespeare plays. Tired and content after her day's excursion, Miranda realized she needed to adjust to the change in climate. She would miss the rain and humidity of home, but she was looking forward to bright, sunny days. That night she slept soundly for the first time since moving.

A couple of days later, she was still feeling restless and decided to take a day and drive to the Oregon coast. Driving along the rugged coastline, she found something which called to her spirit. She located a quiet spot on the beach, and sat for hours just watching the waves breaking against the rocks. It was wild and elemental...and stirred something deep inside her. As she sat watching the waves ebb and flow, she thought back to the many times she and Cindy went to the ocean with their parents. Her memories took her back to so many times where she and Cindy ran, laughed, and splashed in the freezing water until they couldn't take it anymore. She could see her mother's smiling face as she sat watching them play. Their dad would often roll the legs of his pants up and join them, racing with the twins to beat the waves to shore.

While she was growing up, they spent a lot of time along the Oregon coast. The climate anywhere along the Oregon coast can be really rough at almost any time of the year. However, the further south you get, the milder the temperature. Florence, Oregon was one of their favorite places. She remembered, with nostalgia, the hours she and Cindy spent racing up the sand dunes only to come sliding back down on a sand board. They would either slide down sitting up, or face first on their stomach. It was easy to forget how hard it was to climb to the top because the slide down was always so much fun.

As far as the eye could see, there were mounds of sand drifting one into the other, seemingly into infinity. Some dunes were so tall and endless, it seemed impossible to reach the top. Sometimes the twins would spend hours, scrawling their names in the sand or drawing countless pictures. Other times, they would just lie on their backs, feeling the soft breeze on their faces and enjoying the sound of the surf; which seemed so close at hand, but was in actual fact, quite a distance away.

Other times, they went down to watch the gray whales. She still remembered the awe she felt watching those big, graceful creatures gliding through the water or tumbling playfully with their young. More than once they watched, fascinated as the whales breached; coming completely out of the water, arching high into the air, and then slapping the water with their fins or tails as they came back down. Once, Miranda's whole family was blessed to see a huge gray whale twirl as it breached high into the air; and watched water spray high into the air, while listening to the sound its tail made as it slapped the water. Even though they were a distance away, the waves from its descent caused their boat to rock wildly.

Miranda wasn't sure which was her favorite; the whales or the sea lions. She could still remember standing far above the caves, watching absolutely fascinated as hundreds of Steller sea lions appeared below them. She could still hear the noise they made as the huge males bellowed and moved about among the many females. It was always so much fun to watch them splash and swim in the ocean, and then make their way back up the rocks to lie in the sun and sleep. She and Cindy were always thrilled by the new babies which were born in the early summer.

The ocean always gave her a feeling of peace and serenity, and this trip was no exception; she decided to spend the night and drive back home the next day. Early the next morning, she found a quaint little seaside restaurant and ate a leisurely breakfast. The rest of the morning she enjoyed a quiet and peaceful time just visiting the little gift shops and walking along the beach.

She loved watching the seagulls flying and darting above her head; rushing to see what the sea might have deposited on the sand as it retreated once more. She watched the tremendous power of the ocean as it surged into shore, only to immediately begin its journey out to sea again, unending and tireless. It was at this moment she felt more in harmony with herself and her life. For a little while, she was able to put thoughts of Roger out of her mind. Miranda was delighted by the tranquility she felt. She knew she would return here as often as she could.

The ocean seemed to call to something deep within Miranda's soul and make her stronger. Driving back to Medford, she felt as if something changed. She knew now she could move forward and get on with her life. She looked forward to her very challenging career, which would just have to be enough for now. Maybe this was a start, and she would find something exciting up ahead.

Chapter Nineteen

Dining alone at Rodolfo's Italian Restaurant one night, Miranda looked up to watch a couple make their way into the restaurant. Somehow the man looked familiar, but she couldn't quite place him. The woman he was with was very striking. Her hair was a glorious auburn color, full of body and cascaded over her shoulders. She was wearing a dress which drew every male eye in the place. The front dipped almost to the waist, barely covering her breasts, and the skirt flowed as she moved, revealing her beautiful body. She would be noticeable anywhere. They made a handsome couple, as she moved gracefully at his side.

Why did Miranda have this feeling she knew him? Since coming to Medford, Miranda couldn't remember meeting anyone even remotely like him. He could be someone she met somewhere else, possibly on a business trip. For the few seconds she was able to watch him, Miranda sensed a man of authority; of leashed power. He was wearing a navy-blue suit, beautifully tailored, but before she was able to figure out who he was, they turned and followed the hostess to their table. Because they were seated out of her sight, she was unable to study his face. She only got a brief glimpse of him, but he seemed so familiar somehow. Something about him seemed to ring a bell in her mind, but why?

Miranda dressed very carefully for her first day at work. Because she had lost so much weight, a lot of her clothes were still too big, or just didn't look right anymore. Wanting to make a good first impression, she bought a beautiful new dress with an empire waist. It was full and flowing and swirled about her legs as she walked. Because of the way it was made, it concealed the fact she was still so thin, but she was unable to do anything about the slightly drawn look to her face. Even though she was trying, she still found it hard to eat as much as she should. Glancing at herself in the mirror, she decided she looked fine. Even though, to offset the paleness in her cheeks, she was wearing a little more makeup than usual.

Miranda was extremely curious to meet her new boss. She knew his name was Mr. Chandler, but she really didn't know anything else about him except that he possessed a good sense of humor.

* * *

On the way to work that first morning, Miranda's mind drifted back to when she first got the call to come down to Medford for her interview for the position. The secretary, who called, told her she would be speaking with a Mrs. Martin. When she arrived at the office building in Medford, she learned Mrs. Martin was the president's secretary; and Mrs. Martin explained that Mr. Chandler was out of town.

"I suppose I'll need to come down again to meet him?" Miranda stated.

"I doubt it," Mrs. Martin answered. "Mr. Chandler and I have both gone over your resume, and he thinks I will get enough information to decide if you are a good fit for this job. He's extremely busy at the moment, but we both think your background and experience put you at the top of the list of candidates."

"Which doesn't leave you off the hook," Mrs. Martin smiled. "Mr. Chandler gave me some questions to ask you because he can't take the time right now to meet you."

With a sigh of relief, Miranda said; "Thanks. I'll be glad to answer anything you need to know. I really want to work here. I've worked in all areas of Barnes and Cummings in Eugene, and I know I will be able to handle whatever you throw at me!"

"You sound very confident," Mrs. Martin smiled. "I like your enthusiasm!"

For the next hour, Miranda answered questions. Mrs. Martin asked about the work Miranda was involved in, the departments she was familiar with, and her education; how she handled internal issues, and government questions. The hardest question Mrs. Martin asked her was; "Why did you choose to change jobs and move to Medford?"

"I felt I learned as much as I could in Eugene and realized promotions would be hard to get. We have a unique group of people working in all the departments. They love their work, and very seldom leave to work elsewhere. As you know, the management of Barnes and Cummings is topnotch, and retirement benefits are fantastic, so employees tend to stay. I just felt I needed a chance to grow and learn more, and this job will give me a lot more experience and opportunities." Miranda said, realizing much of what she said was true. She did want a more challenging career, and she hoped she would earn this new job.

She was at home in Eugene on Tuesday evening, a week after her interview. The phone startled her when it rang, and when she picked it up a male voice asked:

"Is this Miranda Carlson?"

"Yes," she answered. "May I ask who is calling?"

"Mr. Chandler from Barnes and Cummings," he said. His voice was strong and masculine, with a slight lilt to it. There was a warmth she liked immediately, although she wasn't able to tell anything about his age.

"I've spoken to Mrs. Martin and looked at your work history. Both of us think you will be a good fit for our office," he said. "So, if you want the job, it's yours."

Her hands trembling, Miranda slumped back against the couch. She was so relieved. She would be able to leave Eugene and get a chance to work hard and get her life back. She wouldn't have to be around Cindy and Roger. Tears filled her eyes as hope filled her heart.

"Are you still there?" a voice asked.

Upset at herself for her lack of attention, Miranda spoke quickly. "Sorry, I'm so thrilled, I forgot to answer!"

"It's perfectly OK. I assume you want the job?" A quiet chuckle caused Miranda to laugh as well.

"Of course, I do! Thank you." As Miranda hung up she realized she felt good for the first time in a long time.

She wondered what he would be like to work for. She hoped he would be a tough and demanding boss, as she planned to throw herself into her work. Convinced it would help her get beyond her pain, and help her forget, she planned on working very hard.

* * *

Now, as Miranda walked down the hall of Barnes and Cummings in Medford, she felt a few eyes following her progress. Looking up, she met the smile of a very good-looking young man. She could see the admiration in his eyes. She smiled back and continued on her way.

Mrs. Martin met her at the door and led her to Miranda's new office. Miranda was overwhelmed. This office was nothing like the one in Eugene. It was spacious and impressive. A large leather desk and chair sat under the window. Scattered about the desk were several items she would need. Near the desk was a tall, modern lamp and against one wall were a couple of comfortable looking chairs, as well as a single chair on either side of the desk. Along one wall was a bookshelf stocked with books. Miranda walked over and examined the titles which consisted of medical and pharmaceutical journals and books. She felt her spirits lift and felt a thrill of anticipation.

Miranda's feet sank into the plush carpet as she crossed the room to look out the window. They were four stories up and she looked out over the beautiful nearby park. She could see children playing beneath the shade of a number of large, stately oak trees. As she watched, she realized seeing the children run, jump, and chase each other around the trees, made her sad. Even though she tried, she couldn't help but think of the children she wouldn't be able to have with Roger. A couple of gray squirrels raced down one trunk and sprinted across to another tree. She saw the limbs quiver as they chased each other almost to the end of a limb. Their antics made her smile, despite herself. Sighing softly, she turned back into the room.

"This is just wonderful, Mrs. Martin. I have to say, I didn't expect anything like this."

"Call me Karen," Mrs. Martin said with a smile. "I hope we can work well together, and even become good friends."

"Thanks Karen, I hope so too," Miranda said with a smile. "When will I be able to meet Mr. Chandler?"

"He's in Chicago for the next couple of days, but he should be back by Wednesday. In the meantime, let's get you settled-in and acquainted with everything. I'll take you around, show you the building, and introduce you to everyone."

As Miranda followed Karen, her spirits lifted and she felt a thrill of anticipation.

Barnes and Cummings was a very big pharmaceutical company. There were several branches around the United States and an office in France. Miranda knew Mr. Chandler traveled a lot. During the interview, Karen told Miranda she would be doing some traveling as well, whenever he needed Miranda to go with him.

Being able to travel was one of the reasons Miranda was so happy about getting the job. The more her mind was active and busy, the less time she would have to think about what her life could have been like...if things would have turned out differently.

Chapter Twenty

Miranda was surprised, and yet a little relieved, when Cindy didn't call after getting home from her honeymoon. After moving, Miranda left her new phone number on their answering machine, as promised, but Miranda guessed Cindy must have a lot to do. "Oh well, they are newlyweds after all," she muttered.

Several times during the week when she knew Cindy should be back home, Miranda went to pick up the phone to call her. She even got as far as dialing the number more than once but her nerves caused her to hang up. She missed Cindy so much. She longed for a return to their easy, loving friendship, or "twinship," as they both laughingly called it while growing up. Because she missed Cindy and Roger, it was hard for her to know how to act like everything was normal, so she kept putting off calling.

A couple of days after starting her new job, Miranda realized she had to give Cindy a call. As she picked up the phone and heard Cindy's voice, tenderness almost overwhelmed her. "Miranda, is it really you? I thought you were never going to call. I almost called you several times, but something always interfered. How are you? I've missed you so much!" Cindy said.

"I'm fine, hon. Just awfully busy trying to get used to a new job. And the weather! It's so different here. So sunny and warm! It will take a bit of getting used to, and I'll probably miss the rain, but I'm loving it so far. How are you and Roger? Will you have a while at home before having to take a trip?"

"I think so," Cindy sighed. "They said I would have to go to New York in a few weeks, but it's just for three days. It will be hard to be apart, but Roger knew I would have to travel and he's fine with it."

"How was your honeymoon?" Miranda asked finally, knowing she couldn't keep putting off the question.

Miranda listened grudgingly on one hand, but thrilled for her sister as well, as Cindy rhapsodized about their honeymoon on St. Thomas Island. According to Cindy, it was everything she ever dreamed it would be. As she described the warm tropical nights with their soft breezes, Miranda could almost feel the warm sand beneath her feet, smell the scent of the ocean, and hear the sighing of the wind as it stirred in the trees. She sighed in envy as Cindy told her about playing in the ocean, taking romantic boat rides, and sipping long cool drinks while lounging beside the pool.

"Strolling along and looking at the shops was a fabulous experience because there were so many different things to choose from, and everyone is so friendly. I laughed at all the different tactics they use to try to get you to buy their wares. Miranda, you would have gotten such a kick out of some of the tricks they pulled," Cindy giggled. "By the way, even though I was on my honeymoon, I didn't forget my favorite person in the whole world, next to Roger, of course. I brought something very special back for you, and I think you're really going to like it."

"I'm sure I'll love it." Miranda said.

What a paradise it must have been, thought Miranda, as she imagined them swaying to music amidst the magic of millions of stars glittering overhead. Instantly, the thought took her back to one very special night, but she quickly shut the images out of her mind. She forced herself to listen to Cindy's chatter about Roger and what an exciting and passionate lover he was. Desperately, Miranda sought to put thoughts of Cindy and Roger's lovemaking out of her mind, but it was very difficult. She didn't have to imagine his passion because she experienced it for herself. Pain filled her chest, as despite her desperate struggle not to remember the night she and Roger almost made love, images crept back into her mind anyway.

"Are you still there?" Cindy's voice broke into her thoughts. "You're awfully quiet."

"I'm envious," Miranda sighed. "You make it sound so romantic."

"Oh, it was. I wish you could have been there. On second thought," she laughed, "just forget what I said. I think three would have been a crowd, don't you?"

"I'm afraid so." Miranda hated the envy in her voice, but she couldn't help wishing she was there with Roger, as "his" wife. But, despite it all, she was truly happy for Cindy; and Roger as well, because she loved him, and wanted him to be happy.

"It really was so marvelous that I hated to come back down to earth. Of course, the honeymoon isn't over just because we came back home," Cindy laughed complacently.

"I hope not. You should be able to make it last at least a couple more years, right?"

"Right! At least the next fifty years. Now when are we going to get to see you? Soon, I hope?" Cindy asked.

"I'm afraid it won't be for awhile. After all, I'm just getting settled into a very hard job."

"Well, I hope it won't be too terribly long. I miss you, Randi, so much."

"Randi!" That sure brought back memories! She hadn't heard Cindy's old nickname for her in a long time. It reminded Miranda about how she had shortened Lucinda's name to Cindy when she was three years old. Miranda wasn't able to say, "Lucinda," so Lucinda became Cindy to everyone. Touched, Miranda suppressed a sob threatening to surface.

"I miss you too, very much. But since my job may involve some traveling, I will probably be really busy for awhile learning everything I need to know. It may be a few months," Miranda replied.

"Oh, no!" Cindy cried. "Not so long, surely."

"I'm afraid so, but we'll be able to talk on the phone as often as we want to. You can always come down to see me."

"I know, but because we were both gone for two weeks for our honeymoon, Roger and I will be really busy with our jobs for the near future. I know it's not that far to Medford, but it's going to be awhile before we can come down, but we'll try really hard to figure it out. I miss you terribly," Cindy cried, "I'm never going to get used to not having you around when I need to talk to someone."

"I know how you feel. I've been pretty lonely myself. But don't forget, now you have Roger to talk to." After talking a few more minutes, Miranda hung up, sad and unhappy.

Even though Roger was not home to say "Hi," to her, all the old pain and feelings rushed back over her. Thinking about Cindy's honeymoon and how Cindy described the nights, it made her so lonely and miserable. She cried herself to sleep, wondering if the ache would ever go away.

Chapter Twenty-One

The next couple of days were very busy ones for Miranda. She was getting acquainted with all the different areas and departments she would be working with. It was going to be hard and very demanding, which was just what she needed.

Karen took her around to meet the people from various departments. She found out Andre was the name of the man who smiled at her the first day she was in the building. After Karen left her back at her office, she logged into her computer and started learning about the various departments in the company. A few minutes later, she looked up as someone knocked lightly on her door. She walked to the door and opened it to find Andre standing there. Surprised, she asked, "Do you need something?"

"Sure," he grinned. Before she could say anything, he sauntered past her and went to stand by the window. "Beautiful view. He swept his hand out to indicate the park down below. Wish I had one like it, but alas, I'm just a small cog in a big wheel," he chuckled as he turned to smile at her, and Miranda saw the twinkle in his eye.

Miranda tried to keep from smiling back, but couldn't hold back a giggle as she stared at the handsome young man in front of her.

Grinning back at her, he said; "I know you probably don't know anyone in town, so would you like to get something to eat after work?" She gave him a surprised look, but he just smiled. "I know.

Fast work, huh? But hey, I'm twenty-five and single with nothing to do this evening. How about it?"

Miranda walked behind her desk and sat down, not quite knowing how to take him. "You don't know a thing about me so your question really surprises me."

Leaning forward from the seat he had taken at the front of her desk, he said teasingly, "I know a beautiful woman when I see her. What else do I need to know? Besides I want to get ahead of the stampede that will be heading your way when the other guys see you." His face turned serious for a moment. "I know, I'm nuts, but I really would like to take you out and get to know you. What do you say?"

Miranda never knew anyone could be quite so impetuous. To say the least, it shocked her a little. She was hesitant to go out with a complete stranger.

"Why not?" she asked herself. *"It's about time for me to start doing something besides going straight home to an empty apartment every night!"*

"I'd love to," Miranda blurted before she could talk herself out of going. She didn't want to spend another night alone in her apartment with nothing to think about but Roger. The best way to get on with her life was to surround herself with people. She wanted things to do to keep herself busy and her thoughts at bay.

She enjoyed a wonderful evening. Andre was quite charming with his light chatter and complex personality. Instead of taking her to a nice, quiet restaurant as she expected, he surprised her by taking her to a noisy brew pub called Caps and Taps. Miranda wasn't a big beer fan, but she accepted a light ale along with a hamburger and fries, which tasted a lot better than she remembered.

"Now that we are no longer hungry, come with me," Andre tugged at her hand as he led her to a long table with a light sprinkling of powder on its surface. There were eight round pucks sitting on one end.

"What's this?" Miranda asked suspiciously.

"Shuffleboard. Haven't you ever played it?" Andre asked.

"Never," Miranda answered. "What do you do?"

Taking her to the end of the table with the pucks, Andre demonstrated the game by pushing the puck lightly to send it to the other end of the table. "Try to get the puck to slide onto the scoring section without letting it go too far."

Miranda put her hand over the puck and sent it sliding down to the other end. It went flying past the scores and dropped off the end. Laughing, Andre handed her another one. "Just not so hard this time."

Giggling, Miranda tried over and over and finally got the hang of it. After that, it was a no-holds-barred competition. Laughter rang out as they both tried to best the other one until they were exhausted. After ordering another beer, they headed over to where some people were playing darts. Miranda learned very quickly how easy it was to miss the target! But, she was a quick learner, and soon had the darts hitting the scoring area rather than missing the board and hitting the wall.

She turned to Andre with a gleeful smirk when she managed to hit the bullseye. "Ha, beat you," she chuckled.

"You sure did," Andre said as he hi-fived her. "Now, how about a game of pool?"

Laughing, Miranda shook her head. "I'm tired and I have a busy day tomorrow. We should get home. Andre, this has been a lot of fun. Thank you. You must know me already; because you seemed to know I needed a fun night out," Miranda smiled. She took his elbow as he navigated her through the crowd.

"Of course I know you," he teased. "I figured you out the first time I laid eyes on you! Why do you think I asked you out?"

"You're just a little bit crazy, or conceited. Only time will tell," Miranda teased back. She couldn't help but like this man!

Andre turned serious for a moment. "Can we sit and talk for a few minutes before we go? I'd like to get to know you a little better. I know you have a competitive side, but I'm sure there's a lot more to Miranda than meets the eye."

"Just a few minutes, and then we need to go, OK?" Miranda agreed.

Andre's eyes twinkled whenever he smiled, but despite herself, Miranda found herself comparing his face to Roger's. Andre's mouth was full and generous with a small, straight nose, and very large brown eyes which matched the brown tint of his hair. While telling her a humorous story about his first job, he reached up to push back a lock of hair which fell into his eyes. Miranda felt a lump come into her throat because his gesture reminded her so much of Roger. Roger pushed his hair back the same way the first time she met him; and she remembered teasing him several times about getting his hair cut because it always seemed to be in his eyes.

Dropping her eyes for a moment, to hide the tears which unexpectedly clouded her vision, she listened silently while Andre told her about his family; his parents lived in Medford, as well as his three brothers and three sisters. He was one of the younger boys. Laughing, he said they were a pretty rough and tumble bunch and were always up to something. While describing some of the things which happened while they were growing up, he instinctively seemed to sense her mood, and attempted quietly to draw her out. Trying very hard to shake off the way she was feeling, Miranda said she hoped she would get to meet his family sometime.

Reluctantly Andre said, "I guess we'd better get going. It's getting late and we'll both be tired tomorrow if we don't get some sleep."

Miranda found herself glancing at him as he drove her home. She really liked him and was surprised and happy he had asked her out. She really did want to get to know him better and hoped he felt the same. She sensed that he had a wonderful, close relationship with his family and she envied him for that.

Andre gave her a hug as he said goodnight. "I'd like to do this again sometime if you're interested? I had a lot of fun."

Miranda stepped back as she said, "Andre, it was wonderful and interesting, and I would love to see you again, besides work, that is," she smiled.

A huge smile warmed his face as he said teasingly. "I can't believe my luck. See you tomorrow."

Miranda found herself smiling as she watched him walk to the car before going inside. As she locked the door and got ready for bed she realized that she actually felt happy.

Chapter Twenty-Two

Wednesday morning, she dressed carefully because she was finally meeting her boss. She put on a simple, black wool skirt with a graceful, braided, cord belt. To this, she added a dramatic ivory blouse with voile-puffed sleeves. Stepping into three-inch black heels, Miranda felt she was ready for anything. Braiding her hair into two long French braids, she then wrapped them around her head, giving herself a slightly exotic look.

Making sure she arrived early, she found plenty of things to occupy her time. Slightly nervous, she kept waiting for her buzzer to sound. It was around nine o'clock before Karen finally rang to let her know Mr. Chandler was ready to see her.

"Miranda, Mr. Chandler would like to see you in his office," Karen said.

"I'll be right there," Miranda replied. Her stomach felt a little fluttery and nervous. She didn't even know how old Mr. Chandler was. He could be a very young man, or a very old one, for all she knew. *"Why didn't I ask Karen?"* she asked herself.

Over the last couple of days, talking to various staff members, she got the impression he was very well liked and respected. She heard nothing negative about him.

Miranda tapped lightly on the door and after hearing a brusque; "Come in," pushed open the door to his office and walked part way into the room. A man was standing at the window with his back to the room. Miranda's first impression was he couldn't be very old because his hair was still jet-black, slightly overlong, just brushing his neck and curling slightly. She couldn't help but notice his broad shoulders tapering to slim hips. She sensed a caged restlessness about him as he stood there with his hands resting in his pockets. The gray suit he wore only seemed to enhance his masculinity.

He must have heard her enter because he turned slowly to face her. Steel gray eyes stared into startled hazel ones. *"Who was he? It couldn't be!"*

Suddenly, she remembered the man from the restaurant. *"Brian! He's the one I saw! I can't believe it! Why on earth didn't I recognize him?"* Miranda pondered. It was no wonder he seemed so familiar to her. *"Was Brian her boss? How on earth could this coincidence have happened?"*

"Miranda, of all people to appear in his office!" Brian felt as if he were seeing a ghost. Throwing questions at her, he asked; "What are you doing in Medford? I don't remember telling you where I lived. How did you ever find me? Did Roger tell you where I worked?" He seemed completely stunned to see her.

"I guess I'm your new assistant, Brian, assuming you're president of this company! I certainly didn't know you worked for Barnes and Cummings!"

"You!" Brian exclaimed, startled. Then as if his legs were suddenly weak, he sat down and motioned her to a chair. "I knew my new assistant's name was Miranda Carlson, but I just never put the two together. As I didn't get a chance to meet Cindy prior to the wedding, I guess I didn't pay much attention to her last name when Roger mentioned it. It certainly never occurred to me the woman I hired could be Cindy's sister..."

He seemed at a loss for words... Then he stood up and paced for a moment. "Miranda! I can't believe it," he said almost to himself.

"Yes, it's me, Brian. Hard to believe isn't it? I certainly never expected anything like this to happen." Then she chuckled. "Did you?"

Her laugh was contagious, and Brian found himself smiling. "Not in a million years. Well, we have a lot of work to do, so I suppose we should get started, don't you?"

"Absolutely," Miranda said as she took a seat, notebook in hand.

"Your job is going to be a challenge, but I'm sure you'll be up to it, Miranda. Your resume certainly was impressive, and your former boss, Franklin, gave you a glowing recommendation. I'm sure once we get accustomed to each other's working habits, we'll be able work together and get a lot accomplished."

"I'm sure we will. I've spent a couple of days getting acquainted with everything, and it all seems wonderful. As you said, it's going to be quite a challenge, and I'm really looking forward to working here," and as an afterthought; "With you...Of course, it'll be quite different from what I'm used to doing, but I think I'm going to enjoy the experience. I'm looking forward to my new responsibilities."

"Great. I'm looking forward to working with you, now that I've gotten over the shock of who you are," Brian smiled. They worked for a couple of hours and chatted for a few moments about various aspects of the job before Miranda got up to leave.

"How are Cindy and Roger doing?" Brian asked casually. "Have they returned from their honeymoon?"

147

"Yes, and from what Cindy tells me, it was quite wonderful," she replied.

He noticed her smile slipped a little at the mention of Roger, and he hated that his question brought up bad memories for her. Did she remember the night they spent together? It didn't seem likely because she didn't appear to be nervous around him, and she made no mention of seeing him after the wedding.

Brian walked her to the door, reaching around her to open it. As he did so, he inadvertently touched her shoulder. Startled, Miranda turned to stare up at him for a moment, seemingly quite puzzled about something. He couldn't help but wonder what she remembered, if anything, and really wished he knew the answer.

Chapter Twenty-Three

Seeing Brian again stirred up memories for Miranda. Vague, shadowy memories she couldn't put her finger on. Again, she questioned whether Brian was at her apartment. How would she ever know? There was no way she could ask Brian about it. If it wasn't him who was there; and only her imagination, he would think she was crazy. Now, since finding out he was her boss, she felt embarrassed thinking he might have seen her so messed up after the wedding. Were those loving arms, she still remembered, real; or something she dreamed up? Somewhere, in a part of her memory, she still heard the murmur of soft, quiet words. What made her start having these thoughts again? Was it meeting Brian again, or was it all just some kind of crazy dream?

For months, she was plagued with dreams of Roger, waking up in a haze, hoping the dreams were real; her heart breaking when she realized she was just dreaming.

She must have experienced the same dreams the night Cindy married Roger because vague memories or hallucinations kept playing with her mind. Tying to fall asleep, her mind spinning in a million directions, she could almost feel hungry, demanding lips on hers; her body aching with desire; hands molding her breasts and lips hot on her throat. Roger had never truly made love to her, so why did these feelings seem so real? She could certainly remember how alone she felt when she woke up that morning; unable to function.

Miranda knew her erotic dreams came from her desire for Roger, but somehow these feelings seemed so real. Miranda didn't understand why the next morning she felt like she had spent the night in someone's loving arms; someone who really cared about her? These haunting feelings just kept plaguing her, hovering just beyond her reach. Her instincts told her these impressions were real, not just a figment of her imagination, but how could they be?

Why did seeing Brian again stir up such thoughts? She loved Roger, so why should seeing Brian make her feel this way?

Miranda knew there was something she should remember, but she didn't know how to do so. When Brian touched her shoulder a few moments ago, she felt a certain tension enter her. Her mind went back to the wedding and she could still feel the way her arm tingled at his touch. What was it about Brian that puzzled her so much?

"I have to stop thinking about this or I'm going to go crazy!" Miranda muttered as she tried to concentrate on work. "Brian is my boss and I have to be professional. I certainly don't want to lose this job just because I'm confused, do I?"

She sat at her desk for several moments, unmoving; thoughts and questions tumbling through her mind. Finally, unable to come to any conclusions, she went back to work. Several times during the day, Brian summoned her to his office to go over work which needed to be done. She was really pleased with how well they worked together, but knew it would take a few days to really settle in and develop a routine.

Miranda found it was really hard to change the habits of a lifetime, and she longed to tell Cindy about Brian and her new job. Confiding in Cindy was second nature to her and even though it was now hard for her, she still wanted to share her life with her best friend. After work that evening, she placed a call to Cindy.

After chatting for a couple of minutes, Miranda said excitedly; "Cindy, you're not going to believe what happened this week. It will blow your mind!"

"I can't imagine, but it must be huge for you to be this excited." Cindy laughed. "Let's hear it. I can't wait!"

"If you'll just let me get in a word edgewise, I'll tell you," Miranda exclaimed. "You are really not going to believe this! I was so shocked, I thought I might pass out!   I just found out today, my new boss is…Brian."

"I don't understand… Who is Brian?"

"Don't be silly! You know who Brian is! Roger's best man!"

"You've got to be kidding!" Cindy exclaimed. "And, why didn't you know who your boss was? I assumed you met him before you moved to Medford?"

"No, I thought at the time it was a little strange they gave me the job without meeting him. His secretary, Karen, said he was just too busy to interview anyone, so basically, he let her interview me and she asked me a lot of questions he gave her. I got the impression he trusted her judgment and hired me from her recommendation."

"How odd! Do you like him?" Cindy asked.

"Very much, so far. Today was such a shock when I walked into his office and realized Brian was the one who hired me. He's been traveling and just got back today, but so far he's really nice to work with."

"Would you like to be the one to tell Roger? I'm sure he'll get a kick out of this, and will probably give Brian a hard time the next time he sees him. I thought he was very nice, the little I saw of him."

Not expecting the question, Miranda didn't answer as her heart started to race.

"Miranda? Are you there?" Cindy questioned.

"...Yes, Cindy, I'm here. No...You tell Roger because I have to eat something and get to bed. I have to get up early in the morning. We'll talk again soon."

"Sure, but I have lots to tell you. Sure you can't talk a little longer? I miss you so much," Cindy said.

"I miss you too, very much, but I really have to go. Why don't you call me this weekend? I'll have plenty of time to talk then," Miranda suggested. "I love you, Cindy, and can't wait to hear all your news."

After hanging up, Miranda ate a light supper and got ready for bed. After talking to Cindy, she felt sad and lonely. She missed Cindy, Roger, and all her friends, and they seemed so far away tonight. The nights were still hard to get through. She was really tired of not getting enough sleep and hoped her new job, new friends, and the warm weather would help in some way. She wasn't surprised at how much she missed Cindy; and she longed for their former relationship. She could only hope time would heal the past. Miranda knew it must be really hard for Cindy, especially as she had no idea why their relationship had changed, but she was no dummy. She had to know something was different.

Miranda still found herself dreading nighttime even though she was sleeping better, and although not having as many bad dreams, she still had them. Sometimes her dreams turned into horrible nightmares, where she was constantly searching for Roger but he was just beyond her reach. Cindy was always there to lead him away from her, laughing and jeering. She would wake up crying and begging him to come back to her. She prayed for the time when she could think of Roger without wrenching pain breaking her heart. She hated the emptiness, the loneliness. Waking up to an empty apartment wasn't much better; leaving her feeling cold and alone.

Awake, she knew the dreams had no basis in fact. Cindy would never have let her go through so much pain and anguish. Cindy, whose heart was so full of love, would never have gotten involved with Roger if she had known Miranda loved him.

Time would give Miranda a chance to evaluate her relationship with Roger and Cindy from a distance in order to see them more clearly. Miranda knew she was strong and had no doubt she was going to get though all of this and find her own path someday. In the meantime, she had to be brave, focus on her work, be kind to Cindy, and reach for her own happiness.

Chapter Twenty-Four

To keep the isolation at bay, Miranda threw herself into her job and making new friends. Andre was wonderful. One night he called to say his mother would like to have her come for dinner.

His parents were just as Andre described them. His dad's name was Martin and he was warm and friendly, welcoming her kindly. Shelly, his mother, asked Miranda to come into the kitchen and talk while she finished cooking dinner. She was a warm, generous woman and put Miranda right at ease. They were soon laughing about some of the antics of the Kramer kids. Andre's brother, Ryan and his wife, Linda, came in a little later. They were really nice and she enjoyed meeting their two beautiful children, Tanya who was three, and Jeremy who was seven. It took both children a while to warm up to Miranda, but after dinner, Tanya climbed into Miranda's lap wanting to play with her. Andre's two sisters would not be able to join them tonight. Hopefully, Miranda would meet them some other time.

She met Chris, Andre's youngest brother, and the only one still at home. He was fifteen and she took to him right away. He seemed so much friendlier than most kids his age and soon Miranda was talking and laughing with him.

After a wonderful dinner, it seemed natural to help clean up. Miranda was glad when Shelly didn't object and make her sit down. Shelly seemed to sense Miranda was unhappy in some way. When Shelly asked about Miranda's family, Miranda found herself talking openly about her mom and dad, explaining about how close they were before the accident.

Sympathetically, she gave Miranda a warm hug. "You just call me anytime you get to feeling lonely, and we'll talk, OK? If you would like to, we'll go out to lunch sometime when you're not too busy."

"Sounds lovely," Miranda said sincerely, returning her hug. Miranda couldn't remember feeling so close to anyone for a very long time and it felt good. The rest of the family seemed to like Miranda and made her feel very welcome. After not having parents for several years, it was comforting to be around such a warm and accepting family.

Since Miranda was alone, they included her in their Fourth of July celebrations. It was fun watching all the fireworks and helping light them. She didn't realize there were so many members to Andre's family until she saw them all together. They didn't appear to be like a lot of big families who were always fighting and squabbling. Miranda felt a lot of love and affection between all of them, and they sure knew how to have fun together.

Since they were always pulling practical jokes on each other, they thought it was only fair to include Miranda. Coming around the corner of the house, she found herself right in the middle of a water gun fight, and she didn't have a water gun to defend herself with! Since it didn't seem quite fair, someone gave her one, and before long she was as wet as the rest of the gang. Before it was over, someone took the hose after everyone.

Later, at dinner, Miranda started to eat her dessert but her fork struck something hard. Since it was coconut cream pie, she didn't want to hurt Shelly's feelings by mentioning it so she kept quiet until she heard giggling. Looking up, she saw they were all trying to keep from laughing. It seemed one member of the family, namely Chris, buried an olive in her pie, but of course, the whole family was in on the joke. This seemed to be par for the course with this family!

Andre mentioned how his whole family really loved to play sports, and soon enough, she found herself in an exciting game of touch football. Since she grew up without a brother, sports were not something she knew much about. She gave it her best effort, laughing and challenging all the others, and ending up with some interesting bruises the next day.

Miranda enjoyed meeting his two sisters, Sue and Billie. They were both older than Andre, but they seemed to have inherited everyone's sense of fun as well.

In a very short time, Miranda felt like Andre was the big brother she always wanted. He was peaceful as well as fun to be with. She didn't feel like she needed to cover up the way she was feeling when she was with him. She knew, if she ever needed anyone to talk to, he would be very easy to confide in. There were times when she experienced really dark moods and Andre appeared to understand.

One Friday after work, Miranda called Cindy, and Roger was the one who answered the phone, and because of it she had felt confused and unhappy all day.

"Miranda? Wow! It's good to hear your voice. I don't think I've spoken to you since the wedding. How are you doing?"

"...Ro...Roger!" Miranda stuttered. Gaining control, she said; "It's good to hear your voice, I'm fine. How are you?"

"Just fine. Cindy told me about your job and the fact that you're working for Brian. I can't believe I was that dense. I should have told you that Brian worked for the same company you did. I guess it never occurred to me with everything that was going on, and Brian didn't come up early like I thought he would. Cindy told me about your job change and move to Medford, but I just didn't put two and two together."

"That's OK, Roger. I didn't have a lot of time to explain details of my move to Cindy, so she really didn't know much. How's your job going?"

"Going great, as usual. Thankfully, I haven't done much traveling since we got back, and neither has Cindy. I'm afraid that's going to change next week because we both have to go out of town for a few days."

"That's to be expected with both your jobs, and I'm sure it won't be easy. I'm glad things are going well. May I speak to Cindy?" Miranda asked, anxious to end the conversation.

"Sure. It was nice to talk to you, Miranda. I hope we'll get to see you soon. We both miss you."

"...I miss you both," Miranda said struggling with tears. "Bye, Roger."

She reluctantly answered the phone a while later when it rang. When Andre said hello she was hoping he just wanted to talk and she could make it short, but that was not the case.

"Miranda, do you feel like going for a bike ride? It's so warm and pretty out tonight; I thought you might want to get out."

"Not tonight, Andre." Miranda answered shortly.

A short silence came from Andre's line before he asked, "Is everything OK?"

"I'd just rather be alone tonight."

"Do you think that's a good idea, Miranda? Getting out will be good for you, and I have a good joke for you. Come on, Miranda. Let's go out and breathe some good fresh air and refresh our brain cells. We're going to need them tomorrow."

Trying to keep from laughing, Miranda said, "I give, Andre. Come and get me!" She couldn't hold back the giggle that escaped.

"Be there quick as a wink!" Andre said hanging up.

Going for long walks together, Miranda and Andre seemed to be able to talk about anything. Sometimes Miranda wondered what was wrong with her. Why couldn't she love Andre? He was so good for her. He made her feel safe, cared for, and she was able to tell him private things about her life. Maybe Roger had spoiled her for any other man and she would always be alone. She wanted to be loved and cherished, and hoped someday she would be able to love someone else.

One Saturday, she and Andre decided to have a picnic at a nearby park and then go for a hike afterwards. Miranda almost called Andre to cancel because she was feeling depressed, but at the last minute decided it would be good for her to get out of her apartment. It was a gorgeous fall day and the leaves were starting to turn colors. She knew staying home wouldn't be the best idea and hoped being with Andre would lift her spirits. Miranda tried to be cheerful, but he sensed something was bothering her and asked what was wrong.

"I don't know, I guess sometimes I get nostalgic for home."

"I'm sure you do, but you seem a little more quiet and retrospective today than usual. Is something else going on?" Andre asked.

"I really miss someone who was very important to me," Miranda finally said.

"Important, how?" Andre questioned, "Is it a friend you got into a disagreement with so you aren't close anymore? Or...something more serious?"

"There's a man in Eugene whom I love, and sometimes I miss him so much. We dated for a while and I thought he felt the same, and was just taking his time to get to know me. But I was wrong. Very wrong!"

Andre saw the tears gathering in her eyes and he pulled her over to a bench and put his arm around her. "I had no idea, but I've sensed you were struggling with a loss of some kind, since I met you. Was it recent?"

"A few months ago." A sob escaped as Miranda said, "I will always love him. I gave him my heart and soul but he never knew."

"I don't understand! Why couldn't you tell him how you feel? Maybe you just need to tell him."

Miranda laid her head on his shoulder with a sigh. "He loves someone else and they are married."

"You mean the piece of garbage didn't tell you he was married?" Andre asked angrily.

Miranda jerked away and shook her head. "No, No! You don't understand. He's a wonderful man. He wasn't married when we dated. He met someone and simply fell deeply in love with her, and I couldn't let him know I loved him too."

"I don't understand why you didn't take a chance and tell him. It might have made a difference."

Miranda got to her feet and paced for a moment. "It hurts too much to talk about, but there wasn't a chance after he met her. I've accepted that the man I will always love, will never belong to me. It will get better, but I will never forget him."

"May I tell you about something I went through? I think I know how you feel," Andre asked quietly as he got to his feet as well.

Pacing back and forth, he explained; "A couple of years ago, I met a wonderful woman. She was a vivacious redhead, fun-loving, and smart. Finally, getting up the nerve to ask her out, I was surprised when she accepted. We dated fairly often for about a year. I was madly in love with her after the first month, and begun to think she returned my feelings. I bought a ring and was ready to ask her to marry me, when she told me she met someone else."

"Feeling like I was slowly dying, I went on a weeklong drinking binge. With the help of my family, I was finally able to pull myself together, but it still hurts to think about her. You're the first person I've met since who makes me think it's possible to forget her, and find someone else to share my life with."

Joining him, Miranda slipped her arm through his. "It's awful isn't it? Does the pain ever go away?"

"Yes," Andre answered. "After a while, you'll only think of him once in a while and not all the time. Thoughts of him will probably stay with you the rest of your life, but you won't feel the kind of dreadful pain you feel right now."

He went on; "I assume he will gradually start to recede from your thoughts for longer periods of time, and become like a memory, an elusive face which becomes hard to remember."

Since Andre didn't know she was talking about her brother-in-law, he didn't realize she could never truly be free of his memory.

Hugging her to him, he gave her a sympathetic kiss. Miranda's arms slipped up around his neck, and she buried her face in his chest. Holding her tightly for a few moments, Andre pressed his face into her hair.

Although Miranda didn't feel any of the overwhelming fire and passion she felt when she was with Roger, Andre was so nice. He was a very peaceful man and was just what she needed now. Peace! She never again wanted to experience the kind of black despair that can take away your desire to live.   As Miranda stirred, Andre's hold eased. She reached up and cradled his face in her hands for a moment. "You're a good friend, Andre, and I hope I never take you for granted."

Laughing, Andre teased; "How can you take someone for granted who doesn't let you?" Stooping, he picked her up in his arms and twirled her around until breathlessly she begged him to let her down.

"Not until I get a kiss!" Putting her lips to his she gave him a quick kiss, but unwilling to let her get away with teasing him, he pulled her tighter against him, his lips warm and tender. Finally, he released her, and let her slide to the ground. Miranda found herself wishing she could forget about everything else for a while, and just lose herself in his kiss.

"Thanks Andre," she smiled. "You are just the tonic I needed." For the first time in a long time, she was able to sleep peacefully, a warm smile on her lips. The next morning, she woke up refreshed, ready to tackle whatever the day brought.

Chapter Twenty-Five

One afternoon, Brian stopped by Miranda's desk and sat down casually on the edge of her desk. Startled, she looked up from what she was doing to find his eyes studying her.

"Did you want something, Brian?"

"I was just wondering what you're doing tomorrow night. I'm having a few of my friends over for dinner and thought you might like to join us. Since you're new to Medford, I was afraid you might find the evenings lonely sometimes, and was hoping you might like a distraction."

"Brian, that sounds very nice. I'm afraid I do find the evenings get a little long sometimes. What time would you like me to be there? I'll need a map to get to your place, of course."

"Already done," he said casually as he dropped a hand-drawn map onto her desk. "I'll see you at six-thirty or seven, OK?"

"I'll be there, and thanks again, Brian."

After work, she went shopping for just the right dress. She found it in a deep blue dress, with an inset of lace which covered the top of her lovely breasts but left a shadow of their image. Its simple design showed off her figure to perfection. A slit up the side showed a graceful length of thigh. As she surveyed herself in the mirror, she was very pleased her hips were once again softly rounded, making her realize she was finally regaining some of the weight she lost.

Pulling the front of her hair to the crown of her head, she secured it with a matching bow, leaving soft tendrils of hair curling gently around her face. The rest she left hanging to her waist in the back. As she applied a light mascara, and a pale shade of lipstick, she noticed some of the hollows in her cheeks were beginning to fill out once again, leaving her face looking almost normal. Miranda was one of those fortunate women who didn't need to wear a lot of heavy makeup because her complexion was great. Moving with a sensuality she wasn't aware of, she gave her reflection a last glance before leaving.

As Brian's house was out in the country, it took her about forty-five minutes to get there, and she really enjoyed the drive. At this time of the year, the farms were beautiful. She could see corn standing tall in the fields, waving gently in the breeze. She passed peach and apple orchards, their scent mingling with the fresh air. Although it was long past strawberry-picking time, she could still see beautiful green fields of plants. She remembered, with nostalgia, the many times she climbed tall ladders to help pick big juicy cherries; which seemed to grow everywhere in Oregon. At this time of the year, flowers of all types and colors were evident at every turn in the road.

When she arrived at the address he gave her, she thought how well the house suited Brian. Sitting on a knoll, facing the East, was a beautiful, rustic cabin. It was very large and seemed to fit right into the landscape. One day in the office, Brian told her a little about his house. He explained how he became very tired of living in a crowded subdivision and decided to have a house built. Quite by accident, he discovered five acres of beautiful woodland with a small, but beautiful lake. The lake was in the back of the house and he stocked it with rainbow trout. He also built a small boathouse by the lake which held a 15 foot boat.

The flower gardens in the front were pure magic. She could see every type of flower and shrub imaginable, and everything was beautifully landscaped. She stopped half-way up the drive just to take it all in. She couldn't remember ever feeling this way about a house before. It almost felt as if Brian's house welcomed her with open arms. She was still gazing raptly about her when Brian answered the door.

"Your home is so beautiful, Brian! I never imagined anything could be so breathtaking. It seems so perfect!"

"Thanks," he said. "I'm used to it, but I agree. It is lovely here. It's nice to see it through someone else's eyes. I sometimes forget how lucky I am to be able to live out here. Come on in and I'll introduce you to my friends."

The inside was just as impressive, and yet, Miranda felt the warmth and love which had created this home. The door opened to a large main entrance. It was immediately obvious he was a collector of antiques. She stared around her at the beautiful old furniture which seemed to be everywhere. There was a high-vaulted ceiling in the main foyer, with stairs leading up to a balcony.

The bedrooms looked down on the main living area, where there was a magnificent lighted fan hanging from the ceiling, and a huge fireplace, just waiting to be lit, on a cool winter evening. In her mind, she could picture two people lying stretched out in front of a blazing fire; sipping champagne, and listening to soft, romantic music, fingers intertwined, and lips touching. Just thinking about it brought images of Roger to her mind. Turning away, pain briefly filling her eyes, she followed Brian into the sitting room where his friends were waiting.

Introducing her to his friends, Brian said; "Jennifer, Michael, Allen, and Sharon; I would like you to meet my new assistant, Miranda. She has been invaluable since she started working for me. Allen and Sharon are married and have a wonderful, new, baby boy. Jennifer and Michael are both single, but still looking."

Laughing, they all shook her hand and welcomed her to Medford.

"What would you like to drink, Miranda?" Brian asked.

"Vodka and orange juice would be fine."

The dining room was huge. Once again, antiques were in evidence. At the far side of the room was a large dining room table. Miranda walked around it reverently, running her hands over the chairs. The table was made of solid oak. The chairs' padded seats were rich velvet. The arms and backs of the chairs were elaborately hand-carved with rosettes and finished with claw feet.

An extraordinary chandelier hung above the table. She was fascinated by the multicolored sparkles it threw on the ceiling, walls and floors, as the sun bounced off the crystals. The whole room was surrounded by bay windows. Just outside one of the windows was a huge maple tree which rustled in the wind. Its leaves were throwing shadows into the corners of the room, lending it an air of mystery.

Miranda discovered a cute bay window in an area off the dining room with a cozy little eating nook. She could just imagine a small family sharing a warm, intimate breakfast there before the start of the day. It startled her to find she actually envied the woman Brian would someday marry and share this wonderful house. Wondering why Brian's house made her so nostalgic, she slowly made her way back to the others, trying to shake off this feeling of coming home.

Dinner was everything to be desired. Brian's staff did a wonderful job of serving and the cook made a mouthwatering stroganoff. They were served a full-bodied, red Bordeaux wine called Saint Claret. Miranda couldn't remember tasting a wine quite like this and she loved it. The salad and vegetables were made to perfection, topped off with a fabulous French cheesecake smothered in local cherries. With dessert they were served a wine with a sweet, flowery quality. When Miranda asked what it was, Brian told her it was called; "Chateau A'Yquem."

Sipping a digestif later, Miranda felt so contented. Surprisingly, she was really enjoying herself. As she joined in the laughter and conversation, she was very happy for Brian's invitation.

After showing such an interest in his antiques, when dinner was over, Brian asked if she would like to see the rest of the house. Happily, she left the others to follow him. When she arrived, she noticed a collection of small colorful boxes and was curious to know about them.

"They're bandboxes from the eighteenth century," Brian explained. "Originally, they were used to transport and store elaborately starched ruffs and other personal finery. Later, people used them for storing jewelry, ribbons, hair pieces, etc. It's surprising they were not broken or destroyed, because they are very fragile."

Carefully holding one in her hand, she examined the design. "I find them   charming," she said. Setting the one she was holding down gently, she asked, "What about this candle stand? It looks like the base is a combination of scrolls. Where was it made?"

"It was made in southern Germany between 1725 and 1750 and as you can see, it's crafted from gilt and carved wood. The base is what makes it so unique."

"What about this lamp? It sure is different."

"It's called a mosque lamp and its origins are Turkish sixteenth century, with an oriental influence!"

"Could this possibly be what I think it is?" she questioned excitedly. "It looks like a window seat but the shape certainly is curious."

"It is a window seat and was possibly made by Duncan Phyfe from New York in about 1816. The base is mahogany with caned seat and sides. It's one of my favorites."

"How on earth did you ever collect all of these? It must have taken you years!"

"A lot of extensive travelling, and yes, a lot of years searching for just what I wanted. Anytime I travel, I manage to find a day or two to search for something unusual."

"But the cost of shipping!" She protested. "It must be astronomical."

"It is, of course, but to me it's all worth it, to be surrounded by so much history."

"Thanks, Brian, for taking so much time to show me your wonderful antiques! I don't know very much about them, except to know I find them captivating. Just think of the time it took our ancestors to make just one small item, whereas today, we turn out hundreds of machined pieces of furniture and they aren't unique at all! It's a shame isn't it?"

"Yes, it is. One of the reasons I collect antiques is so I can preserve just a little bit of history. Now we'd better get back to the others, but some other time, I'd like to show you some of the others pieces."

"I can't wait to see the rest of your collection. I'd especially like you to tell me about the desk and chair," she said, pointing to a tall piece of furniture on the other side of the hall.

Taking her arm as they walked back to the others, Brian said casually, "You're a very good listener, and I get the feeling you're really interested."

"Oh, I am. I've always been interested in old things. I read a lot of historical books just because I like to know how people lived before aircraft with jets."

"I know what you mean. Our lives are so fast paced, stepping back into history once in a while makes you feel like it slows down just a little, doesn't it?"

"Yes, it does," she sighed.

"Thanks, Miranda. It's been fun showing you around," Brian said.

As evening was turning to darkness, all six of them sat out on the balcony overlooking the lake. They were able to see the last of the sun as it sank slowly on the horizon, sending shafts of glorious rays everywhere. For a moment, it sat like a big golden globe, and then sank silently beyond their sight, leaving a trail of wondrous colors behind. As they watched, entranced, the first stars suddenly appeared, twinkling in the sky. These were followed soon by millions of others. Fancifully, Miranda thought she saw a shooting star cross the sky, but it was probably only the lights from a plane.

Watching the shadows at the edge of the woods, Brian said musingly, "Almost every evening I see deer come out of the woods to eat the grass in the meadow. I never get tired of watching them. They seem so delicate and timid, and at the slightest noise, they leap silently away and are gone as quickly as they came. I love watching the raccoons come right up on the porch, and it's fun to leave food for them. They're really cute; the way they take food in their paws and scurry out of reach. You can see their eyes, like coals, glowing in the dark... I know better than to leave any food out though. They can make a mess," he laughed.

"I wish we were able to live out like this," Allen said quietly. "I hope to be able to, by the time Ryan is old enough to run and play. I hate to see children cooped up in town, unable to enjoy the outdoors."

"I agree with you," Brian said. "I thought this would be the ideal place to raise children when I have some of my own."

"Hey, is there something you aren't telling us?" Sharon and Jennifer chorused.

"Maybe," he grinned teasingly, "and you two will be the first to know."

"Is it someone we know?" Sharon asked. "Come on, out with it!"

"Aw, I was just teasing. There's no one special, yet," he said. But they all noticed how his eyes seemed to linger on Miranda's face for a moment, making them wonder.

Michael suddenly pointed to the moon, which just appeared in the sky. It was just a sliver at this time of the month. Sitting up there among the stars, it was like a small miracle. Brian walked over to where Miranda was standing and leaned his elbows on the rail, wishing he could put his arms around her instead. She was so beautiful tonight.

"It's all so splendid, Brian. I envy you. How can you ever bear to leave all of this and go in to work every day?" Miranda asked almost sadly, as it seemed to Brian. "If it were mine, I wouldn't ever want to leave it."

A light breeze ruffled her hair as she turned to look at Brian. Surprisingly, a strange expression on his face was quickly hidden.

What did his look mean? Once more, it gave her a feeling she and Brian shared something, but again, whatever it was, sat just beyond her reach, in the shadows of her mind.

Shaking herself mentally, she forced her attention back to the conversation.

Around nine o'clock, Brian turned on a stereo which seemed to fill the entire room with sound. Dragging her to her feet, he took her lightly in his arms.

"I hope you don't mind dancing with me," he said softly.

Shaking her head, she gave herself up in the enjoyment of the moment.

They spent the next couple of hours just having fun. Miranda danced with both Michael and Brian. She laughed a lot at Michael's corny sense of humor. He told her about the company he worked for. They made small farm equipment and he kept her laughing at some of the funny things which happened while he was working.

Sharon and Allen ran their own business, a small appliance store, and Sharon did most of the bookkeeping. She also helped with the customers, between taking care of the baby and helping Allen. It was rough going at first, but it was now a going concern, and they were thinking about starting a second store in Klamath Falls.

Jennifer was a buyer for a local clothing store chain and travelled all over the country. She often went to France for their fashion shows. She got them laughing so hard their sides hurt, as she described some of the clothing which came out every year. She said there were strange, even weird styles sometimes, which were actually bought by some chains. Laughing, she said she always wondered if they were ever sold. Her sparkling eyes betrayed how much she enjoyed her job. It made Miranda wonder if she knew Cindy, but she chose not to ask.

"Would you ever want to do anything else?" Miranda asked, trying to stop chuckling.

"I really doubt it. I have too much fun to go back to a mediocre life like the rest of you."

"Mediocre," they all chorused.

"Sure, dull, daily routines," Jennifer said, jumping up and dodging around the couch. Michael raced after her, catching her and tackling her, as she collapsed onto the couch, laughing helplessly.

"Are you kids ready to act like adults?" Brian asked teasingly, after watching their antics for a few minutes.

Miranda was having so much fun it was well past midnight before she could bring herself to leave.

"Brian, thank you so much for having me tonight. Your friends are wonderful and made me feel welcome. I've enjoyed myself so much."

"I'm really glad. I was hoping you would like my friends even though they can be a little unconventional sometimes. I can tell they all liked you, too. Let me get your jacket and I'll walk you to your car. Please be careful driving home. Keep an eye out for deer because there are a lot of them out at night," Brian cautioned.

During the evening, Sharon and Allen asked Miranda to come to their house for dinner the following week, and Michael asked her to go to a movie with him on Wednesday.

"It's been so nice meeting all of you. Thanks for being so kind to a lonely stranger," she said smiling.

"It was really nice getting to know you, too. See you Wednesday," Michael said holding her hand lightly for a moment.

"What was that all about?" Brian asked as he walked Miranda to her car.

"What was what all about?" she asked teasingly.

"You know what!" he said a little grumpily. "Michael saying he'd see you on Wednesday."

"Oh, that! Michael just asked me to go to a movie with him."

"Fast worker," Brian muttered under his breath.

"What did you say? I didn't hear you."

"Nothing," he said sheepishly. "I was just wondering if you would like to come out some weekend and take the boat out on the water. We could have a picnic in the meadow across the lake."

"I would love to, very much," she replied.

He opened the car door for her, then bent down and gave her a quick kiss. His lips felt firm and tender, causing her heart to beat a little faster. She looked up at him in surprise.

"Just for making tonight so special. I hope you don't mind," he grinned.

"It's a little late to ask, don't you think?" she grinned back at him.

* * *

A few weeks later, she took him up on his offer of a boat ride and picnic. It was a beautiful day; the weather was sunny and warm. As she relaxed beside him on a blanket, she realized she hadn't thought about Roger all day. Turning on her side, she leaned up on her elbow to gaze down at Brian, whose eyes were shut. Teasingly, she trailed a piece of grass down the side of his face, causing him to slap at it. Trying to keep from laughing, she tried it again, only to have him suddenly grab her wrist.

With a swift twist of his body, she suddenly found herself lying on her back with Brian leaning over her. Bursting into laughter, she glanced up to find him grinning down at her. He slowly lowered his face until their lips touched gently. She returned his kiss for a moment, then, slightly breathless, she pushed him away, laughing. Getting slowly to her feet, she unconsciously rubbed her wrist, feeling the same strange tingling she experienced at the wedding.

At home later, she realized how much she enjoyed the day with Brian. Today, she saw a different side to him than the one she always saw at the office.

Chapter Twenty-Six

One Sunday, because Miranda was bored and lonely, and everyone she knew seemed to be busy; she decided to go for a long hike, taking along a backpack and food. Since she lived alone, she called Karen to let her know what she was doing. Not knowing exactly where she was going, she could only give her the general area. She wanted someone to be aware of where she was headed. In case she didn't make it back, they would know where to start looking for her.

Starting out early, she headed into the woods. There were some nice hiking trails and her maps showed her where she was going. For a long while she walked fairly level, but gradually she found herself going uphill. She stopped from time to time just to get her breath, and sit, and enjoy the scenery. It was so quiet and serene, it seemed to commune with her spirit.

As Miranda walked along, she thought about her life here in Medford. Her job was very demanding, as she wanted it to be, but it took a lot out of her. There were nights she still found it hard to sleep. This meant she went to work tired, making it hard to be pleasant and friendly to everyone. As a result, this was taking a heavy toll on her strength. Today, she was hoping to regain some of the serenity she so badly needed. Her relationship with Brian and Andre helped a lot. Working with Brian and doing things with Andre helped quiet her mind for short periods. She was also going out with Michael once in a while. However, she found herself keeping an emotional distance from all of them.

174

Miranda knew she needed closure with Roger before she would ever be able to love another man. That meant she would have to face him; and reconcile her feelings with what her future would be. She knew she couldn't go on loving him if she ever wanted to have a happy future. Just how to accomplish that was a big question mark in her mind. There was no doubt in Miranda's mind that soon she needed to go home and see Cindy...and face Roger.

Miranda was eating and sleeping a lot better now, but she still found herself very unhappy and miserable at times, especially at night. Although she made a few new friends, they all were very busy people with demanding careers and children. She couldn't expect them to keep her occupied, and didn't want to impose on them either. Reading books and watching television only took up so much time, so she often found herself at loose ends with nothing to do. Maybe today she could make some decisions about what to do to help fill in some of her leisure time; such as volunteer work and joining a club of some kind.

As she turned a corner in the path she came upon a baby fawn with its mother nearby. Charmed, Miranda knelt down in the long grass, silently watching them for what seemed forever. Suddenly, as if sensing something, the doe raised her head and sniffed the air. Whatever it was must have disturbed her, because both she and the fawn bolted, bounding gracefully through the woods.

Throughout the morning, she saw various other small animals, but nothing like the deer and her fawn. Miranda walked through a pine forest with the smell so potent and fragrant she stopped just to relax and enjoy the peace she felt there. For a while, she lay back on the bed of pine needles and listened to the rustling in the trees as the wind swept gently through them.

About midmorning, she walked out of the woods into a beautiful meadow. She could see the wind moving softly through the long grass, and there were so many beautiful wildflowers in bloom it took her breath away.

Taking a blanket out of her backpack, she spread it on the ground. Gazing about, she slowly ate some of the food she brought with her. With so much beauty around her, how could she possibly feel any sadness? Yet, she was sad. If only for someone special to share all of this with! She thought back to the day she spent with Brian on the lake. Miranda felt happy then, and she found herself wishing he were here with her today. Or Andre! She should have called and asked one of them to come with her...

Miranda realized she was very tired, but it was a good feeling. She lay down on the blanket to rest in the shade of a giant tree, its leaves effectively blocking the sun. She listened to the lilting tones of the birds singing, and from time to time she could hear sounds of small animals rustling in the bushes. She was even sure she could hear the gentle crooning of a meadowlark, and listened enthralled to the chattering of the squirrels, wondering what they were saying to one another. It was so peaceful here. During her walk, her hair gradually worked out of the bun she put it in, and tendrils were falling around her face. Reaching up, she took it loose, causing it to tumble over her shoulders in glorious disarray. When she lay back down to sleep for a while, it covered her like a soft, silken blanket.

Chapter Twenty-Seven

Halting suddenly, wondering if he was living a dream, Brian rubbed his eyes as if to clear them before moving slowly toward where she was asleep. He thanked whatever impulse caused Karen to call him and tell him about Miranda's hike. Missing her like mad, he decided to see if he could find her. Following the directions Karen gave him, he eventually came upon what he thought were her tracks. He was hoping he hadn't made a mistake in directions, but then he came out of the woods to find her sleeping like a baby, the epitome of all his dreams.

Bewitched, he stood there, unable to take his eyes off her. What a vision she made lying there, like some woodland sprite of the forest. He knew he would remember this scene for the rest of his life. Not wanting to wake her, he sat down a short distance away, and leaned his back against a tree. He wasn't sure why he was so drawn to Miranda and why he was unable to keep from thinking about her. He missed her when she wasn't with him, and often his eyes would search for her at work, hoping to be able to catch a glimpse of her in the hall.

A thrill filled his body as he sat quietly watching her. She was so lovely! He longed to go over and lie down beside her, take her in his arms, and just hold her. If only he had the right! He knew Miranda liked him, but he often caught a glimpse of suffering in her lovely eyes, when she didn't know anyone was watching. He sensed the kind of pain she suffered was not something that could be easily forgotten. From the anguish he saw in her eyes the night of Cindy's wedding, he knew she must love Roger with all of her mind and soul.

He often wished he knew her story and why Roger was her whole world, even though Roger loved Cindy.

From the very beginning, he was drawn to her. He instinctively knew Miranda was a very brave and tenderhearted woman. After watching her struggle with her pain, unwilling to let anything mar Cindy's wedding day; he realized she was sacrificing her own happiness for some reason. He watched her struggle through her own unhappiness, keeping it secret from Cindy, Roger, and everyone else. He wanted to know the kind of love he sensed Miranda was capable of giving. If she were his, he would never ever let her go! In his dreams, he often saw them together, laughing and happy, making a life together. If only dreams could come true! Sighing, he knew he was probably wishing for the impossible.

Slowly sitting up and stretching languidly, Miranda gazed around her. When she rose to her feet, Brian just stared. She was beautiful. Stunning! Her golden hair flowing past her waist made her seem like some goddess rising from the earth. She must have heard his gasp because she swiftly turned in his direction. Her hand flew to her mouth as she suppressed a scream. Frightened eyes started at him for a moment until she realized who it was.

"What on earth are you doing here? You almost scared me to death!" she exclaimed.

"I'm sorry! I didn't mean to startle you. I was just sitting here waiting for you to wake up, but it didn't occur to me that I might frighten you. You just seemed so peaceful that I didn't want to disturb you."

Blushing she said, "You still haven't answered my question as to why you're here and how you found me. This is an awfully big country, so how did you just happen to pick this place?"

"I don't know, just luck I guess." Laughing, he told her about Karen's call. "She was worried you might get lost and no one would ever find you again. She knew I couldn't do without your beautiful face at the office every day."

"Hah! I bet! She was just afraid she would have a lot more work to do if I didn't show up." Laughing with him she said, "Isn't this just the most gorgeous sight you've ever seen?"

"Yes," he sighed, but he wasn't looking at the landscape.

Even though she didn't say so, Miranda was thrilled Brian found her. For the next couple of hours, they completely enjoyed themselves, as they lingered for a time in the meadow. They took off their shoes and waded in a wonderful little stream they found nearby. Even though the water was icy, it was invigorating. Later, sitting quietly on the bank, they talked drowsily about anything which came into their heads. It was starting to get a little late, and even though they both hated to leave, they knew it wouldn't be long before the sun started to go down. Neither one wanted to get caught up here in the dark. As they started back down the trail, Brian put his arm around her waist to help her over a fallen log, and because she didn't seem to mind, he kept it there. As they walked along, he tucked her snugly against his side, close enough to feel her soft, warm body against his. He found himself longing for something, as yet nameless.

Dusk was falling as they neared the edge of the woods. She stopped all of a sudden… He almost tripped over her!

"Wha..." he started to say, but she put her hand over his mouth.

"Sh..." She whispered, "Look over there."

Looking where she pointed, he saw a small herd of deer. A massive buck with a huge rack on his head was standing just beyond, guarding them. Standing with their arms around each other they watched them for several minutes. Reluctantly, they finally turned to go. Not wanting to release her so soon, he bent and kissed her. His lips were warm and generous and she found herself returning his kiss with more ardor than she intended. After a moment, she pushed out of his arms. Shyly, she moved away a short distance and pretended to be watching the herd. She was surprised to find her heart was beating a little faster, and she felt flushed.

"I'm sorry if I upset you, Miranda," Brian said contritely. "You are just so beautiful, and we've had a lovely day together, I couldn't resist... Forgive me?"

"There's nothing to forgive, Brian. I'm just feeling a little shy I guess," Miranda said as she turned and smiled at him.

"Then I guess we'd better get going as the sun is close to going down and it will get dark pretty fast. It's not too far to where we left our cars," Brian said as they started walking.

At the car, Miranda turned to Brian and gave him a hug. "It was so nice of you to come looking for me. You turned a quiet day into a special one. Thank you."

"I'm glad I came," Brian said as he turned and walked to his car. Once there, he turned and watched as she drove out of the parking lot.

Waving as she left, Miranda said, "See you Monday."

"Nice and early," Brian said.

Chapter Twenty-Eight

Cindy and Miranda were calling each other at least twice a week. They both craved the twin connection which had tied them so fiercely together since birth. During the last few calls, Cindy begged Miranda to come up to see them.

"You can fly up easily and be back at work on Monday. Please, Miranda. I miss you! I understand why you haven't been back home. You must be extremely busy and under a tremendous amount of stress trying to adjust to a new job. I'm really sorry for putting pressure on you to come home for a few days, but is there any way you could break away and come see us?"

"It's been tough. I have to learn so much more about the management and technical side of Barnes and Cummings. I've had a lot of reading and training to do and it's exhausting, but exhilarating. I wish you guys could just take a quick trip down to see me," Miranda said wistfully.

"Roger and I have talked about coming down more than once, but our schedules have been so busy we haven't been able to come," Cindy replied. "If I don't have to work on weekends, he does; making it impossible to get away. It would be a lot easier if you could come up to see us this time."

"I miss you too, Cindy. I'll think about coming home soon, I promise," Miranda said.

"Soon? Is there any way you could come next weekend?" *Cindy began to wonder if there was something Miranda wasn't telling her.* "After all the chaos of my engagement and wedding, I've thought about you a lot. I've also realized I neglected you horribly, and I'm ashamed of myself. After looking at our wedding pictures several times, I got the impression you were sad in a lot of them. When I thought about it, I realized you were not your usual, smiling, cheerful self. Your pictures even look like you lost weight. Miranda, are you keeping something from me? You're not sick are you?" Cindy asked worriedly.

Stricken, Miranda said hurriedly; "Of course not, Cindy. What could be wrong? My job is going well, and I've just been busy, that's all. Of course I was very sad about leaving you, and that's probably what you picked up on. Remember, I was very busy before the wedding, and I know I wasn't eating right; hence the weight loss!"

Anxiously Cindy asked; "Well, are you taking care of yourself now?"

"Of course. I'm busy during the week, but I..." She stopped herself, because if she said she had a lot of free time over the weekends, Cindy would be hurt because she hadn't been up to see them sooner. To cover her blunder she said quickly; "By the way, I've made several new friends and they've been keeping me busy. I told you about Brian. Well, he asked me over for dinner one night with some of his friends. He lives out in the country and his home is spectacular!"

Distracted, Cindy said; "He did? I'm glad he's nice to you. Roger told me about their friendship. They have been friends for a long time. I still think it's a crazy coincidence he turned out to be your boss! Roger thinks so too!"

"I know, isn't it though? Anyway, I met someone at Brian's who has asked me out a couple of times. His name is Michael, and he's lots of fun. Of course, there's Andre. I've already told you about him. We see each other quite often. So... you see, you don't have to worry about me, I'm really quite popular!"

"Ha! Of course I knew that, but it still doesn't mean you can't make a quick trip up to see your favorite sister, does it? After all, I'm the only one you have!"

"I know that, silly! Let me think about it, and I'll call you back on Wednesday and let you know what I've decided. If I can make it this weekend, will that satisfy you?"

"Sure, but you'd better be coming!" Cindy ordered.

"And what will you do if I don't?"

"Kill you when I see you, I guess!" Cindy giggled.

"Well, that would accomplish a lot! Then you wouldn't have a sister to nag anymore." Laughing, they both hung up.

Trembling, Miranda sank down onto the couch. "That was close," she thought. "I'm going to have to be more careful from now on, or Cindy will know something's off. I guess I don't have any choice. I'll have to go up this weekend, whether I'm ready for it or not," Miranda decided.

For the next couple of days, Miranda could think of nothing else. She didn't want to go. She longed to see Cindy, but the thought of seeing Roger again so soon scared her.

Cindy and Roger had moved into a big, rambling ranch house he inherited from his grandmother. Cindy told Miranda she and Roger talked about buying a new house, but decided to live in his grandmother's house instead. There were a lot of improvements to make, but they both thought it would be fun to tackle.

Miranda would have loved to find an excuse to keep from staying with them, but since the house had plenty of bedrooms, she couldn't think of one.

Suddenly, a crazy idea occurred to her and she jumped to her feet; pacing the floor nervously. Maybe it would work! "I'll just take somebody with me. Instead of flying, I'll drive up and that will give me an excuse to bring a friend along," Miranda thought.

Miranda was upset at herself and she wanted to understand why she was so intimidated by this. In her heart, she knew she should have moved on and made peace with losing Roger, but the hurt was still too close to the surface. She knew seeing Roger again would be painful and probably send her back into a dark hole if she wasn't careful. She wanted to continue healing, and move on with her life, not wallow in the past.

The more she thought about it, the more she liked the idea of taking someone with her; even though she was sure Cindy would not understand. Miranda made her decision. She looked for Andre at work the next day to ask if he would want to go with her.

"Hi, Andre. I've missed seeing you for a few days. You must have been busy," she said, stopping him in the hall.

"No more than usual," he smiled. "What's up? You want to do something fun next week?"

"Actually...I was hoping you were free this weekend. I'm going to make a trip to Eugene and thought you might like to go with me?"

"Rats! I have a commitment I can't get out of, or I would definitely take you up on your offer. I really want to meet your twin! Imagine two of you in the same room. Wow!" Andre smirked.

Miranda couldn't help but laugh. "You're funny! I know Cindy would love to meet you as well. I've told her about you."

"I can't imagine what you said. That's I'm devilishly handsome, smart, intriguing, and rich?" Andre chuckled.

"All of the above. See you later," Miranda grinned as she walked away.

Miranda pondered what to do next. She thought of Brian, of course, but was a little afraid to ask him. He was her boss after all! "Yes, he kissed me a couple of times, is really nice to me, but he will probably still think it strange if I ask him to go," Miranda mused. "Well, why not?! After all, he is one of Roger's best friends, and might be glad to get a chance to go and see him. Might as well give it a try! Nothing ventured, nothing gained, as they say," she thought.

Finally, screwing up her courage, she called him after work. She just couldn't go by herself. She couldn't ask Michael because they were just getting to know each other after a few dates. So that left just one person!

"Hello?"

"Brian...Hi... This is Miranda."

"Miranda, what a surprise! Didn't I just see you a couple of hours ago? What can I do for you?"

"I know this is going to sound odd, but I have a favor to ask." Hurriedly, before she lost her courage, she explained about her trip to Eugene. "I know this is presumptuous, but Brian, would you consider driving up with me?"

There was a short silence on the other line. Brian knew what she must be going through at the thought of having to face Roger again so soon. After a minute he said, "I'll be glad to go with you. When would you want to leave?"

"You would?" Miranda exclaimed. "That's great! I want to leave about six Saturday morning. Will that be all right? I'd like to come back Sunday evening, but it might be a little late." Under any other circumstances, she would have left after work on Friday, but the thought of spending two nights under the same roof as Roger was more than she could manage.

"That'll be just fine," Brian said. After talking a few more minutes they hung up.

Miranda called Cindy back to let her know what she was doing. Cindy was really surprised when Miranda told her Brian was coming with her.

"Why did you ask him? I can't understand why you don't just fly up. You could be here longer and not have to drive," she said curiously.

"Just chalk it up to one of my idiosyncrasies," Miranda laughed. "You know how I like the outdoors and I've always liked the trip between here and Eugene. It will be very relaxing. Since it's been a hard week, the drive will do me good, and Brian should be great company."

"I really don't understand you sometimes, sis; but if that's what you want to do, I really can't argue with you. After all, you are coming and that's what I was after. I'm sure Roger will be very glad to see Brian again. See you sometime before noon on Saturday."

Brian arrived at her house on time Saturday morning. Miranda was waiting anxiously for him and she ran down the steps to meet him. "Just park your car in my space after I back out," she called.

"Wait! Why don't I drive my car? It's probably more comfortable for a trip than yours will be."

"Sure, sounds great. I don't mind being comfortable," Miranda teased.

The first part of the trip, Miranda was extremely quiet. Understanding how she must be feeling, Brian drove silently, concentrating on driving. To keep it from getting too awkward, he made a passing comment once in a while, to which he usually got a nod or a short answer. Finally, he asked if she would mind if he turned the radio on, and hoped the soft lilting sounds of the music would soothe her nerves. He was worried about her.

As they were nearing Roseburg, Miranda asked Brian if he would like to stop and have a cup of coffee. "Sure, that would be nice. I have a great idea, if we have time to spare. Have you ever been to the Colliding Rivers' Viewpoint?"

"No, but I've always wanted to. Brochures I've read say it's a rare and beautiful sight."

"It sure is. In fact, it's the only place in the world that such a phenomenon occurs. From the viewpoint, you can see the swift, deep waters of the North Umpqua River funnel into the whitewater chute. From there, it rams head-on into the rapids of the sparkling Little River as it comes in from the South. It's a magnificent sight just to see the clash the two rivers make as they meet. Then, to be able to watch the much larger North Umpqua churn its way directly westward, is pure joy. I saw it a few years ago myself. Do you think we have the time to drive the extra distance to see it?"

"Sure, why not? It sounds neat, but let's get a cup of coffee first, OK?" Miranda said. "Roseburg is one of my favorite spots. Even though Roseburg itself doesn't have a huge population, it's surrounded by valleys and farms and the county spreads out over a wide area. Here, we are between the mountains and the coast, and it's not very far to the Oregon Dunes."

"I assume everyone in this area knows about Zane Grey because he wrote so much about this area in his books," Miranda said, as she settled into a booth. "I've read the books he wrote about the North Umpqua River and Steamboat Creek and they are so informative."

"I've never read any of his books," Brian said.

"Then you've missed some wonderful stories about the settling of the West. If you like to read, you might enjoy reading 'Rogue River Feud.' Zane Grey had a cabin on the Rogue and his attachment and fascination with this epic river makes it the primary focus of this book. I grew up reading most of his books, and once in a while I still grab one to read."

Chapter Twenty-Nine

Later, standing at the viewpoint, they were both awestruck by the beauty and turbulence below them. Eyes shining, Miranda turned to Brian. "It's beautiful, isn't it? It's amazing how the water rushes through the chute and just smashes into the whitewater. I could stay here all day but we really have to get going. Cindy is going to wonder why we aren't there."

Back on the road, they passed a lot of signs advertising wineries in the area. Brian said; "We'll have to stop and taste some of their local wines the next time we come through. I understand they are becoming quite famous and have been winning awards for their excellent taste."

"I've been reading about the local wines myself," Miranda said, but silently wondered what he meant by "next time."

As they got closer to Eugene, Miranda became very quiet. When Brian tried to draw her out, she would respond to his comment, but not continue the conversation which was a little unusual. Miranda was always a good conversationalist, and she could carry on an intelligent discussion with almost anyone, but she was also a very good listener. When she looked at him, he could see the strain growing on her face. Her eyes held a look of panic in them, and he didn't know what to do. Somehow, he needed to calm her down before she got to Cindy's or her sister would know something was wrong. After watching the interplay between Miranda and Cindy at the wedding, and becoming aware of how far Miranda must have gone to protect Cindy in the past, he somehow knew Miranda wanted to continue to protect her.

"Miranda, we're almost there, so let's take a short break and relax before we go any farther. Is that OK with you? I wouldn't mind stretching my legs. How about you?" Brian asked.

Numbly, Miranda nodded. When Brian stopped the car, she just sat without moving. She was sorry she was being such bad company for Brian, but the closer she got to Eugene, the more scared she became. What if she couldn't pull this off and Cindy found out she loved Roger? So far, Miranda was able to keep her secret hidden from Cindy, and she just needed to keep on doing so. Miranda felt she should keep up a front for Brian as well, but right now she seemed incapable of doing so. She needed to pull herself together. She just had to! This weekend was going to be hard enough without her falling apart before she even got there.

Coming around to her side, Brian opened Miranda's door, and taking her hand, helped her out of the car. Keeping her hand in his, he walked with her to a small stream meandering its way through the meadow.

Concerned, Brian said quietly; "Miranda, I don't know what's wrong, but I know something is; because you seem to be very upset. If there's anything I can do to help you, I'll be glad to listen."

Shaking her head, she sat down by the edge of the stream, and stared out over the lazily moving water. Brian watched her quietly. She seemed mesmerized by the movement of the water, as she sat without speaking. Brian didn't know that she was mentally gathering her courage to face Cindy and Roger. Finally, taking a couple of deep breaths, Miranda rose to her feet.

"Brian, thanks for being so kind, and not asking questions. This isn't something I can talk about yet, but it's going to be very hard for me to face my sister in a little while. Let's just say, your being here has made it easier for me. I think I'm all right now, so we can go if you're ready."

Putting his arm lightly around her shoulders, Brian walked her back to the car. Turning her slightly to face him, he said gravely; "I can't begin to imagine what you're going through, but I've grown to care what happens to you. If you ever feel like you can talk to me about this, I'm a good listener, and I'll be there for you."

Touched more than she could say, Miranda put her arms around him and snuggled close for a moment, drinking in some of his strength. Almost reluctantly, she pulled away. "If I ever get to the point where I can talk about this, you'll be the one I come to," she said quietly. "I bet Cindy is going crazy wondering where we are. We're much later than I told her we would be."

When they arrived, Cindy and Roger ran out to meet them. Giving Miranda a bone-crushing hug, Cindy said, "I didn't think you were ever going to get here! What took you so long?"

"Oh, you know me, sis. I couldn't help but stop to enjoy the scenery every once in a while."

Slowly, almost reluctantly, she turned to face Roger. Brian, who was watching, saw her face pale slightly. "Hi Roger, how are you?"

"Come here and give me a hug, you crazy lady," Roger said teasingly. "It's good to see you. It's been way too long!" Feet dragging, she moved toward him. He put his arms around her and she turned her head into his shoulder. It felt so good, so right. She held him tightly for a moment. Then, turning her head, she kissed him lightly on the cheek and moved back out of his arms.

"It's good to see you, too," she said softly. As once before, she saw a slightly questioning look on his face.

"Oh, God!" she thought. She hoped she hadn't given herself away.

When she turned around, she found Brian there, blocking her way. Taking her arm lightly, he said, "I'm sure glad Miranda asked me to come with her. It'll be good to catch up on old times, Roger. It's been awhile since we've seen each other long enough to reminisce." Grinning, Roger agreed, slapping Brian on the shoulder.

Brian could feel some of the tension drain out of Miranda, and when he looked down at her, she managed to smile at him.

Cindy fixed a nice lunch while they all talked; Brian and Roger catching up with each other, and Miranda and Cindy discussing the last few months. Cindy talked a little to Brian about his life, as well as asked some questions about his work at Barnes and Cummings. Even though Brian observed that Miranda was a little quiet, no one else seemed to notice.

Roger and Brian went off by themselves for a little while so Cindy and Miranda would have a chance to be by themselves. "I thought we'd all go to dinner and catch a movie tonight. Does that sound good to you?" Cindy asked.

"Sure, that sounds great. Is there anything exciting or new with your job since we talked last, Cindy?" Catching up on each other's lives took most of the afternoon. The guys joined them after a while and they had a nice visit.

Brian noticed Roger glance at Miranda more than once with a puzzled look in his eyes. Hoping Roger wasn't beginning to realize how Miranda felt about him, Brian tried successfully the rest of the day to keep Roger's attention away from Miranda. He was surprised at how much he wanted to protect Miranda from being hurt. He vividly remembered the night he had spent with her and didn't want to see the same suffering in her eyes he had seen that night.

Chapter Thirty

As she got ready to go out that evening, Miranda found herself thinking about the day. She was doing alright, and having Brian here was wonderful. He was very thoughtful all day, and curiously, filled in any awkward silences. He seemed to sense that she needed him. Surprisingly, she caught herself thinking about him at times, instead of Roger.

Cindy explained that the restaurant they were going to was new and very popular with the young crowd. "Bruxie is very trendy, has a wonderful, diverse menu, and a mix of bands five nights a week. They serve a variety of original dishes in a casual, yet modern environment. The Grey Valley band is playing tonight. They play a mix of jazz, light rock, country music, and contemporary. Sometimes we just sit and enjoy the music but we love to dance; so most of the time we end up on the dance floor, don't we?" Cindy asked, smiling at Roger.

Roger grinned at Cindy as he opened her door. "I doubt we will ever just listen to music. Both of us love to dance too much." He slipped his arm around her as they walked into Bruxie.

Brian offered Miranda his arm as she stepped out of the car. He was aware of a slight trembling in her hand where it grasped his elbow. He glanced at her face and noticed how pale her face had become.

"Miranda, are you OK?" he asked quietly.

"I'm fine Brian, but thanks for asking. Let's go enjoy dinner. I'm a little hungry." Miranda smiled up at him, and he gave a sigh of relief. She was a very brave woman and he admired her so much.

While they were waiting for their food, Brian asked; "Miranda, would you like to dance?" Roger and Cindy were already on the dance floor.

Smiling, she took his hand and they slid smoothly into a waltz. Brian turned elegantly, his body in tune with the music; their feet moving in sync, Miranda's body following his every movement. When the music changed to a foxtrot, they transitioned easily, Brian guiding her across the floor as if they had danced together for years, his steps moving in perfect rhythm with hers.

Miranda felt herself letting go for the moment; of her worries, her pain, and her sorrow over losing Roger. She simply followed his footsteps as they moved across the floor. He was a wonderful dancer, and she remembered the fun she experienced at his house. Tonight, however, was a little different. Needing his strength, she held him a little tighter than usual. She felt his heart beating steadily against hers, and it gave her a feeling of security.

Looking up at him, she smiled. "Brian, this is so nice. I love dancing with you."

Smiling back, he pulled her a little closer, and she felt his heart beat a little faster. Dropping her head on his shoulder, she closed her eyes and gave herself up to the music. It felt good to be held like this.

It was funny, but it seemed as if some of the pain she felt over losing Roger was gone. She knew she still wanted him. Just looking at Roger still made her heart beat faster and her breath catch in her throat. Curiously, it just didn't feel quite as crushing. The pain wasn't as intense. "Am I getting over him?" she asked herself; although there didn't seem to be an answer to her question.

The rest of the evening was great. During the movie, Miranda cuddled against Brian and he put his arm firmly around her. It felt good, and sensing Cindy watching them, Miranda glanced over at her. Cindy raised her eyebrows and gave her a wicked grin, and a thumbs up sign. Miranda knew there would be questions later, but right now she felt so good she just wanted things to stay this way for a little while longer.

Arriving back at the house, Roger suggested; "Brian, I know Cindy would like to spend some time with Miranda so why don't we go out on the porch and have a beer before we go to bed?"

"Sounds good to me," Brian answered. "I know Miranda misses Cindy a lot and I assume they have a great deal of catching up to do. Miranda talks about Cindy all the time."

As the guys headed into the kitchen to get a beer, Miranda went up to her bedroom to freshen up. She wasn't surprised when Cindy joined her. "Is there something you're not telling me?" she asked Miranda teasingly.

"Whatever do you mean?" Miranda asked quizzically. *As if she didn't know what Cindy was talking about...*

"You know what I mean! What's going on between you and Brian? Is there something I should know?"

"Of course not! Brian is my boss and we are becoming good friends, nothing more."

"Are you sure? It looked like more to me."

"Yes, I'm sure. I think Brian is a very physical man, and he likes to be close to women. He's very tender, gentle, and caring; and he's been very good to me."

"Well my advice to you, 'little sister', is to get hold of him and hang on. You two make a neat couple. Your fairness against his dark coloring...He seems too good to be true and I certainly wouldn't let him get away if I were you. Now if I weren't married..."

"Well you are, so just forget about it," Miranda said teasingly.

"Oh, by the way, I almost forgot to tell you something," Cindy threw over her shoulder as she started to leave the room. "Roger said he would like to talk to you privately for a few minutes. Could you meet him in his office?"

Paling, Miranda just stared at the door after Cindy left. What on earth could Roger want to talk to her about? Almost too afraid to find out, Miranda made her way down to Roger's office. Knocking timidly on the door, she pushed it open slightly.

"Cindy said you wanted to talk to me?"

"Yes, please come in and close the door," Roger said, coming toward her.

Taking her arm, he led her over to the couch. Sitting down beside her, he seemed at a loss for words for a moment. Miranda was getting more and more apprehensive. "Roger, is there something wrong with Cindy that you're afraid to tell me about? You seem so serious."

"No, Miranda. There's a question I need answered. This has been bothering me since the wedding and I want to ask you about it. I'm just not quite sure how to say it."

Now Miranda was sure she knew what was coming, and jumping to her feet she moved agitatedly about the room. Turning toward him, she said frantically, "Please Roger, just leave it. For both our sakes just don't ask me."

"I have to know, Miranda. Are you in love with me?"

Miranda slowly sank down on the sofa and put her hands over her eyes. Unable to stop the tears that flooded her eyes, she pleaded; "Please Roger! Please don't ask me."

Reaching for her, he pulled her hands from her eyes. Taking a tissue from the side table, he tried to wipe the tears, but they just kept coming. Taking her in his arms he rocked her gently, murmuring, "I'm sorry Miranda, but I just had to know. For all of our sakes, this is something you can't keep hiding."

Panicking, she pushed him away blindly. "You can't say anything to Cindy, Roger! You just can't! It would destroy her. I told her you didn't mean anything to me, and you can't ever tell her anything different. Promise me! Please, Roger," she pleaded frantically.

"All right, Miranda. I won't tell her, I promise." Sighing, she sank against him, and he held her tightly until she quieted. "I'm sorry, Miranda, I didn't know. I don't know what I would have done differently, but I wish I had known."

Lifting her head, she moved slightly away from him. "You wouldn't have done anything differently, and I wouldn't have let you. You loved Cindy from the first moment you saw her, and there's no way I could have come between you."

"But what you must have suffered! Having to watch your sister get married to the man you loved. How were you able to keep up such a front and not let her know? As close as you two are I can't believe it was possible."

"I honestly don't know how I have been able to, either. That's why I was so afraid to come today. Having Brian with me is a lifesaver. If it weren't for him, I'm afraid Cindy would know something was wrong. He calmed me down before I got here, and has been there for me all day."

"I thought there was something funny about his being so protective of you. Does he know how you feel?" Roger asked.

"He knows something is wrong, but I haven't told him what it is. He's a smart man. If you were able to see through me, I'm afraid he might be able to figure out what is bothering me, too. I hope he doesn't. I feel so foolish as it is, and I don't want him feeling sorry for me."

"Don't ever feel that way, Miranda. I am so sorry I hurt you because I never meant to and I am at a loss as to know what to say to help you."

"There's nothing you can say, Roger. I just pray that someday I find someone as wonderful as you whom I can share my love with. I want what you and Cindy have."

Putting his arms around her, he held her tightly for a moment. "I hope you find that too, Miranda, and I will be praying for that day. I'm sorry I upset you, but I've been worrying about you all day. For my own peace of mind, I just needed to know what was wrong."

Tiredly she said; "I'm not OK, but someday I will be. Go back to Cindy, but please don't let her know anything's wrong, OK?"

"I'll be very careful," Roger promised. "I'm sorry Miranda."

Totally exhausted, Miranda made her way to her bedroom. She changed into a floor length, silk nightgown. Letting her hair down, she sat down to brush it. She looked a mess. Her eyes were red and swollen and she was glad no one saw her coming back to her bedroom. What would she have told Cindy if she ran into her on the way back? The thought sent a shiver down her spine. It was unthinkable. She found her hand trembling thinking about Roger and Cindy together in their bedroom. What would Roger say to Cindy? Miranda knew Cindy would be full of questions, but Roger promised, and she knew he would keep his promise.

Climbing into bed, she tried to sleep, but was unable to settle down. She kept thinking about Roger. She loved him so much, and even more so because of his gentleness with her tonight. He could have laughed at her, or ridiculed her for her love; but that was why she loved him in the first place. She knew the kind of man he was. He would never deliberately hurt her. Tossing and turning, her body burning, she could feel his lips on hers. Oh, how she wanted him! She had to stop this. Roger wasn't hers and would never be. He belonged to her sister and she didn't have any right to be feeling these things. It must stop!

Sliding out of bed, she pulled the matching top over her nightgown. She knew that it wasn't adequate covering, but assumed since it was so late that everyone would be asleep. Opening the door, she started toward the kitchen; thinking maybe a glass of warm milk would help her to sleep.

She stopped suddenly, enchanted by the flood of light coming in through the living room window. Cindy had left the curtains open, and the room was flooded with moonlight. Stepping closer to the window, she could see a beautiful, full moon shinning in the sky, surrounded by millions of twinkling stars. It was such a fascinating sight, Miranda stood there, enthralled. It reminded her of another night, and another moon; a night where she hadn't been so terribly unhappy.

Unknowingly, she cast a spell over the man standing silently in the shadows. Brian had been unable to sleep because the events of the day kept running through his mind. A few minutes earlier, he had come downstairs hoping to clear his mind so he could get some sleep. He was startled when Miranda walked into the room. He started to say something to her, but something stopped him.

Miranda had no way of knowing that the moonlight surrounded her, making a silhouette of her nude body through the thin material of her nightgown. With his heart pounding, and his pulse racing, Brian just stood there, unable to move. Her hair floated around her like a shimmering curtain of gold, sometimes revealing glimpses of her lovely form. As she finally turned to leave, he could see her beautiful breasts outlined against the material of her gown. He wanted to go to her and kiss her until she surrendered to him, but the glimmer of tears in her eyes stopped him.

He knew she must be thinking about Roger; and sadly, he remembered the time he had kissed her and heard her murmuring Roger's name. He couldn't go through that again. He longed to have her in his arms — loving and kissing him — and no one else. He knew he could accept it no other way and until that time came, he would just have to be patient.

He stood silent as she left the room. In the moonlight, he watched as tears filled her eyes and collected like sparkling dew on her lashes, before they finally spilled down her cheeks. She put her hand to her eyes and tried to wipe some of them away, but they just trickled slowly through her fingers. He heard a soft sob as she put both hands over her eyes in an effort to stem the tide, and once again he longed to go to her.

He knew this was something she was going to have to resolve by herself. Nothing he could do would stop the longings she felt for Roger. Only time and space could do that. All he knew right now was that he wanted to be there for her, whenever she needed someone. Brian now knew he loved her.

Chapter Thirty-One

The next morning, Miranda awoke, feeling hollow-eyed and tired. Brian and Roger both saw the shadows under her eyes, but they said nothing. Cindy gave her a strange, searching look, but she didn't say anything until later.

Miranda was determinedly cheerful the rest of the morning. Only Brian noticed how often her eyes strayed toward Roger and the longing which came into them. Miranda was very careful not to let Roger see how often she looked at him. She didn't want to cause him any more pain. For his sake, she tried to be very pleasant, and, after a while, she actually did feel better.

After lunch, as she and Cindy were cleaning up the dishes, Cindy asked her what Roger wanted to see her about the night before.

"Didn't you ask him?" Miranda asked apprehensively.

"Well sure, but he wouldn't tell me. He was acting so mysterious, he's got me curious. He seemed sad and absentminded when he came back to our room."

Thinking quickly, Miranda said, "You must have just imagined it. He was fine when he left me. As far as what we talked about, you do have a birthday coming up soon, so stop being so nosey!"

Nicely sidetracked now, Cindy started trying to get information out of Miranda about her birthday present. She would have to remember to talk to Roger about it, so he would be sure and surprise her. Knowing him, he probably would anyway. A little while later, she took him aside and told him about Cindy's concerns.

"Thanks Miranda, I was having trouble ducking all her questions. Are you all right today?"

"Yes, Roger, I'll be just fine. Stop worrying about me and take care of your beautiful wife." Giving him a gentle smile, she walked away.

Brian hadn't missed their interchange and wondered what had taken place between them. Miranda did seem a lot more calm and happy today.

They put up a croquet set on the lawn and had a rousing game. To his surprise, Brian learned Miranda was very competitive. It was a side of her he didn't know about. She was always knocking someone else's ball out of the way, so she could get ahead. She never ceased to amaze him.

Later, as they played cards, he saw this same competitiveness. Brian took cards with a grain of salt, often playing sloppily, but Miranda took them very seriously, and several times she got on him for being so careless. Cindy and Roger played the same way, and they had a battle going before it was over. Brian was having more fun watching them than playing cards. He was happy to see Miranda with rosy cheeks and sparkling eyes.

After dinner, they sat talking quietly for a little while before Miranda said; "Brian, I think we should get going. It will be dark long before we get home."

"Oh, I hate to see you go," Cindy cried tearfully, hugging her close. "I miss you already. It's terrible not being able to run over and talk to you whenever I want to."

"I know," Miranda said, just as tearfully, "But you have Roger now."

"Of course I do, but it's not the same as having a sister to confide in."

Giving Roger a quick hug, Miranda waved and ran out to the car, with Brian following.

Cindy and Roger followed them out the door. "When will we see you again?" Roger asked.

"Probably when you come down to see me. It's your turn next, you know!"

"That's true. We'll see what we can do," Roger answered.

"Take care of yourself; and Brian, thanks so much for coming up with her. It was really nice getting to know you," Cindy called.

"You too," Brian called back. "I enjoyed myself very much. It was fun watching both of you together. If it weren't for your different hairstyles, I'd find it hard to tell you two apart." Cindy still wore her hair short and curly.

"I have a cuter nose than Miranda," Cindy teased.

"Forgive me, I must have missed that," Brian laughed.

"Hey, you two. Cindy, how dare you? Your nose is not cuter than mine," Miranda joined in the teasing.

Waving, they pulled out of the driveway and headed home. Miranda gave a sigh of relief and settled back in her seat. She was glad Brian was driving so she wouldn't have to concentrate on anything.

"Cindy's really nice," Brian commented. "I really enjoyed watching you two together because your personalities are dissimilar in many ways."

"I'm not surprised you noticed. I was always the domineering one when we were growing up. I guess I bossed her around a lot, but she never seemed to mind. Mom often got on me and told me to stop being so bossy, but I guess it was just part of my nature." A smile lurked in her eyes, as she said, "Now she's all grown up and married, so I can't tell her what to do anymore."

"I know how that goes. It was a lot that way with my brother and I, but we all have to grow up sometime and start our own lives. It must have been hard for you to leave her to come to Medford. By the way, how did Cindy and Roger meet, anyway?" Brian asked casually. He often wondered how both sisters fell in love with the same man.

"I met him first and we dated for awhile. When I finally introduced them, it was love at first sight." He could hear the sadness in her voice. Reading between the lines of what she said, Brian realized she was probably already in love with Roger before he met Cindy.

Putting on some soft music, Brian drove steadily. Miranda stopped talking and when he glanced over at her, she appeared to be asleep. He knew she must be very tired, because it was after midnight when he saw her downstairs the night before. Just thinking about it made his breath quicken. He hadn't gotten much sleep himself. In fact, it was almost dawn before he finally went to sleep.

Miranda wasn't asleep, but she felt very lethargic, unable to move. She was mentally and emotionally drained. She lay there quietly with her head against the window and her mind a void. She was too tired to even think.

She roused herself a little later to ask if he wanted her to drive.

Smiling at her gently, he said, "You seem very tired and I'm doing fine. Why don't you lay down with your head on my lap and sleep for awhile."

Too tired to protest, Miranda loosened her seat belt so it wouldn't cut into her when she laid down, then slid over and put her head on his lap. She was thankful for the nice, comfortable bench seat in Brian's car. "Thanks Brian," she murmured, "This feels good." She put her hand up on his leg to cushion her cheek, and was soon sound asleep. He could feel her breathing softly, and let out a deep breath.

"Brian, what have you done to yourself? You've got to be crazy!" he thought.

It was almost more than he could abide, feeling her softness against him. Unable to resist, he let his hand linger on her hair for a moment, stroking it softly, and then gently touched her face. She sighed and moved slightly which was almost his undoing. He could feel his body responding to her soft movements and he tried desperately to think of something else. Rolling down the window, he let in some cool night air which seemed to help a bit.

When it became more than he could bear, he stopped the car for gas. His heart was racing; he felt hot, and his body was alive with longing. Touching her shoulder gently, he said; "Miranda."

Startled, she looked up at him, and then sat up quickly almost bumping her head against his chin. Her face flamed and she looked away from him for a moment. When she regained some composure, she glanced at him shyly.

"I'm sorry. What must you think of me?"

"Don't you remember? It was my suggestion. You looked so uncomfortable trying to sleep sitting up, and you looked so tired."

"Well, I must have been awfully tired because I don't remember. Thanks for the nice cushion," she chuckled. "I feel a lot better now."

"I'm glad you do," muttered Brian under his breath, "because I sure don't." Grimacing, he got out of the car. After filling the car with gas, he walked around for a few minutes. By the time he got back to the car, he was in control of himself.

"Brian, before we leave, would you like something to drink to help keep you awake?" Miranda asked.

"Sure, a coffee, black, would be good."

"OK, back in a moment," Miranda said as she headed into the station.

Miranda said she felt good enough to drive the rest of the way, so Brian walked around to the other side. Taking a deep breath, he slipped into the seat.

Teasing, she said, "Maybe I should offer you my lap for the rest of the trip?"

"No thanks," he said more sharply than he intended, "I think I'll pass..." And under his breath; "That would be more than any man could take."

A little hurt at his tone, Miranda asked, "Did you say something?"

"I said the car's a little short for me. I'd be cramped."

Laughing, she said. "Duh! I guess it would be a little uncomfortable."

"More than you know," Brian thought.

They finished the rest of the trip with Brian dozing some and talking at other times. She seemed to sense when he wanted to talk and when he wanted to be quiet. She was such a restful person to be with. Some of the tension eased from his body, but he would be glad when they arrived back at her place.

When they got to her apartment, Miranda and Brian both got out of the car. As Brian came around to walk her to the door, Miranda said; "Brian, you'll never know how much I appreciate this. Someday, maybe I'll be able to tell you how much it meant to me."

At the door, she turned to him and lightly kissed his cheek, but this time, despite all of his good intentions; it was Brian who turned his head so that their lips met. He meant for it to be a quick, goodnight kiss, but the minute her lips touched his, it turned into something more. All of the tension of the evening had built up inside of him and before she realized what was happening, he drew her into his arms. His lips were firm and urgent on hers. She stood motionless for a moment, her heart pounding, before her arms crept up around his neck. He made an inarticulate sound in his throat and his kisses became hungrier. Exploring the shape of her lips with the tip of his tongue, he teased them apart, until her mouth opened to his, flooding her with a desire she had never felt before.

Clinging to him, she wanted nothing more than to forget everything and give herself up to this mindless longing she felt. But some shred of sanity held her back and she wrenched out of his arms, panting. Her breathing was ragged, and she searched his face in the shadowed darkness surrounding it. The sounds of the traffic were blocked out, and she could hear nothing except the sound of their harsh breathing.

"Goodnight, Miranda," he said, and then strode back to his car.

Watching blindly, Miranda unknowingly touched her lips with her fingers. She had been kissed before, but never like this. She couldn't remember ever being affected like this before, not even when Roger kissed her. What was wrong with her anyway?

Trembling, she struggled to wrap her mind around what just happened. As she got ready for bed that night, her mind returned again and again to their embrace. She could still feel his lips burning against hers because they had left a fiery imprint wherever they touched.

Unable to get to sleep immediately; not surprisingly, it was Brian's face and not Roger's she saw. For the first time since Cindy's wedding, Miranda found herself thinking about someone besides Roger. Miranda couldn't get Brian out of her mind and he was all she could think about for the next few days. She couldn't stop remembering the warmth, tenderness, and passion between them during their trip, and she placed her hand over her heart which was beating a little faster than normal.

Brian didn't fare any better, and he was the one who came to work for a few days looking tired and worn out. Neither one of them could bring themselves to mention what happened. Consequently, nothing was said, but it stayed there between them, unspoken, but real.

Chapter Thirty-Two

One Friday, after a very hard week, Brian came and sat down on the edge of Miranda's desk. She was just getting ready to leave for the .weekend. For once they didn't have to work a few hours on Saturday as they had been doing for a while.

"What are you doing this weekend?"

"Nothing special. Why?" she asked.

"Well, we've been working long, hard hours and I thought a break would be nice. Would you like to go to the beach with me?"

"Yes," Miranda said eagerly. "I absolutely love the coast, from Newport down to the California border. There is nothing like driving along the rugged coastline and getting to witness the power of the Pacific Ocean. Someday I hope to get up to Astoria and drive further up the Washington side. My parents never took us that far up the coast. To answer your question, yes. I would love to go to the coast with you. What do you have in mind?"

"What would you think of taking off for Gold Beach Saturday morning, spending the night, and coming back on Sunday evening?" Brian asked. "We could drive down to Brookings and then up Highway 101 to Gold Beach. It's been a long time since I've been to Brookings. I don't know about you, but I could use a break from work. We've had to work way too many Saturdays and I'm just plain tired. Should we play hooky for once?" he teased.

"That sounds like...fun," she said a little slowly. Miranda wasn't quite sure how to broach the subject of accommodations because of what had happened between them after their trip to

Eugene. She didn't want to embarrass him by asking his intentions, but neither did she want to be put in an embarrassing situation by not asking.

As if reading her mind, Brian grinned and said, "Separate rooms, of course."

"Of course," she said smiling. Now, since that was cleared up, she was really pleased Brian wanted her to go with him.

Miranda was a little nervous Saturday morning, but when Brian arrived, she was ready and waiting. Her gaze swept over him. Most of the time, she was used to seeing him in business suits, although she had seen him dressed in oxford shirts, with the sleeves rolled up, and black casual pants. Today was different. Miranda's heart reacted to him in snug-fitting jeans that hugged his body, and a matching grey shirt with the sleeves rolled up revealing muscular arms. With his shirt partially unbuttoned, she could see silky black hair peeping from his shirt collar.

She found herself slightly breathless, and for some reason, wanted to reach out and touch him. Flustered, she dropped her eyes. She now knew that she wasn't immune to him; and knowing what it was like to be held and kissed by him, wasn't helping either. Since she still loved Roger, she was trying to understand why she was so attracted to Brian. In her mind it didn't make a lot of sense.

Trying to turn her thoughts elsewhere, she walked over to his car. This wasn't the same car he drove to Eugene. It was a beautiful, gunmetal grey Lamborghini, built for speed. It looked sleek and powerful. She thought how appropriate the color was. It matched his eyes beautifully. "What a fabulous car," she said. "I've never ridden in one even remotely like this car, so this is going to be fun."

Smiling, Brian reached down and opened the door for her. "I hope you enjoy the experience," he smiled. "I'm sure looking forward to this weekend away from work. What about you?"

"Absolutely," Miranda said as she settled into her seat. As he maneuvered the powerful car into traffic, Miranda admired the way he sat relaxed behind the wheel.

After driving for a few minutes, he glanced over at her. "Have you had much chance to get out and explore Medford?"

"Yes, while I was waiting for my things to arrive, I drove around and became acquainted with the area," she answered.

"What about new friends? I know you met mine, but have you had a chance to meet many others?"

"Yes. Actually, Andre — from the lab — and I have become good friends. We've seen quite a bit of each other. I've also enjoyed lunch a few times with Lindy and Kayla from accounting. They are very nice. I have a passing acquaintance with some of the other staff."

Brian listened quietly as she continued, "I started attending St. Sebastian's Methodist Church and met some very nice people there. A few weeks ago, Marsha and Kyle Stewart asked me over for dinner. They invited two other couples and we had a wonderful time. They like to play hearts so Marsha invited a young man named Steven to be my partner. We've seen each other a couple of times since then. He's very nice."

"Well you sure seem to be getting around. I'm glad you've been able to make so many friends. I know it can get very lonely when you're new in town."

Brian felt a stab of jealousy because she was going out so much with other guys. He had noticed her in the hallway a couple of times with Andre and that was one of the reasons he asked her to go with him this weekend. He wanted to be the only one in her life when she got over her feelings for Roger. He wanted to make some memories with her so that if there was ever a chance, she would turn to him.

As they drove along, Miranda kept glancing at him. He was a fascinating man. She observed him being very strong and aggressive when it came to business, but she saw another side to him as well. He wasn't afraid to be kind and gentle; and she knew from experience that he was tender and caring as well. She admired the way he handled his professional life. He was never harsh or mean, but he was exacting and tough when he needed to be. She really liked the Brian she was getting to know.

Watching him surreptitiously, she noticed his beautifully-shaped hands. She was growing used to his face, but she never grew tired of watching the expressions that flitted across it. She often found herself wishing she knew what he was thinking. Sometimes at work, she would look up and surprise a very strange expression in his eyes, a mixture of pain and longing.

Because they sat close in the car, Miranda felt his legs brushing against hers from time to time. Her eyes were drawn to his powerful thighs; the muscles rippling across his legs as he changed gears. Restless, all of a sudden, Miranda glanced up to find his eyes fixed on her.

Their glances locked for a moment, and Miranda found it hard to get her breath. Once again, she wanted to reach out and touch him. Brian must have sensed something of what she was feeling because a smoldering look of passion came into his eyes. Looking away, hardly knowing what she said, she made some inane comment about the country they were passing through.

Brian sensed her disquiet and starting talking quietly. They passed the next couple of hours pleasantly. Topics ranged from sports, to politics, to childhood experiences. They had some heated debates on several topics. As they got better acquainted, they discovered some differences in what they liked and disliked. Fishing was a sport that Miranda had never tried. She always thought it looked boring, but after listening to Brian tell some of his experiences, she decided it was something she would like to try sometime.

It was fun discovering some of the things that they looked at differently. For instance, Roger already knew Miranda was an avid card player but Brian felt it was a waste of time. Brian loved the opera, but Miranda would rather see a rip-roaring comedy.

They already knew they both loved the outdoors; hiking being one of their greatest pleasures. Miranda's parents travelled a lot with her and Cindy when they were growing up. They spent a lot of time just hiking and seeing the country. Miranda and Cindy had grown up loving the ski slopes. Both she and Cindy still went whenever they could find the time. When she told Brian about skiing, Brian said he had tried it a few times but said he wasn't sure if he'd ever get the hang of staying upright.

"I doubt I would ever get the hang of skiing. The one time I tried it, I got the skis on; and confidently started out thinking I kinda had it figured out. Whoops! Down I would go, legs sprawling, time after time. My friends were laughing so hard they almost fell themselves. I spent more time sitting or lying down in the snow than skiing," Brian grimaced and then burst into laughter. "You should have seen me!"

His laughter was contagious and Miranda found herself giggling as she pictured him; confident, proud Brian sprawled in the snow. Chuckling, she said, "I guess I don't remember that because we were pretty young the first time mom and dad took us. It probably hurts a lot more when you try to learn as an adult!"

"I guess," Brian said ruefully.

Both of them had been to several of the national parks, including The Grand Canyon, Yellowstone, Grand Teton, and Glacier National Park, not to mention Crater Lake. Brian had always wanted to hike down the Grand Canyon, but Miranda said she would rather go somewhere where she could see waterfalls, lakes, and rivers and not have to exert so much energy.

Chapter Thirty-Three

Stopping for lunch, they took a leisurely stroll into a nearby park. Brian asked a local restaurant to pack a picnic lunch for them before they left; so they sat down by a small stream to enjoy their picnic.

The stream meandered slowly through the woods, babbling and murmuring happily as it flowed over the stones. Miranda loved to sit quietly and watch the constant movement of the water as it dipped and gurgled, drifting in and out of hidden crevices. If Miranda looked closely enough, she could see small fish swimming merrily along in little ponds.

The weather was balmy and warm on the way to the coast. Brian was so happy the day wasn't rainy, dreary, or cold; the way it often turned out to be.

They both hoped the beach would have one of its rare and glorious days. "I hate it when you decide to take a day off and come to the coast only to find it's so foggy you can't see anything, and it's cold and miserable, as well," Brian said. "Brookings seems to be the exception. It can be in the seventies in January and February and some people call Brookings 'Oregon's Banana Belt' because of warmer temperatures."

"I understand that nearly all the lilies marketed in the U.S. are cultivated in Brookings, and one year my parents brought us to the annual Azalea Festival over Memorial Day weekend," Miranda added to what Brian had said. "It was so beautiful with all the colors and a lot of the azaleas were trimmed into different shapes. I've often thought about coming down to watch the Southern Kite Festival in July, but have never made the time."

Brian added, "In contrast, Gold Beach is sixty feet above sea level in mountainous, timbered, scenic terrain. It can get so cold and windy, that even a heavy coat isn't enough."

At other times, though, there are days where it is sunny, balmy, and pleasant. "It's looking like we will get lucky," Brian commented as they got closer.

"I hope so," Miranda said. "It was beautiful the weekend I came down."

Arriving at Gold Beach, they found it was indeed, beautiful. A light jacket was all they needed. After checking in at their motel, which was right on the beach, they met out by the ocean.

Brian reached out, as if it were a natural thing to do, and took Miranda's hand as they walked toward the waves. They both stood for a few minutes just watching the movement of the ocean as it ebbed and flowed. Today, the waves were fairly high and there was a light breeze.

Releasing his hand, Miranda turned her face into the wind. Holding her arms at shoulder height, she started turning in big circles; windmilling her arms. It was so peaceful and yet so primitive. She felt like she was communing with nature. With her hair loose and flowing in the wind, she was beautiful beyond anything Brian had ever seen. He could almost imagine her as a sea goddess; bewitching all those who saw her. She certainly had bewitched Brian, almost from the first moment he saw her.

After watching for a few moments, Brian joined Miranda with her wind dance; whirling, dancing, and laughing at her antics. But, what he actually wanted to do, was take her in his arms and kiss her. The combination of the wind, sand, and the ocean made him want to embrace life and live it to the fullest.

Brian was glad to see Miranda so happy and excited. He hoped this trip would help her put the past behind her and start to build a new life for herself. He knew for certain that he wanted to be part of her future; in whatever way she would let him. Brian was willing to put in all the time it took to help her heal, and he wanted her to know he was there for her. Just being with her right now was reward enough.

With a sense of anticipation, he caught her in midstride and threw his arms around her and twirled her in a circle. Both collapsed breathlessly onto the sand and lay flat on their backs for awhile.

"Hey, how would you like to go get one of those fancy kites? I never get tired of watching them dip, caper, and swirl like a mad dervish in the wind," Brian said, after taking a moment to catch his breath.

"Yes, let's do!" she said, jumping to her feet and grabbing his hand. Laughing, they raced back to the car. A little while later they came out of the store with a beautiful dragon kite.

For the next several hours they were like youngsters; sometimes running down the beach with the kite, even taking off their shoes to run in the waves. The water was so icy cold that they could only stand it for a minute or two. Shivering, they would race down the sand to get warm, collapsing on the sand to catch their breath.

After a while, Miranda and Brian sat quietly watching the waves roll in and smash against the rocks, or walking along hand in hand exploring the tide pools. It was exciting to discover all the little sea creatures hidden in the crevices of the rocks. There were places along the beach where they climbed up on the rocks to watch the waves roll into the clefts. The tide would bring the waves in so strong that they crashed into the rocks, sending spray high into the air.

They sat for a long time without talking just watching the natural ebb and flow of the ocean. It made Miranda realize how small humans are in the scheme of things as she watched the power of the waves; seeing them smash into the rocks, only to race back out to sea, soon to return. Later, Brian and Miranda raced the tide, to see if they could make it across a shallow place before the waves could reach them.

Out of the blue, Miranda misjudged how far out she was when the water receded, and she raced to beat a big wave coming in. Brian heard her screaming his name just as the wave hit her and knocked her off her feet. Running as fast as he could, he grabbed her as the waves were getting ready to knock her over again.

"Miranda!" he gasped as he helped her up, quickly getting out of harm's way. "What made you get so far out? I should have been watching so I could warn you." Then, he couldn't help laughing. She looked like a drowned rat standing there, dripping wet. He wasn't so dry himself. He found himself laughing uproariously.

"Brian," she said piteously, "I'm freezing!"

Belatedly, realizing she needed to get out of her wet clothes and get warm, he grabbed her hand and ran with her as fast as he could back to her motel room. Once inside, she just stood there shivering. Her teeth were chattering so hard she couldn't speak, and water was dripping everywhere.

Standing like a statue, Brian couldn't take his eyes off of her. The water had plastered her blouse to her and since she hadn't put on a bra, her breasts stood out enchantingly. Her nipples were swollen from the cold and straining against the fabric because of her rapid breathing. His mouth was so dry he had to swallow. His breathing became shallow and hoarse.

"Brian...! Brian...! What's wrong with you? Can you get me a towel, please? Can't you see I'm freezing to death?" Miranda finally croaked.

Coming out of the fog he was in, Brian picked her up and carried her into the bathroom. He quickly turned the hot water on and thrust her under the shower.

Sputtering, she blubbered, "Now you're trying to drown me!"

"I don't want you to get pneumonia! Are you going to be all right?"

"Sure," she stuttered, still shivering. "I'll...be just...fine."

"Then I'm going into the other room. Here are a couple of towels. Please stay under the hot water for awhile.

Dragging his eyes away from her, he left and went into the bedroom, shutting the door. He was breathing as if he had run an uphill race. His heart was pounding and his body felt like it was on fire. His manhood was straining against his jeans.

By the time Miranda came out, wrapped in a towel, he had himself partially under control. But the sight of her long, slender legs and thighs barely covered by the towel had him straining to keep that control.

Muttering that he would let her get dressed, he almost ran out the door.

Once inside his own room, he collapsed into the nearest chair. "Wow!" he muttered, "If this keeps up I'm not going to survive today, much less tomorrow."

Even though he was just about as wet as Miranda, he wasn't cold. His skin felt like it was on fire. Hurriedly getting out of his wet clothes, he stepped under a cool shower. A little later, he was still shivering from the cold, but the shower hadn't done much to shake the image of her from his mind. Knocking on the door between their rooms, he asked if she was OK.

She said, "Yes, but I can't quit shivering so I'm going to climb into bed and try to get warm."

On the other side of the wall, Brian paced like a caged tiger; the picture of her beautiful body branded on his brain. It didn't take much imagination for him to envision what she must look like; all curled into a ball trying to get warm. It took all of the control he was capable of not to open that door and crawl into bed with her. How he longed to curl up with her, bringing her into the warmth of his own body. Even the thought of it made him start to throb again. Finally, grabbing a jacket, he left his room and spent the next hour in hard walking and jogging along the beach. When he returned to his room, he was too tired to do anything but lay down and rest, falling into a deep sleep.

Chapter Thirty-Four

That night they went to a local seafood restaurant and had a relaxing dinner. Afterward, they took a moonlit walk along the beach. Unresisting, Miranda let him take her hand. The sky was filled with millions of twinkling stars and the moon was big and luminous; seemingly suspended right over their heads. The sounds of the night surrounded them. They listened to the swish of the waves breaking against the shore and both felt as if their senses were heightened. They were very much aware of each other.

Feeling Miranda's hand start to shake, and hearing a strange sound coming from her, Brian turned quickly to see what was wrong. Instead of finding anything wrong, he heard giggling. As he watched curiously, she started to shake with laughter. Asking what was so funny got him nowhere, because she continued to chuckle helplessly; holding her stomach and throwing her head back, as peal after peal of laughter rippled through her. Exasperated, Brian finally took her shoulders and shook her lightly, asking; "Hey, what's so funny? Let me in on it, won't you?"

Shaking her head and clutching her stomach, she collapsed onto the sand. "Oh, I must have looked so funny when that wave knocked me over," Miranda gasped. "I was so cold I thought I would die and you just stood there laughing at me. Then you had the nerve to throw me under the shower with all my clothes on. The water was so hot I thought it would scorch my skin!"

Her humor was contagious and Brian found himself lying on the sand beside her, unable to control his own mirth. "You did look like a drowned rat!" he gasped. Finally, unable to laugh anymore because their sides were hurting, they both lay back on the sand, trying to control the snickers that kept threatening to erupt.

After a while, Brian sat up and looked down at Miranda. She was irresistible and it would have taken a stronger man than he to do so. She looked relaxed and he knew her laughter had been good for her. This weekend had been a good idea.

Staring up at Brian, Miranda wondered what he was thinking. For the first time in ages, she felt a lightness around her heart. Brian was good for her. Reaching up, she put a hand lightly to his cheek. Taking her hand in his, he brought it to his lips and kissed her fingers softly. Running his tongue over the palm of her hand, he felt her shiver. Bending closer toward her, his grey eyes were like a dark night with no moon.

Her breath whispered over his face as he bent closer. Her tongue crept out to moisten suddenly dry lips. She knew he was going to kiss her and she longed for it. Impatiently, she reached up and pulled his face down so that their lips touched, soft as a whisper.

He kissed her tentatively at first, tasting and savoring. His hands came up to thread through her hair, burying his face in it for a moment. His lips returned to trail a line of fire from her chin, her eyelids, her cheeks, pausing at her lips.

Pulling him completely down to her, she took his lips fully, passionately. His hips strained against her, making her aware of how fully-aroused he was. Whimpering into his mouth, her hands moving over his body, she moved sensuously against him. Her body arched to meet the fiery hand that slipped beneath the front of her blouse to cup a bare breast. —Didn't she ever wear a bra?

Miranda was helpless to contain the small cry of pleasure that escaped her. At that moment, a cloud passed over the moon, creating almost total darkness. A shiver trembled over her skin, chilling her completely. She became still and unresponsive.

Sensing the change in her, Brian rolled away from her and sat up. He leaned back on his heels, bracing his hands on his thighs, his body rigid with tension. Pushing himself to his feet, he walked a few paces away. Breathing raggedly, he fought for control.

This had to stop or he was going to hurt her worse than she already was.

Finally walking back to where Miranda still sat, he knelt beside her. She slumped, unmoving with her face in her hands.

Reaching out and touching her gently, he said; "Miranda?"

She didn't look up and he could feel her tremble. "Miranda, please forgive me. I didn't mean for this to happen. You were just so beautiful lying there on the sand, I couldn't keep myself from touching you. I just wanted to bring you here for a weekend of relaxation, and now I've ruined it for you."

Lifting her head slightly, Miranda shook her head and mumbled, "No, it was more my fault than yours."

Tentatively reaching out and lifting her face with his hands, Brian could see tears running down her cheeks. Wiping them gently away with his fingers, he said softly; "I didn't mean to hurt you, Miranda. I'm so sorry."

Stumbling to her feet, Miranda stood looking at him with tear-moistened eyes. "I'm sorry too," she choked. "I just get so lonely sometimes, and you felt so good. I shouldn't have let this happen. It's not fair to you. Thanks for bringing me to my senses."

226

She seemed so vulnerable standing there, that Brian put his arms around her and held her gently, tenderly. She was so warm and fragrant, so responsive; the way she settled into his arms, resting her head against his heart, her hand against his shoulder. She deserved more than she was getting from him and Roger. He would have to be very careful not to let this happen again. He didn't want to hurt her.

Maybe somewhere in the future there would be a time for them but he didn't want to ruin their chance by hurting her now. She had seemed so happy today and he didn't want to put her back into that deep, dark despair he had seen her in after Cindy's wedding.

Taking her back to her room, he touched her face softly and kissed her lightly. "Sleep well, Miranda," he said tenderly.

Chapter Thirty-Five

After a long night with very little sleep, Brian got up around five and went for a walk on the beach. Returning, he found Miranda was also up early. She was engrossed in watching the waves as they rolled in and out. She looked pensive and quiet. "Miranda, are you all right?" he asked.

Turning slowly to face him, she nodded. He could see the pain lingering in her lovely eyes. "Can we forget what happened last night?" she asked huskily. "Pretend it never happened?"

Touching her face softly, he slowly stroked her cheek with his thumb. "Yes, Miranda, we'll forget about it and try to have a nice day, OK?"

She nodded again and he saw the pain in her eyes start to fade a little. She even gave him a tentative smile as she turned and stared out at the ocean. "Do you have any specific plans for today?"

"Not yet, but I had an idea this morning. How would you like to take a jet boat trip on the Rogue River? There's a boat that leaves at 8:30. They have a two-hour stopover with lunch upriver and we can take the return boat at 2:30. I've always wanted to do this and we'll get back in plenty of time to start home. What do you think of that idea?"

"It sounds wonderful. What is the trip like?"

"We'll be in a fairly small boat and I'm not sure how many people it holds. It's a 104-mile whitewater trip. There are experienced guides and they provide a fully-narrated river trip with plenty of stops to enjoy the wildlife and scenery."

"Sure, let's go. What do we need to do?"

"I'll call and see if they have an opening. Hopefully it's not too late to make reservations. Then we should have time to grab a quick breakfast before we go," Brian said. After hanging up, he said, "They aren't full for this trip, so we can go."

When they arrived at the boat dock they grabbed waterproof jackets in the office because they were told they would get wet.

A few hours later they were sitting side by side on the boat with blankets on their laps because it was a little cold. There were several families and couples on the boat with them. Their guide, Mitchell, was very well-informed about the Rogue River and the history of Jerry's Rogue Jets. "This is the original jet boat tour on the Rogue River, and we deliver mail to the town of Agness, Oregon. The mail delivery service started in 1895 and has continued uninterrupted since then," he informed them.

Mitchell had long hair pulled back into a ponytail and a full beard. He wore a red and black checkered flannel shirt, jeans, boots, and a waterproof jacket. He started out by explaining how the jet boats ran on the Rogue River. "They have almost no draft and can operate in 6 inches of water, so they easily fly over the rapids on their way upstream. This gives one the strange sensation that the river is not very dangerous. However," he cautioned, "Things get a lot more bumpy and wet, and you really do get a feeling for the rapids themselves. So," he laughed, "If you don't want to have a bumpy ride outside this boat, I suggest you stay seated and hang on tight!"

Steering slowly at first, Mitchell continued his narrative. "The popularity of the Rogue River has been steadily growing over the years. This legendary river has long been a secret paradise for game fishermen and now I hope you enjoy its long and entertaining history, filled with tales of gold, Indians, and modern-day moviemaking."

"Is there still gold-panning?" someone asked.

"It's one of the favorite occupations of many visitors because gold is washed down from the mountains and lodges in gravel and between boulders," Mitchell responded.

"What about movies filmed here?" Brian asked.

"Many think Butch and Sundance jumped off Hellgate Canyon, but locals say it's just not true," Mitchell laughed. "Parts of 'One Flew Over the Cuckoo's Nest' was filmed here along with several others, though," Mitchell replied to Brian's question.

"Waterskiing, kayaking, canoeing is all enjoyed by visitors, as well as guide trips for the novice who wants to experience the thrill of whitewater rafting. There's really no limit to the number of things you can do on and around the river."

Mitchell continued to entertain them with tall tales and the rich history of the Rogue River and the surrounding valley. He helped them relax as they navigated the swift currents, still waters, rugged canyons, and spectacular whitewater.

The beginning of the trip was interesting and scenic. There were stretches where the water was calm and serene, and Miranda could even see her reflection when she leaned over the side to look into the water. Soon, Mitchell slowed the boat to point out a couple of otters playing in the water. Further on, a mated pair of bald eagles roosted in a large cottonwood tree on the riverbank, and rounding a bend in the river, Mitchell drew attention to a beaver lodge at

Cannery Riffle which was the former site of a salmon cannery. A little farther upstream, he directed their attention to where a black-tailed doe and her two spotted fawns grazed near the river's bank. Traveling around 30 mph, Mitchell always looked for animals, slowing or stopping to share the sights with his passengers.

Further on, Brian said excitedly; "Miranda, look! There's an eagle!" She looked where he was pointing and saw an eagle floating in the air above them; a beautiful sight as they all watched in wonder while he soared through the air. As Miranda watched, it ascended in circular sweeps without a single flap of the wings, until it disappeared from sight.

"Ready?" Mitchell suddenly yelled as he sent the boat into a sudden burst of speed, laughing uproariously as he listened to their screams of shock. "We're going at least 50 miles an hour!" he shouted as he skillfully navigated the jet boat into lots of twists, turns, and swerves for maximum fun. All too quickly for Miranda, they were stopping to stretch and take a bathroom break at Agness before continuing on to the rapids.

After the break, they all climbed back aboard and anticipation increased as, above the noise of the engine, they began to hear the sound of the rapids up ahead. Clutching Brian's arm, Miranda asked fearfully; "It sounds awfully loud, are you sure we can get over the rapids safely?"

"These boats take this trip every day. If it wasn't safe, they wouldn't be doing it."

The scenery was gorgeous and thrilling to Brian and Miranda as the river carried them upstream. Then, without warning, they were propelled into the whitewater.

Scared, Miranda huddled against Brian for a moment, but soon the excitement got to her and she was straining to see what was happening. The boat dipped and swirled as it made its way through the water. Water splashed up on all sides of the boat, getting their shoes wet as well as their arms and legs. It was a thrilling, wondrous ride and once they were clear of one of the rapids, Miranda couldn't wait for the next one.

"I hope you are enjoying the ride so far," Mitchell spoke into the microphone loud enough to be heard above the river. "I'll try to tell you a little about this part of the country as I navigate. The Wild and Scenic River designation begins — included in the Wild and Scenic Rivers Act — west of the city of Grants Pass; where Applegate River flows into the Rogue River. The river turns north, flowing through the scenic Hellgate Canyon, and then bends sharply west of Grave Creek, where the Wild Section of the Rogue River begins. Here, the powerful river cuts through the rugged terrain of the northern edge of the Klamath Mountains."

Mitchell became very busy trying to navigate a particularly tricky section of the river before continuing his narrative. "Then the river churns through the steep rock walls of Mule Creek Canyon and the boulder-strewn Blossom Bar Rapids. The 34-mile Wild section features predominately Class III or less rapids, and includes breathtaking rapids at Mule Creek."

Just above the Agness Bridge, Mitchell pointed out where the Rogue was joined by the Illinois River, which he explained was a wild and scenic stream as well.

"We're passing Foster Creek; which is the usual takeout point for whitewater rafting trips." Everyone became a little nervous and excited as Mitchell steered the powerful jet boat into the Wild Rogue Wilderness.

Suddenly, they were hanging on to the side of the boat as Mitchell dodged giant boulders and swept past brush-covered islands. Each time it appeared they might have a perilous collision; Mitchell swung the boat sharply to the left or right. A beautiful double waterfall tumbled from one rocky canyon wall just before they reached Blossom Bar.

As they neared Blossom Bar, Mitchell spoke above the thundering roar of the falls; "We'll be turning around here because Blossom Bar is the most hazardous of any Rogue rapid and far too dangerous for the jet boat to navigate. You can see the massive power of the river flowing through these huge boulders. This power creates a churning, twisting, Class IV rapid, and it has taken several lives as boaters tried to navigate it over the years."

"At the top of the rapid," Mitchell explained, "Boaters must make a left-to-right move to avoid a lineup of jagged rocks called the Picket Fence. The consequences of getting swept into the Picket Fence can be a nightmare."

As he talked, Brian and Miranda and everyone else on the boat were awestruck by the power flowing down the canyon. After a short stop, Mitchell turned the boat around to run the Devil's Staircase.

Before starting the return journey, Mitchell warned they were in for the thrill of their lives; and they would definitely get wet. Bracing themselves for what was coming; Brian and Miranda soon understood that the 345-foot elevation gain between Gold

Beach and Blossom Bar wasn't half as thrilling as the descent of Devil's Staircase.

"There may be a little bump here!" Mitchell exaggerated, as he navigated the hellish cataract. Sixty seconds later, there wasn't a single person aboard the boat who wasn't drenched from head to toe. Thankfully, all were covered in rain gear, and the sun, along with the drying effect of the boat's velocity, soon had them drying out; except for wet, sloshy shoes, a source of much grumbling, as well as amusement, among the passengers.

Chapter Thirty-Six

Much too soon, they returned to Agness where they stopped for lunch at Cougar Lane Lodge. Taking her hand, Brian laced his fingers through hers as they walked up the ramp. Her hand felt so small in his. Playing with her fingers, he glanced down at her. This had been a wonderful idea. Her cheeks were glowing and she had a sparkle in her eyes.

She looked up with a smile. "I'm starving. What about you?"

"Me too. I think I could eat a horse right about now," he said laughing.

"Well, I don't know about a horse, but maybe a small cow!" Giggling, she preceded him into the restaurant.

After lunch, Mitchell guided them back to Gold Beach, but he had some more thrilling moments for them. They were all relaxing and enjoying the scenery when he suddenly slowed and shifted the boat into reverse. Then he sharply turned the steering wheel and locked the boat into a 360-degree spin. The boat's prow dipped and someone shrieked as a sheet of cold water sliced through the air getting most of them wet all over again. Screaming and laughing along with the others, Brian and Miranda felt lucky because they didn't get soaked. After the excitement died down, Mitchell got the boat back up to about 35 mph and continued telling them some more of the history of the area. Tired and happy, they settled back; listening to Mitchell and watching for more wildlife.

Someone spotted a giant osprey nest cushioned on the very top of a bare tree. It was hard to imagine how it could remain in such a precarious position, especially with some of the strong winds that whistled through this canyon. "Sometimes you are able to see black bear along the way, primarily during Salmon season," Mitchell informed them.

Suddenly Miranda shouted, "There's a bear!"

"Where?" everyone shouted back.

"On the shore!" she pointed excitedly, almost standing up. Brian grabbed her coat to drag her back into her seat. "Do you see it, Brian?"

Then she shouted again, "There's a young bear, too! Look, Brian!" Eyes shining, she turned to Brian. "I can't believe it! This is the best!"

Mitchell slowed the boat to a crawl as everyone craned to see the two bears. Brian chuckled at Miranda's enthusiasm. After watching for a few minutes, Mitchell continued on to Gold Beach.

As they disembarked, Miranda said, "Brian that was fabulous. Thank you so much for suggesting it. This will be something I'll never forget."

Tired but happy, they started back to Medford. After driving silently for a while, Brian asked, "Have you ever wanted to travel to another country?"

"I've thought about going to Paris with Cindy."

"But you've never gone?" Brian asked.

"Work always got in the way, I suppose," Miranda sighed.

"Is there any other place you would love to see?"

"Oh yes. Indonesia. It's hailed as the Isle of the Gods, and has always fascinated me. I've read that the serene, unspoiled beauty of Indonesia's natural landscape and its unique culture and hospitality makes it a wonderful country to visit. I really would love to go someday," Miranda said.

Brian smiled at her as he said lightly, "Maybe you will."

They talked quietly about the day, but in the back of both of their minds was the attraction they felt for one another; and what had happened the previous night. Aside from taking her hand today, Brian hadn't attempted to touch her again. Miranda couldn't understand why she felt a sense of loss. After all, they had both decided not to pursue what had happened last night. Thanking Brian for a wonderful weekend and watching him drive away, Miranda went thoughtfully inside.

Loving Roger the way she did, why was she so drawn to Brian? Why did he make her breathless and wanting all the time? —Because she did want him, in every way a woman could want a man.

Miranda had always wanted her husband to be the first man to make love to her. That was one of the reasons she was so glad Roger had stopped her from making a big mistake. She had wanted him to be the first, on their wedding night.

But now, even after what had happened last night, she found herself wanting Brian to kiss her today. She loved it when he held her hand, or put his arm around her shoulders. This wanting to be touched by Brian all the time disturbed her. She had felt this way with Roger, but the feelings with Brian were much stronger, more intense.

Miranda didn't understand how she could still love Roger and be sexually attracted to Brian. She longed desperately for her mother, so her mom could explain what was happening to her. After a lot of thought, she finally decided that she would just have to be more careful around Brian, and not let anything like that happen again; at least until she no longer wanted Roger.

When she arrived at work on Monday, there was a new professionalism about her. She was warm and friendly as always, but Brian sensed that she had put a distance between them. Even though it hurt, he had to believe that this was for the best, right now. He would need to keep his distance until something changed. But knowing this didn't stop the dreams he kept having; wild, wonderful dreams where he came awake with the feel of her still in his arms. He could almost feel her close to his heart, her glorious hair spread enchantingly across his pillow. At times, he thought he could even smell her fragrance. Trying to break the spell she had over him, he threw himself into his work even more than in the past.

Chapter Thirty-Seven

Brian had made several trips to some of the other offices over the last few months, but until now, he hadn't needed Miranda to go with him. Karen always accompanied him on the previous trips. Miranda kept hoping she would be able to go with him soon because she was getting anxious for a change. She had been employed about six months when he informed her that he needed to make a trip to Washington, D.C.

"Miranda, because of the seriousness of the negotiations I will be conducting, I want you on this trip with me. We will be meeting with several government agencies and it's very important that we be well-prepared. As you know, we have been working on a new type of longer-lasting pain reliever, and we'll be trying to get FDA approval for the product we have developed."

The next few days were extremely busy for all of them. Karen would also be going with them. The evening before they were to leave, Miranda was getting excited about their trip. She really loved her job, and to her surprise, found she was sleeping well. She had also regained all of the weight she lost, and most of her nightmares and dreams had disappeared.

For the first time in a long time, she was beginning to feel that she might be able to get over Roger. Knowing he would never completely disappear from her mind, she now found herself thinking of him as Cindy's husband. That had been so hard to do for such a long time, but now it didn't seem to hurt as much. She still loved him, but knowing he could never belong to her helped her to put her love in the right perspective.

Brian was taking the company jet, which was a beautiful, sleek and powerful Learjet. Traveling this way was much more comfortable than taking a commercial flight. As she and Karen boarded the plane, Miranda was surprised to realize she was happy.

Brian was already there and he gave her a sharp look. Today, everything about her seemed different. There was a sparkle in her eyes and a sense of excitement about her. It was the first time he had ever seen that look in her eyes. They seemed to be free of the pain he so often saw lurking in their depths.

Could she finally be getting over her feelings for Roger? He knew she was seeing Andre fairly regularly and he wasn't surprised to feel a sharp stab of jealousy. He should be happy she had found someone to take away some of her pain. Instead, he was wishing it could be him.

After the plane started and they were in the air, Brian offered them a drink. Sipping her gin and tonic, Miranda looked up to find Brian watching her. For a moment, she thought she saw that same look of pain in his eyes she had glimpsed before. It was gone in an instant and she thought she must have imagined it.

The look that came into them instead left her breathless and unable to look away. Her heartbeat quickened and color rose under her skin and flooded her face. That same look of passion, she had noticed more than once, was in his eyes, and darkened them to the deepest grey, almost black. Swallowing, her throat suddenly dry, she finally managed to look away.

Karen, unaware of what was going on, suddenly broke the tension with a comment, making them all laugh.

A little flushed and restless now, Miranda kept glancing at Brian from time to time, but he seemed to be preoccupied with the papers he was going over and didn't look at her.

Only she didn't realize the number of times he looked at her when she wasn't watching; or of the restlessness which invaded his body. She was so beautiful and he found it increasingly harder to keep his hands off of her.

She didn't know this, of course, but the past few weeks had been very difficult. He was sleeping very badly at times. He found his mind dwelling more and more often on the feel of her in his arms; her lips burning against his and the way her body responded to him. Knowing that Miranda might have been thinking of Roger when he kissed her didn't change how he was feeling. Just knowing the fire and passion she was capable of was enough to make him want her. His love for her was growing stronger daily and he would give anything to know how to make her forget Roger; and turn to him.

Now sitting across from her, he wanted nothing more than to be able to take her in his arms and kiss her again and again. He felt a terrible longing for her and suddenly he found it difficult to breathe; his heart pounding in his chest.

By the time they landed in Washington, D.C., he had some semblance of control over himself. A plan had formed in his mind, and, as soon as he could, he would implement it. "Oh, if it only works," he thought. "It might bring me more pain than I can bear, or it might bring joy beyond my wildest dreams." It was a tremendous gamble, but Brian was willing to take it.

Miranda sensed something different about Brian that night at dinner. It was a mixture of elation and tension. After the waiter brought their drinks, Brian asked if she would like to dance. Karen chose to have dinner in her room to watch her favorite television show, so they were dining alone.

As Brian helped her out of her chair and led her to the dance floor, an inexplicable feeling came over Miranda. Brian's hand seemed to burn where it touched her arm. As his arms went around her, she felt her heartbeat quicken and she knew she was where she always wanted to be; in his arms.

Their steps matched perfectly and it felt so good to be held by him. His heart started to beat faster against her breasts and his hands slipped slowly from her waist to move restlessly from her shoulders to her hips. As his hands molded her closer to his body, she could feel the heat and tautness from his thighs.

Miranda felt the coolness of his breath against her cheek as he bent his head toward her. He softly kissed her cheek, and then moving slightly, found her lips. Her eyes closed as his lips moved against hers. They seemed to burn where they touched. A shiver went through Miranda and she pressed her body closer to Brian, her lips responding eagerly to his. Her mouth opened eagerly, seeking his probing tongue. Her body was suddenly on fire with longing.

The music ended, and Miranda became aware of where they were. Breathlessly, she pulled away from him, wondering how they could act this way on a public dance floor. Could she possibly be starting to fall in love with Brian?

Sensing her withdrawal, Brian took her hand and led her from the dance floor, ruefully realizing they should have been more circumspect since they were in public. Miranda excused herself quickly and went to the ladies room. She stared at her reflection in the mirror. Her cheeks were rosy and her eyes sparkled. Her thoughts were jumbled and her mind uncertain about what was happening between her and Brian. Why shouldn't she find some happiness for herself? Didn't she deserve love just like everyone else? She didn't feel she would ever love anyone the way she loved Roger, but she certainly was physically attracted to Brian; and if she were honest with herself, she knew what she was feeling went beyond just physical attraction. Leaving the ladies room, she hoped her future included Brian.

When she returned to the table, there was a change in Brian. He was withdrawn and moody. He toyed with his food and wouldn't meet her eyes. They talked quietly about various things, but the atmosphere was strained.

Striving to keep the conversation going, Miranda asked, "Brian, tell me about your family. I know you have a brother, but is he your only sibling?"

"No," Brian answered rather tersely. "My parents live in Medford but they are in Europe right now."

When he didn't add anything, Miranda asked; "What's your brother's name? Does he live here?"

"Nathan. He lives in Chicago. He and his wife Marisa have one boy." Unsmiling he added, "My sister's name is Grace, and she and Gabe have two girls. They live in Omaha. Why all the questions, Miranda?"

Offended, Miranda didn't say anything for a moment wondering what she had said to upset him. He wasn't acting at all like himself. Was he regretting kissing her? "I just wanted to get to know more about your life," she responded finally.

"Sorry," Brian said. "Why don't you tell me a little more about your family?"

Since he already knew about her parents, she spoke about being raised by Aunt Patricia after her parents died. "After Cindy and I went to college, Aunt Patricia moved away to be close to her other sister. She comes back to see us a few times a year, and Cindy and I have both visited her several times. We have some distant cousins, but we don't see them often because they have their own lives to live. We've never really had a chance to get to know them very well," Miranda explained.

"Our mother was an only child, but Dad had two sisters. Consequently, we've always wished we had more family. Mom miscarried after we were born, and I've always been sad I didn't have another brother or sister. Cindy was thrilled to learn Roger has a big family and they have all accepted her; and she seems to get along well with all of them."

"What's your mom..." she trailed off when she realized that Brian wasn't really listening and seemed anxious to go to his room.

"Brian, is something wrong?" Miranda asked uncertainly.

"No, just tired. I'm ready to go if you are," he said getting up from the table.

He was silent as they walked to the elevator and he said a quiet goodnight and left her at the door.

As Miranda prepared for bed, thoughts tumbled through her mind. She realized she had been giving Brian mixed signals for a long time. She always responded to his caresses and returned his kisses, but something always caused her to pull away. She knew why she was doing it, but that didn't make it right. Roger had hurt her so badly with his rejection and lack of insight that she was afraid of getting hurt again. She remembered all the pain and humiliation she had felt when he turned to Cindy, never realizing how Miranda felt about him. She also realized her decisions had played a big part in what happened, and she alone was responsible for Roger having no idea how she felt about him... But, knowing how happy Cindy was, she knew she would not have done anything different. She knew she must make some changes, or Brian might walk out of her life.

The next few days were extremely exhausting and they were completely caught up in business. Coming back to the hotel at night, they would have a quick dinner and then return to their rooms. She missed the easy camaraderie she and Brian had developed, but couldn't blame him for pulling away. Talking to him was always easy, but now he completely withdrew from any personal contact with her. In fact, he seemed to go out of his way to avoid her touch. If her hand or body accidentally brushed his, he would quickly pull away and put some distance between them.

Miranda found herself lying awake at night trying to understand herself, and knowing she had to make some decisions about what she was going to do. She knew she was responsible for Brian's sudden withdrawal from her, but, his avoidance hurt her terribly. She had come to count on the easy friendship which developed so quickly between them. She missed it and wanted everything back the way it had been.

She had seen Brian with other women from time to time, not to mention the woman she saw him with when she had first arrived in Medford. Maybe there was someone special in his life and he was feeling guilty about this attraction between the two of them. She didn't know why the thought of him with another woman would hurt so much, but it did.

Chapter Thirty-Eight

Miranda became increasingly aware of Brian over the next few days. As they flew home to Medford, she found her eyes straying more and more often toward him. What was this fascination she had with him?

When she thought of Roger now, he seemed more and more vague in her mind. Why was this? Was Brian beginning to take his place in her mind and heart? Was she to go through that same agonizing pain and torture again because of another man? No! This time it would destroy her!

She knew now what she must do. She would make her career a priority in her life and put all thought of Brian out of it. Andre was undemanding and fun to be with, and so were Michael and Steven. She would concentrate on having a good time with them and forget about anything serious, at least for a long time. She was determined to think of Brian only as her boss from now on and act accordingly. There would be no more of these romantic interludes between them; if she could help it.

Arriving at work on Monday after their trip to Washington, D.C., Miranda made her way to her desk. Her new resolution was in place. She was going to concentrate on her job from now on.

Brian sensed her withdrawal when he called her into his office later that morning. She seemed extremely professional in her greeting, but he could see unhappiness in her eyes. He knew that his actions during the last week had really upset her. Many times he had looked up to find her watching him, a puzzled look in her eyes. Even though what he was going to do frightened him, he knew that he had to act right away, or he might never have another chance.

"Miranda, there's something I would like to ask you." Brian said.

She looked up wondering what it could be.

Without hesitating, afraid if he did, he would never have the nerve to do so again, he plunged right in: "I first realized something was wrong at Cindy's wedding. That's why I watched you so closely. After driving to Eugene with you and seeing the turmoil it caused, I think I now know what it is. You are in love with Roger, aren't you? I think you gave him up so your sister could be happy and I don't think she has any idea how you feel. Am I right?" he asked.

Miranda felt as if a chair had been pulled out from under her. She turned white and started to tremble. "Why would you ask me something like that?" she whispered. "What could it possibly matter to you?" What he said next took her breath away.

"Because, Miranda, I would like for you to marry me." Gasping, she looked up at him. Was she hearing things? Had he really said he wanted to marry her? Why?

Slowly, Brian started to talk; "Miranda, I am 34 years old. I have met and dated a lot of women. I have been around a lot, and yet in all these years, I have never known a woman that I wanted to ask to marry me. Ever since I met you, you have been on my mind. I saw the way you felt about Roger, and I could sense your pain. Even though I can't begin to understand what happened, I respect you. I think you are a wonderful, giving woman. Now that I know you better, I believe you sacrificed your own happiness for that of your sister."

"A lot of the women I meet are restless and unsure of what they want out of life. They can be very self-centered and unfeeling; used to getting what they want. Many of them come from rich families and have never had to work for a living; and wouldn't know what to do if they did have to. Either that, or they are career-oriented to such an extent that there is no time for a man in their lives, except on a temporary basis. When I get married, I want it to be a lasting relationship. My wealth has always been a problem because I never know if a woman is interested in me, or in my lifestyle and prestige."

"After working with you and getting to know the real person over the last few months, I've found myself drawn to you. We get along well with each other and have a lot in common. Even though you may find this hard to believe, you are the first woman I've ever asked to marry me. I know we're not in love with each other, but from the way you've always responded to me, I think there is hope for our future. I won't ask anything from you that you aren't ready to give until you say different. We can have a platonic relationship for a while, if that is what you want. I know you still love Roger. I just want to take care of you and give you some kind of happiness. Maybe we can find it together? What I'm asking for right now is a companion and friend, and I think we are already friends."

Miranda sat there in complete silence while Brian talked. She was stunned by what he had to say. Even in her wildest imagination, nothing like this had ever happened. When he stopped speaking, she got up and quietly walked out of the room.

After she left, Brian paced the floor. What had he done? Thinking back over what he said made him drop his head in his hands. He had sounded like someone hiring a maid, not asking the woman he loved to marry him! Flinching, he knew he had come across cold and unfeeling. She would never accept a proposal like that. If only he could do it over again. How stupid! Stupid! Stupid!

Miranda was dazed. After deciding she would never let another man hurt her, out of the blue here Brian was, asking her to marry him. Would it work? She liked him very much, and she wanted him physically, in every way. As he had said, they did get along well together; and good marriages had been built on less than that. She and Brian were good friends. She knew she would have to like and respect the man she married. She and Brian did respect each other, and that was a good basis to start from.

She had been around Brian enough over the last few months to know he was a good man. She knew he was honest and trustworthy, and she could do a lot worse. She could end up marrying someone out of loneliness and make a terrible mistake. Was being attracted to him enough? Suppose he found someone else and fell in love with them after marrying her? She could be terribly hurt again. What should she do?

Through a long, sleepless night of tossing and turning, her mind spinning and wondering what she should do, Miranda finally made her decision.

Walking into Brian's office the next morning, she found him once again standing by the window. His body seemed tense and strained as he turned slowly toward her when she came in. He seemed like a man under a tremendous burden and his eyes looked anxious and tired. She watched as a look of real pain fleetingly contorted his rugged features. It was gone so quickly she wasn't sure what she saw.

"The answer's yes." Miranda said quickly, before she changed her mind. "If you still want me."

He was around the desk before Miranda realized he had moved. His arms went around her and she could feel the slight tremor in his hands. His heart was beating so rapidly she could feel it against her breasts; and he seemed to be struggling under a tremendous burden. He held her so tightly for a moment she thought he might crush her. Releasing her slightly, he brought his hands up to her face and tilted her head back.

He looked deeply into her eyes for a moment before his lips closed firmly over hers. She resisted for a moment and then a tremor raced along her flesh. Once again her mouth opened eagerly to his, inviting him to take what he wanted. His hands ran over her arms and shoulders with a sudden fierce passion.

She felt him pluck the pins from her hair and let it fall in shining waves to her waist. He thrust his hands into it and murmured something she couldn't understand. She felt as if her body were on fire. As she had done once before, unknowingly, she brought his hand to her aching breasts. Her body was trembling so badly, she felt she would fall; if he were not holding her up.

Suddenly realizing what was happening, he seemed to wrench himself away from her. Turning his back for a moment, he tried to get hold of his emotions. When he turned around she had slumped into a chair and tears were streaming down her face.

"Miranda, I'm so sorry." He got down on his knees beside the chair and pulled her head into his shoulder. "I didn't mean to hurt you that way again. I was just so happy when you said you'd marry me that I lost my head for a minute. I promise it will never happen again, unless you want it to. Please believe me, Miranda. Will you still marry me?"

When Miranda looked up at him, her eyes drenched in tears and a stunned look on her face, he thought she was the most beautiful sight he had ever seen. Unable to speak, she nodded her head instead.

Chapter Thirty-Nine

Miranda couldn't believe it. She loved Brian! She didn't know when this had happened. She didn't even know how it had happened. All she knew was that the love she felt for Roger was tame compared to the way she now loved Brian. She now knew why she had always responded to him the way she had; and why she always hungered for his kisses and longed to be in his arms. She never wanted to be parted from him again, and if that meant sacrificing her needs she would do it gladly, just to be near him. He was her life. She needed him so much it hurt.

Knowing all this, she desperately wanted to tell him that she loved him, but after what he had said when he proposed, she wasn't sure how he would react; because all he wanted was a companion, a friend, and a lover. How would he feel if he knew how deeply she loved him? He wanted her. There was no doubt about that. But that was so different for a man. A man could want a woman without a deep commitment, without love.

Remembering his words; "We're not in love with each other," made her tremble. Was she making a terrible mistake? No! Miranda knew she would be willing to settle for what he could give, rather than be alone without him. She already knew what being alone was like. It seemed like she had been alone forever. She didn't want to live that way any longer. Her decision made, she got slowly to her feet and gave Brian a shaky smile. He seemed to be very shaken, too.

"When shall we get married?" he asked. "Soon? My parents will be home next week and I can get my brother and sister here anytime. What about Cindy and Roger? I know you would like for them to be here."

Miranda nodded, still unable to take it all in. "A month will be fine with me if you don't want a fancy wedding," she said. Walking out, she left a stunned Brian to sink slowly into his chair. He couldn't take it all in. She had actually said she'd marry him in a month! He couldn't believe it had really happened! He reached down to pinch his arm to see if he was really awake, or having another one of his dreams.

After leaving Brian's office, Miranda stopped by Karen's desk. By the look on Miranda's face, Karen knew something had happened. "Karen, you're not going to believe this, but Brian and I are getting married."

Absolutely stunned, Karen just stared up at her for a moment. Then jumping up, she ran to Miranda and gave her a tight hug. "You two are so perfect for each other! I had secret hopes you would get together, but I never, in my wildest dreams, thought it would happen. When are you getting married?"

"In a month, if you can believe that! I know it's soon, but we decided we didn't want to wait."

"Wow! That is soon, but I think it's wonderful. I'm going to run in and congratulate Brian."

Stopping her, Miranda said, "Karen, I need a little time to myself to absorb what has happened, so I'm going to leave the office for a little while. I'll be back later this afternoon, OK?"

"Sure. I'll tell Brian."

A few minutes later, walking slowly through the park, Miranda's mind couldn't seem to take in what just happened. All she knew was that now she had a reason to get up in the morning. She no longer felt miserable and unhappy. She felt like singing and dancing, and her love for Brian put a spring back in her step, a sparkle in her eyes.

Sinking slowly onto a park bench, she thrilled at the beauty around her. She listened to the singing of the birds and the chattering of the squirrels and felt as if she heard them again for the first time in a long time. Thrill after thrill went through her as she thought of Brian as her husband and all that it might bring in the future. She wanted his children. She wanted to share his laughter and love. Even though he didn't love her now, she had no doubt he would grow to love her. She would fill his life with so much happiness and joy that he would be unable to keep from loving her in return.

Without him, day faded into day, without much meaning. This was the way she had been living for so long, but now it was so different. She now had Brian! Spreading her arms wide, she embraced life, free of the burden of loving her sister's husband. No matter what lay ahead for her and Brian, she would be content because she had been given her sister back. She would no longer have to hide her feelings from Cindy. The jealousy was gone. She was totally and completely happy for her and Roger. What a wondrous thing her love for Brian was! When she returned to the office later, it was with a new serenity.

The next few days were hectic for both Miranda and Brian but he took the time to take her down to get a lovely swirl diamond and sapphire white gold engagement ring. Miranda loved it. She chose the sapphire because she was drawn to its brilliance; and the jeweler said it symbolized wisdom, virtue, good fortune, and royalty. She still wasn't sure this was happening. She was marrying a man who didn't love her. He did want her, she kept reminding herself. Maybe that would be enough. Maybe someday, he would come to love her. It was a chance worth taking.

Chapter Forty

A couple of days later, Miranda was walking to her car when she heard her name called. It was the end of a busy day and she wanted to get home. Turning, she saw Andre approaching. She had just left Brian in his office so she could go home and get ready for him to pick her up for a meeting with the wedding planner. Since they had such a short time to plan the wedding, they were anxious to find out if Rebecca from *Heart's Desires* would be able to meet their needs. As Andre approached, Miranda noticed Brian leaving the office. She smiled and waved at Brian before turning to Andre.

"Hi. How are you?" Miranda asked.

"I'm just fine, but I haven't seen you lately. You must have been busy," Andre replied.

Miranda smiled as Andre drew her into a hug. Neither of them noticed Brian's car as it left the parking lot.

"I haven't seen you since you got back from Washington, D.C. How was it?" Andre asked.

Miranda moved out of his embrace as she answered; "It was very busy, but we got a lot accomplished. We think the formula you were working on is going to be approved for the second stage of tests."

"That's wonderful," Andre applauded. "It's been a really challenging drug but I hope it will eventually be approved. There are a lot of people who need a drug like this one."

"I understand. We talked to a lot of people, and attended several hearings on the findings and possible side effects. Everyone seemed really enthusiastic about the results from the trials."

"That's really good to hear. Are you doing anything tonight? I would love to take you out to dinner if you're not busy," Andre said.

Hesitating, Miranda took a deep breath. "Andre, there's something I need to tell you."

"It must be important. You sound kinda serious."

"We haven't told anyone but the family because I asked Brian not to say anything yet, but Brian and I are engaged. I think you have a right to know." She held out her hand to show him her ring.

"Wow! Congratulations, I guess. When did this happen? I didn't even know you two were seeing each other," he asked heavily.

"We weren't," she replied, "But when we met at my sister's wedding, there was an instant attraction. It all came together after Washington, where Brian asked me to marry him. Andre, I know this is a surprise, but I'm hoping you'll be happy for me." She reached out and touched his face gently. "You are my friend, and I hope it can stay that way."

"I was more than halfway in love with you," he said gravely, "But now," grimacing, "I'll have to go find someone just like you."

Miranda gave him a little shove and said, "Good luck, there's not anyone else like me." Then laughing, she said, "I take that back. You haven't met Cindy yet, but I'm afraid she's married!"

"I know, and that stinks!" Grinning, Andre started to walk away. Turning back, he asked, "When is the wedding? I hope I'll be invited."

"Of course you will be, if you really want to come. The wedding's in three weeks."

"That's fast! I'll be there. Congratulations again, Miranda. I wish you happiness." Lightly touching her hand, he walked away.

Miranda dashed home to get ready for Brian. Talking to Andre had taken up too much of her time.

Brian picked her up but he was quiet and seemed to have something on his mind. When they met Rebecca, they had so many things to consider and decisions to make that Miranda didn't think any more about his mood. She just figured he would tell her if anything was bothering him.

Later, on the way home, Miranda asked if he wanted to stop and get something to eat. "I know wedding planning is not something most men enjoy, and I doubt if you are the exception," Miranda laughed. "Sorry to put you through all of that."

"No problem," Brian said. "It's all part of the process. Are you happy with the arrangements?"

"Yes. Rebecca seems very capable of pulling everything together on such short notice."

"I think I'll pass on dinner if you don't mind," Brian said. Miranda waited for him to explain, but he stayed silent until he stopped at her apartment.

When he came around to open her door, Miranda asked quietly, "Is something wrong, Brian? Earlier this afternoon you seemed excited about planning the wedding but tonight you seem less than enthusiastic."

"That was before I saw you in Andre's arms." Brian said drily.

"What...?" Miranda asked shocked. "What on earth are you talking about?"

"In the parking lot..." Brian let the words hang in the air.

"I was just talking to Andre. He's my friend. Brian..." she said tentatively. He turned toward her and she was shocked to see he was angry.

"What's wrong, Brian? I don't understand. Why are you mad?"

"What were you and Andre doing? Why were you hugging him?" he asked.

"I wasn't. He hugged me," she said. Now he was starting to make her angry.

"Well, it didn't look like that to me," Brian stated as he said a sharp goodnight and walked back to his car.

Watching him leave, Miranda muttered, "Well, what was that all about?"

Thoughts churned in Brian's head as he drove home. Who did she think he was? He wasn't someone to be trampled on! She had kissed Roger after he and Cindy were married, and now she was doing the same with Andre after promising to marry him. Maybe he didn't know her as well as he thought he did. Or maybe he was wrong, and just reacting to the insecurity of their situation.

Miranda was a beautiful woman, not only physically, but he saw an inner beauty that he had rarely seen in other women. He knew she was the woman he wanted to marry, and he didn't like being jealous. He slumped into his chair and felt pain tearing through him. He couldn't stop the tears that filled his eyes; that slowly slid down his cheeks. He loved her so much. He wanted her so much! He just had to go on with this wedding and pray she would come to love him.

Later, Brian called her and canceled the date they had planned for the next evening. "I have to make a quick trip to Kansas City to fix a problem they are having." He sounded tired and dispirited, and Miranda wished she could be with him.

"Brian, there's nothing but friendship between Andre and me. We bumped into each other. He just gave me a spontaneous hug, which I've become used to from him. It meant nothing. We're good friends; that's all. I really hope you will believe me, Brian. I want to marry you."

She heard a sigh from him before he said, "I believe you, Miranda. I just need to work some things out in my mind. Give me a few days and we'll talk, OK?"

"OK, Brian. I'll miss you," Miranda said.

"I'll miss you too," Brian said before hanging up.

Miranda had been hoping to go to Kansas City with Brian, but under the circumstances, she realized it was good that she wasn't. Brian was hurt and upset and she needed to figure out how to reassure him that everything was going to be all right. If she could just figure it out herself!

While he was gone, she and Karen decided to have dinner together at an Italian restaurant they both loved. She was lonely for Brian and didn't want to spend the whole evening by herself.

They were just finishing up with their dessert when Miranda looked up and caught sight of a couple making their way into the restaurant. Suddenly, her breath caught in her throat. It was Brian, and the woman she had seen him dining with when she first came to Medford! They were laughing, and she saw him take her arm as they walked to their table.

Karen sensed something was wrong and glanced up. Startled, she turned to Miranda. "Did you know Brian would be here tonight, Miranda?"

"No." Miranda's face had turned white. "I didn't even know he was back from his trip."

When she didn't explain further, Karen leaned over and touched Miranda's hand. "Did something happen between you two?"

"I'm not exactly sure what happened, Karen. One minute we were happy and planning our wedding, and then Brian became really upset with me. He saw Andre hug me in the parking lot and seems to think something is going on with us. You know Andre and I have been friends since I moved to Medford, and I thought Brian understood."

"Brian's always so level-headed," Karen said. "It surprises me that he would react by getting upset. Are you sure nothing else happened?"

"I'm sure," Miranda said.

"When did it happen, and have you spoken to him since? This makes no sense."

"A couple of days ago, and since he was going to Kansas City, he said we would talk when he got back. I decided to let things cool off until I could talk to him in person, not on the phone."

"Brian loves you, Miranda," Karen said. "I'm sure he's going through what a lot of us go through just before getting married, but everything's going to be OK."

"I hope so," Miranda said wishing Karen's words were true about Brian loving her. "Do you know the woman he's with?"

"Yes, but I'm surprised to see them together. I thought they broke up over a year ago. Her name is Blake."

"Do you think they were serious about each other?"

"I'm not sure, but they've known each other for ages and were quite an item for a couple of years," she replied. Suddenly, realizing Miranda was very upset, Karen said quickly; "You don't have to worry about her. Brian's in love with you. He's probably just having a meeting with her about something. I'm sure he'll tell you about it tomorrow. Why don't we just go over and say hello to them?"

"I'd really rather not. Brian's never mentioned her to me," Miranda muttered. "Let's get out of here before they see us. OK, Karen?"

"Sure, but I know there's nothing for you to worry about. Talk to Brian tomorrow, please, and straighten this out before it becomes bigger than it is." Without answering, Miranda made her way quickly out of the restaurant, before Brian noticed they were there.

That night, Miranda paced the floor, unable to sleep. She didn't know what to do. Not seeing Brian for a couple of days had made her very insecure; especially since their fight about Andre.

For the first time in a long time, Miranda cried herself to sleep. She was so scared. Suppose Brian married her and continued to see this woman? She couldn't bear it!

Going into his office the next morning, Miranda confronted Brian. She wasn't going to wait for him to call her. They were getting married soon and she had to know where she stood.

Brian looked up when she tapped on his door. Opening the door, a tentative smile on his face, Brian said, "Miranda, I've missed you so much. I'm sorry about the fight we had. Please forgive me."

Miranda stepped back, saying sharply, "Brian, who is Blake and what does she mean to you?"

Brian gave her a startled look. "Why are you asking about Blake? She's an old friend of mine."

Miranda took a deep breath. "I saw you with her at Bellagrossi's last night, and you seemed very friendly. How do you explain that? You didn't even call to let me know you were back, and I find you with an old friend?!" He couldn't miss the sarcasm in her voice.

"Miranda, I'm so sorry I didn't call you while I was gone! I have no excuse. I wanted to talk to you in person, rather than on the phone; to apologize for my behavior. Before I left, Blake called and asked if I could help her with a problem. I made an appointment with her for last night, and it was so late when we finished, I didn't want to wake you. Blake and I are just old friends, nothing more."

"I'll just bet," Miranda said. "It didn't look much like a business meeting to me." Giving him a hurt look, she turned and quickly left the room.

A couple of hours later, Miranda's buzzer sounded. "Miranda, Brian would like to see you," Karen said.

Miranda was over her anger and now felt sad. She and Brian had never had an argument about anything before becoming engaged. They both needed to stop reacting so strongly and realize they each had a life and friends separate from each other.

Brian met her at his office door. "Miranda, we have to get this all straightened out. We're getting married soon and we can't keep fighting."

"I know," she said. "What's happening to us? We got along so well before we decided to get married…"

"I think it's just anxiety about the wedding," Brian said. "Come here." When she walked over to him, Brian put his arms around her and held her tenderly. "Miranda, I don't want anything to keep us from getting married. Do you?"

Miranda shook her head and he tipped her face up so he could see her answer. "You mean that?"

"Yes," she whispered. His lips found hers gently at first, but at her response, they became demanding. Pulling her tighter against him, he kissed her hungrily. Her arms stole up around his neck, and she returned his kisses eagerly. For a moment, he continued to kiss her, and then he pulled her fiercely against him and held her tightly. They were so close; it was almost like being one person. She could feel his heart hammering against hers. A moment later, gently putting her from him, he gave her a light kiss.

"Let's not fight anymore, please, Miranda? I hate it when we're angry and separated from each other."

She nodded and gave him a misty smile. "I know. I miss having my best friend around. I was hoping you would call. I waited up for you."

"I'm so sorry. Please forgive me, Miranda. I guess I was still hurt over seeing you and Andre together, and was trying to hurt you back. I promise, I'll never do that again."

"I'll hold you to that," she said taking his hand for a moment, holding it gently between hers and smiling up at him. Impulsively, she reached up and kissed him tenderly.

Chapter Forty-One

A couple of nights later, Brian called to ask if Miranda would like to have dinner with his parents. "They are both very anxious to meet you. They want to see you with their own eyes; then they'll believe I'm really getting married." Miranda could hear the laughter in his voice. "My mom's been waiting for me to get married and give her grandchildren for a long time... Oops! That came out wrong. No pressure here, I promise," Brian chuckled.

"I've been anxious to meet them." Seriously, she said, "I hope we do bless them with grandchildren someday. I'll be ready at five."

When she met his parents, she liked them both immediately. His father, Doug, was so much like Brian that she couldn't help but like him. He was a little taller than Brian, his black hair streaked with grey. A few lines showed on his face, but he was still a handsome man. He looked strong and fit with well-developed muscles.

His mother, Mary, was a warm, lovely woman. Her hair was light brown with blond highlights, curling softly around her face. She was slightly built but moved with a lithe stride as if anxious to get something done. As soon as she found out Miranda's parents were gone, she was instantly sympathetic, making Miranda realize that she was soon going to be a part of another close-knit family. Someday it would be a joy to surround Mary and Doug with grandchildren. Miranda longed for that day! To be the mother of Brian's children...what a thought that was!

It wasn't until a few days later that she was able to meet Nathan and Grace, Brian's brother and sister. They flew in a few days before the wedding to spend time with their parents. Nathan was a surprise as he looked nothing like his parents. He was tall and a little bit overweight, bearded, with a slightly rakish look. His smile was infectious and he cocked his head to one side while listening.

Grace, on the other hand, looked like Dad and Mom. She was small and delicate, but with the same dark eyes and black hair as Brian. She had a beautiful smile and an infectious laugh. Miranda liked them both immediately.

Not having been around children very much, at first, Miranda was a little wary around Brian's nieces and nephews. Charlie, at nine, was a somber little boy; more interested in books than in playing. Bella, who was seven, was a little black-haired beauty. She was mischievous, but with a shy streak. She clung to her mother for a few minutes, smiling shyly at Miranda, before running off to play. It took a few days, but they were soon old friends. Little Mandy, who was three, would come and climb into Miranda's lap and give her a hug. Miranda had been right about Brian being good with children. She could see they adored their uncle, Brian.

She saw quite a lot of Brian's family over the next week before the wedding. The more she got to know them, the better she liked them.

Anxious to find the right dress for her wedding, Miranda asked Mary and Grace if they would go with her to Perfect Day Boutique which was the largest wedding store in Medford. She was hoping to find just what she wanted without too much trouble. She didn't have to worry about Cindy's maid of honor dress because Cindy had already found something nice.

267

"What are you looking for in a wedding dress?" Mary asked as they waited for the bridal consultant to finish with a customer.

"Something simple but elegant," Miranda said. "I don't like a lot of fluff and frill."

"Like this?" Grace giggled as she held up a dress with several layers of fluffy white ruffles from the waist to the floor.

"Exactly," Miranda laughed. "I would probably trip over it and fall flat on my face halfway up the aisle." They were all giggling when the consultant finally came over to help.

"Hi, I'm Marcie. Are you looking for a ready-made dress or one we will design?" she asked Miranda.

"Definitely something you already have as I'm getting married in a couple of weeks."

"Wow. Then I hope we can find you something that fits so we don't need to alter it. We wouldn't be able to for several weeks. Have you seen anything you think might be suitable?" Marcie asked a little abruptly.

After trying on several dresses, Miranda was really discouraged. Even though Grace and Mary said she looked beautiful in a couple of dresses, she wasn't satisfied.

"Miranda, I know a little shop called Enchanted down near the waterfront. Why don't we go see what they have?" Mary suggested after seeing the disappointment on Miranda's face.

"Sounds good," Miranda said. "I'd like to find what I'm looking for and it's not here."

"Besides, Marcie isn't exactly helpful is she?" Grace whispered. "I guess she likes to make the big bucks on designer dresses."

"Did you find anything you liked?" Marcie asked as they gathered up their things to leave.

"No," Miranda answered. "But thanks for your help."

"What help?" Mary grinned. "I'm really surprised by her attitude."

"Maybe she's having a bad day," Grace giggled and Miranda couldn't help but chuckle. Grace had a snarky sense of humor that Miranda liked.

She loved the Enchanted Boutique immediately. The owner, Serena, listened to what Miranda wanted and brought out several dresses. "I know you don't have much time, but we'll do everything we can to help you find the perfect dress," she smiled.

Miranda walked out in a Chantilly lace cap-sleeve sheath dress and Mary said softly, "It's perfect."

"I agree," said Grace. "You look like a princess."

The "perfect dress" was tiered with gorgeous bands of point d'esprit and Chantilly lace cascading down the A-line silhouette. A V-neckline and dramatic open back, framed with intricate Chantilly lace straps seemed perfect.

"I love it and it fits perfectly," Miranda said as she twirled in front of the mirror. Hugging Mary and Grace she said, "Thank you both so much for coming with me."

Even though Miranda faced an unknown future, her heart was full because she loved Brian; and that was a good place to start.

Chapter Forty-Two

Their wedding day dawned cold and rainy. It looked as if it would be that way all day. Miranda's spirits dropped to match the weather. Was she making a mistake?

She loved Brian to distraction, but he didn't love her. She remembered his words when he proposed to her. "We don't love each other." Would he learn to love her, or would he turn to someone else after getting bored with her?

While all of these thoughts were racing through her mind, she waited at the airport for Cindy to arrive. Karen had offered to pick Cindy up for her, but Miranda longed to see Cindy, so she decided to go pick her up. It was an early morning flight so Miranda had plenty of time to get ready for the wedding.

Roger had been unable to get away because he was scheduled to attend a seminar in San Francisco. Miranda was uncertain how she felt about this. In one way, she would like to have seen him; and in another, she was relieved. Convinced that the old feelings for him were gone, it would have been nice to be able to see him and put the past where it belonged.

Because Roger couldn't come, Cindy was flying down instead of driving. She would stay for the day and leave shortly after the wedding. Karen would take her back to the airport. Miranda wanted Cindy to come earlier, but her job was keeping her very busy.

It was so good to see Cindy. She looked radiant. Hugging Miranda fiercely, Cindy said, "I am so happy for you! I knew you would find someone, and Brian seems cool. Even though I don't know him like you do, I know you wouldn't choose someone who wasn't perfect for you."

"I haven't really had a chance to get to know Brian very well," Cindy continued, as they walked through the airport. "I was so busy at my own wedding; I just barely got to meet him. And when you two came to Eugene, you were there such a short time that I didn't have a lot of time to talk to him. I did notice, though, that he couldn't seem to keep his eyes off of you," Cindy laughed.

"That's because he couldn't quite figure me out," Miranda smiled.

"I still wish we could have come down to spend time with you and get to know him a little better, but Brian does seem like a very nice man. Roger has told me a lot about him, especially since we found out that you two were getting married. I guess he's really rich, isn't he?" Cindy asked.

"I don't know much about that, as we haven't talked about it, but I guess he is. He once told me that some women wanted to marry him for his money."

"He actually said that to you?" Cindy asked, shocked.

"Sure, and it's probably true, but I'm the one who got him, aren't I?" Smiling, she showed Cindy where her car was parked and put the small bag Cindy had with her into the back.

"According to Roger, Brian is a really good man," Cindy confided. "I guess he helped Roger out of a tough spot a time or two in the past. They've been close friends for a long time."

"Yes, he is very nice! He's warmhearted, charming, amusing, and very handsome. I've witnessed his kind and generous side by

271

observing how he treats his employees. Everyone seems to like and respect him; and his secretary, Karen, just adores him."

"I hope she's not too young and good-looking," laughed Cindy.

"No, she's not," smiled Miranda. "She's a young grandmother with a couple of grandchildren that she adores. She's been with Brian for ages, and I don't think he could get along without her. She's been a very good friend to me, too."

Talking to Cindy put Miranda in a much better frame of mind. Putting all her doubts behind her, she was starting to look forward to her wedding. This would be the start of her life with Brian, whatever it might bring. They would be happy together. They just had to be!

The wedding was to be at four o'clock in the afternoon. By three, the family was all at the church, and Miranda was getting decidedly nervous.

"Calm down, Miranda. Here, have a sip of wine. It should help calm your nerves. It did mine," Cindy said, handing her a glass. "Take a few deep breaths; that will help too. You'll be all right once the wedding starts."

"I have something for you. Remember; 'something borrowed, something blue'? Do you remember that pretty sapphire necklace that Mom gave me for my sixteenth birthday? Wear it today for something borrowed. Maybe it will make you feel like Mother is here with you. If only she and Dad were here," Cindy said, wiping tears from her lashes.

"I know," Miranda said. "I miss both of them so much." Quickly, she wiped away the tears filling her eyes and smiled at Cindy.

"I also have this blue handkerchief Grandma Carlson gave me when I was little. I still have it, and would like you to carry it."

Hugging her, Miranda said, "Thanks so much, these will make today that much more special!"

Sticking her head around the corner of the door, Mary asked; "Miranda, may Grace and I come in?"

"Of course," Miranda said warmly, going over to give them a hug. "I'm glad you guys are here. This is my sister, Cindy. Cindy, this is Mary, Brian's mother, and Grace, his sister."

"There's no doubt you two are sisters," Mary teasingly responded.

"Ditto," Grace chuckled.

"Yeah, we get told that a lot," they laughed.

"Miranda, the only thing I ever wanted for my son was for him to find the right girl. She didn't have to be rich, or beautiful, or famous; just as long as she loved my son. I think he has chosen well, and I would like for you to wear this ring that my grandmother gave my mother on her wedding day. When I got married, my mother gave it to me. I've been keeping it for the girl that Brian would someday marry, and I would like to give it to you on this very special day. Will you accept it?" Mary asked.

"Oh I couldn't," protested Miranda. "It must hold a lot of memories for you."

"It does, but I would like you to have it, please Miranda."

Hugging her tightly, Miranda said, "Thanks Mary, you are so sweet to me. I'll treasure it always and hopefully pass it on to a daughter of mine someday."

"Well...that takes care of 'something borrowed', 'something blue,' 'something old,' 'something...'"

"New!" Karen said from the doorway. "Put this on!" Laughing, she held up an eye-catching garter which they all stared at in awe. It was an elegant, ivory garter crafted of fine stretch lace with an ivory organza flower. Miranda smoothed her hand lovingly over the puff of ivory feathers, ivory simulated pearls, and real Swarovski crystals.

"Wow, Karen! This is so beautiful. I will treasure it."

"Here's the keepsake box it came in," Karen said, handing it to her.

Miranda hugged her warmly. "That is so sweet! Thank you."

"Only the best for Brian's bride," Karen smiled.

Laughing, Miranda said, "Now it looks like I'm ready! Karen, I would like you to meet my sister, Cindy. Cindy, this is the paragon of virtue that Brian relies so heavily on. Remember, the one that I told you about?"

"Hi Karen, I want to thank you for being such a good friend to Miranda. I know it was hard for her coming to a strange place and not really knowing anyone."

"She is easy to be nice to," Karen smiled. "She's a lovely woman."

"Would you two cut it out?" Miranda protested. "You're making me blush. You can say nice things about me when I'm not around."

Laughing, Karen turned to say; "Hi," to Mary and Grace whom she had known for years.

"I think it's about time to start," Mary said. "I'll just run out and see if everyone's ready."

Very shortly, she was back with a frown on her face. "I don't understand it," she said. "No one's seen Brian."

"What do you mean, 'no one's seen Brian?'" Miranda asked, startled. "Where is he? He should have already been here. I talked to him last night and he said he'd be early!"

"Just what I said," Mary blurted. "No one's seen him. Doug called the house and nobody's answering the phone, so we have to assume that he's on his way. Maybe he got caught up in traffic, or thought of something he'd forgotten at the last minute. He'll be here, don't worry."

But they did worry as time slowly ticked by and Brian still didn't show up. Miranda was starting to get scared. There was no sign of him. They tried calling the house again, but there was still no answer.

Mary had started to pace the floor. "What could have happened? This isn't like Brian at all. I know he was very anxious to get married, so I know he didn't get cold feet at the last minute."

"He would have called," Miranda protested. "I agree. This isn't like Brian. If he had decided he couldn't go through with the wedding, he would have told me."

"I didn't think he would do anything like this either, but what could have happened?" his mother asked anxiously.

Nathan and Grace stuck their heads in the door just then. "Mom, it's been over an hour and I think we'd better go home. If something's happened to Brian he might try to call there," Nathan said.

"I'm going to the house and call the police to see if there has been an accident," Doug said. "I know Brian would not be a coward and run out on his own wedding. He's a better man than that."

As Miranda stood there trembling, a picture of Brian and Blake together, with her arm through his, floated through Miranda's mind.

Chapter Forty-Three

Numbly, Miranda changed out of her wedding gown. It had been a wonderful dream, but now it was shattered. How could Brian do this to her? Were he and Blake together?

Cindy's face was pale and she appeared to be stunned. "Let's go home Miranda, and I'll cancel my flight. I can't leave you like this. I'll call the office and tell them I won't be back for a few days. They'll just have to do without me."

In a daze, Miranda let Cindy lead her out to the car. What about her resolution not to let another man hurt her? Oh, why hadn't she stuck to it? Would she never learn? She didn't feel anything right now, but later... she didn't want to think about later...

Cindy glanced at her. Miranda hadn't said a word, poor baby. Cindy couldn't imagine what she must be feeling.

As Cindy was backing out of the parking lot, a man ran up to the car and tapped on her window. "What's happened?" he asked anxiously. "They just told us that Brian didn't show up."

Rolling down her window, Cindy asked; "Who are you?"

"Andre," he replied.

"Andre. I know who you are. Miranda has spoken of you often. I'm Cindy."

"I would know you anywhere," Andre said. Anxiously, he asked again; "What's happening?"

"I'm afraid we don't know any more than you do at this point. Brian simply didn't show up, and nobody knows why. Listen Andre, I know you're concerned. Everyone is, but right now, I have to get Miranda home. She's not dealing with this very well."

Andre bent his head to look at Miranda, who was staring sightlessly out the window. "Miranda," he said gently. When she didn't respond, he said more loudly, "Miranda!" He was shocked at the paleness of her face as she looked at him at last. "I'm here for you, sweetheart. You know that don't you, Miranda? Just call anytime and I'll be there." Dully, she nodded and he had to be satisfied with that. "You call me, Cindy, if there's anything she needs."

"I will, Andre. I promise. I know you care a great deal about her." Glancing at Miranda and seeing her shiver, she said urgently, "Andre, I really must get her home right now."

Andre stepped back and watched as they drove away. He couldn't imagine what would have kept Brian away from his own wedding, especially to someone like Miranda. If he had been the lucky man that Miranda had chosen to marry, he would have gone through hell to get there on time. He hated to imagine the pain Miranda was going through for the second time in her life.

Once inside the apartment, Cindy led Miranda to the couch and wrapped her in a warm blanket. Going to the kitchen, Cindy made her a strong, hot cup of tea with lots of honey in it. She thought that might help with the shock she felt Miranda was in.

"Here, drink this sweetie. It will help," she said.

Miranda mechanically did what she was told. Cindy wished Miranda would cry; she hated to see her so pale and silent—pain etched in her face.

Miranda was afraid that if she ever started to cry, she would never stop. She felt frozen inside. She was like a block of ice...so cold.

Seeing her shiver, Cindy grabbed another blanket and wrapped it around her. Miranda just stared blankly at the far wall. Cindy wondered what she was thinking.

"She is in shock," Cindy thought. "I've got to do something."

Going into the bathroom, she found a bottle of sleeping pills. Coming back to Miranda, she said; "Here sweetheart, take this and it will help you sleep for a while. Sleep will be good for you, and when you wake up, maybe we can sort this all out."

Miranda pushed her hand away, but Cindy insisted; and finally she took the pills. Leading her to the bedroom, Cindy helped her out of her dress and into bed. "Go to sleep, little one," she said soothingly. She brushed Miranda's hair back from her face with her hand, and heard Miranda give a soft sigh. A few minutes later she was asleep and Cindy went to the living room to call the Chandler's.

"Have you found out anything?" she asked Nathan anxiously. "I gave Miranda sleeping pills and put her to bed. I think she's in shock."

"I'm glad you got her to sleep. It's the best thing for her right now," Nathan said. "I'm worried about Mom and Dad. They are completely stunned. And no, I'm afraid we haven't heard anything for sure yet, and I'm not sure if that's good or bad. There has been an accident reported, and we're just waiting for the police to call with the details. We'll let you know as soon as we find out anything. There's nothing we can do until we hear from them."

"I sure hope it wasn't Brian, but that would explain why he didn't show up," Cindy said. "Call me as soon as you hear anything!"

The waiting was horrible, and Miranda was sleeping fitfully. Every once in a while, she would cry out in her sleep, yelling; "No, no!" and "Why, Brian?" thrashing about wildly until Cindy soothed her, calming her down. It seemed an eternity while Cindy sat holding her sister's hand, talking to Miranda quietly whenever she was restless.

A little while later, the phone rang loudly in the silence; making Cindy jump. Dashing to pick it up, she asked breathlessly, "Have you heard anything?"

"Yes," Grace said. It sounded like she had been crying. "Brian skidded on the wet road and ran off the pavement, straight into a telephone pole. They say he's in critical condition. Mom and Dad have already left for the hospital and Nathan and I are just leaving. Oh Cindy, what are we going to do if he doesn't make it?"

Cindy's legs sagged, "Oh no," she protested. "That's horrible! Miranda is still asleep and I won't be able to wake her up for a while because I gave her a couple of sleeping pills. I'll get her to the hospital as soon as I can. Please call if there is any change."

Cindy tried to see if she could wake Miranda, but she was too sound asleep. An hour later she went in and shook her. "Wake up, Miranda! Come on honey, wake up!" Since that didn't seem to be working, she dashed to the bathroom for a cold washcloth and pressed it to her forehead. Groggily, Miranda opened her eyes. Uncomprehending, she just lay there, looking up at Cindy, her eyes clouded and dull.

"I have to tell you something, Miranda. Can you sit up? I need to get you awake."

Suddenly, Miranda cringed and turned her head into the pillow. "Miranda, please..." Shaking her head, Miranda just continued to lie there. Finally, in desperation, Cindy pulled the covers off of her and reached under Miranda's shoulders to lift her into a sitting position. Gently, she turned Miranda's head.

"Honey, something has happened to Brian and I want you to be brave. I have to get you awake enough to tell you."

Dumbly, Miranda just stared at her for a moment, and then slowly slid out of bed. Walking unsteadily, Miranda made her way to the bathroom. She washed her face in cold water, returned, and sat down on the bed.

"What is it?" Miranda asked. "Has anyone talked to Brian? Why didn't he show up for the wedding?"

"Miranda, this is going to be hard for you to hear, but I want you to be strong, OK? Brian has been in a car accident."

With an inarticulate cry, Miranda grasped Cindy's arm. "Is he hurt?"

"I'm afraid so, but we need to get to the hospital as soon as possible. Are you up to it?"

"How bad is he?" Miranda asked, getting to her feet.

"Let's just wait till we get there to find out," Cindy answered.

Quickly, she found a light jacket for Miranda to wear and got her out to the car. There was an unbroken silence while they raced to the hospital. Neither one knew what to say. Miranda was lost in a world of her own. The man she cherished more than anything in this world was hurt and she didn't know how badly. Was she going to lose him before they even had a chance? Oh God, she hoped not.

281

Praying silently, she asked God to spare him; "Please don't let him die. I love him so much!"

They almost ran through the doors and up to the desk. Cindy asked where Brian was. "Second floor, room 239," a nurse said. "He's in intensive care."

"How is he?" Miranda asked urgently.

"You'll have to ask the doctor," she replied.

Hurrying to the elevators, they waited impatiently for one of them to open. Almost running when it opened, they dashed for the waiting room where they saw Nathan, Grace, and Brian's parents. Rushing over to them, Miranda asked breathlessly, "How is he?"

She could see tears in Mary's eyes. Holding out her arms, Mary hugged her tightly. "He's not so good. He has a bad concussion and is in a coma right now. The doctors aren't saying much." She started to cry and Miranda cried with her.

Chapter Forty-Four

It was a long, sleepless night. Frantically, Doug would pace the floor; and when he sat down, Nathan would jump up and take his place. Grace and Mary cried quietly at times. Finally, Mary could take their pacing no more and begged them to sit down. Miranda felt numb, not knowing what to do. She couldn't believe this was happening. She laid her head down on Cindy's shoulders; so thankful her sister was there.

Around one o'clock in the morning the doctor came in. He didn't have any more news, but thought it might help Brian to have someone sit with him. Mary tried to get Miranda to go first, but shaking her head she said, "Mary, you and Doug go see him first, please. I know how anxious you are to make sure he's all right. I'll go when you get back," she said, pushing them gently in the direction of Brian's room.

When it was finally Miranda's turn, she walked into his room and was stunned. He was hooked up to so many tubes and looked utterly defenseless. She had never seen Brian helpless before, and it shocked her to see him lying there so still and silent. Sinking into a chair, she took his hand.

"Oh, Brian! Why did this have to happen to you, darling? You've got to be all right. I need you so much!" Laying her head down beside him, she said a prayer for his recovery.

"Please be OK. I can't live without you!" Tears streamed down her cheeks as she reached out to gently touch his face. The man she was looking at didn't seem like the Brian she knew. The one she had hiked with, laughed and danced with, who was always so full of life. Instead, he was lying here, unmoving, unable to smile at her and tell her everything was going to be all right. She sat quietly beside him until a nurse came and told her she had to leave.

Visions of his laughing eyes, his humor, and tenderness played over and over in her mind as she waited with the others; anxiously hoping the doctor would come soon to tell them he was going to be all right. Nathan went to get them all some coffee, and Grace had fallen into a light, restless sleep before the doctor came to tell them Brian was finally out of his coma.

"It looks like he's going to be all right," he said; "Barring any complications. He has an awful lot of bruising. He has some injury to his pelvis, as well as broken ribs and a concussion, but it looks like he's out of danger. There doesn't appear to be serious injuries to internal organs."

Thanking him profusely, they all dropped into their chairs tiredly. Doug held Mary tightly and said, "Thank God, honey, our son's going to be OK!"

Miranda wept openly on Cindy's shoulder, and Grace and Nathan came over and wrapped their arms around both of them; but underneath the tears, smiles kept trying to break through. They were all so happy and relieved that the waiting was finally over. It had been a long night!

Nathan talked his parents and Grace into going home after they all peeped into Brian's room. He was asleep, but it was drug-induced, so he wouldn't be able to talk to them for a while. Nobody could get Miranda to leave until she had spoken to Brian and reassured herself he was going to be all right. She kept silent vigil in the waiting room until a nurse came and told her Brian was awake. Joyfully, she went into his room. Smiling through her tears, she bent down to kiss him and asked; "How are you?"

Weakly, he tried to smile back.

"Shhh... don't try to talk. I'm just happy to see you awake." She sat quietly holding his hand until he went back to sleep. Only then was she able to go home for a short time for some much needed sleep.

Over the next few days, the whole family, including Cindy and Miranda, spent a lot of time at the hospital. Brian was improving rapidly. He smiled brightly whenever Miranda came into his room and would hold her hand while she read to him. He tended to get restless and bored after a while, but Miranda managed to keep his mind occupied.

Sometimes she read to him out of the newspaper, and they would have lively discussions on various topics. Other times it would be a sports magazine or even the current bestseller. It embarrassed her when it came to the love scenes and she tended to skip over them hurriedly. Brian would always catch her and make her go back and read them right. Chuckling, she would tease him about his active imagination.

He still tired very easily and many times she would be reading and glancing over at him, find him asleep. Putting down her book, she would sit quietly and watch him. She longed to put her arms around him and hold him tight; keeping him safe. She had almost lost him and the thought was almost unbearable. Her love for him grew during those days of watching him slowly get better and stronger, and she could hardly wait for him to be released from the hospital. She hoped it wouldn't be too long before they could get married.

When he felt strong enough, they discussed what had happened on their interrupted wedding day. Brian told her he was in such a hurry to get to the church that he was speeding. When he lost control of the car, he panicked and grabbed at the steering wheel. That was the last thing he remembered before waking up in the hospital. He wanted to know what happened after they knew he wasn't going to show up.

"Did you think I had changed my mind about marrying you?" he asked.

"Well, of course it did cross my mind a time or two," she said teasingly. Then sobering, she said; "I thought I would go out of my mind for a while, and if it hadn't been for Cindy, I don't know what I would have done. After what I went through with Roger, losing you could have destroyed me. Later, when I heard you were hurt, I felt so guilty for even thinking you would back out. I just couldn't imagine you were capable of doing something so awful as leaving me at the altar, but even your mother started to have doubts."

"She did?" he asked, completely taken by surprise. "That amazes me! I thought my mom knew me better than that!"

"She does, but what else were we to think? Everyone was ready and waiting and you were nowhere to be found. We tried calling the house and your phone several times. Of course, we began to suspect you may have been in an accident soon enough. Cindy insisted on giving me a sleeping pill, so I was out of it for a while. They were told there had been a bad accident with injuries, but they didn't know the name of the person or persons in the car. It was a long couple of hours until the police told them you were the one injured in the accident. Until then, they still didn't know what had happened to you."

"I'm just so thankful you are alive and getting better every day." She squeezed his hand tightly and tears came into her eyes. It hurt to think she had come so close to losing him.

Cindy stayed for several days, but now that Brian was on the mend, she needed to get back home. Reluctantly, she left, telling Miranda to keep in touch. "Let me know as soon as you two set a new wedding date," she said. "Maybe this time Roger will be able to come."

"I hope he can," Miranda said, "I'm anxious to see him again and find out how he's really treating you." Smiling, she hugged Cindy and watched her leave for the plane. She would miss Cindy an awful lot. Now that Miranda loved Brian, it had been wonderful having Cindy with her. She was so thankful to be free of those old feelings of envy and jealousy.

Chapter Forty-Five

Then, one day, everything changed dramatically. Miranda wasn't sure how it happened or why. When she came into Brian's hospital room, she sensed a strange atmosphere. As she walked over to the bed, Brian didn't smile or reach out for her hand the way he usually did. Watching his face, Miranda realized he was in a very black mood. "Depression," she thought immediately.

When she reached to take his hand, he deliberately moved it out of her reach. "Brian, what's wrong?" she asked. Everything was getting better and Brian would be going home soon. She could hardly wait. "I know being in the hospital has to be getting to you, and you must be anxious to go home. Is that what's bothering you?"

When he didn't respond to her question, she looked up to find him staring at the far wall, a frown on his face.

Anxiously, she asked; "Have I done something to upset you, or is being cooped up in this room getting to be too much?"

"Get out of my room," he snarled. Startled, she stepped back, staring at him wide-eyed.

"Just get out!" he snapped, scooting down and turning his back on her. Not knowing what else to do, Miranda turned and left the room.

In the waiting room, she dropped into a chair and then immediately jumped up again. Pacing, she didn't know what to think. What on earth was wrong with Brian? Was he just angry with her, or was he mad at everyone?

Going over to the nurses' desk, she asked to speak to the doctor. "I'll let him know, and he'll be with you as soon as possible," the nurse said.

Waiting impatiently, Miranda went over everything that had happened in the last few days. He had kissed her when she left yesterday and seemed happy and content; although, a bit anxious to get out of the hospital and go home. They had even discussed a possible wedding date. None of this made any sense at all, unless, as she suspected, Brian was deeply depressed.

Dr. Marlow came in just then and she hurried over to him. "Doctor, can you tell me if something has happened to Brian? Just now, he practically threw me out of his room. I've never seen him like this before."

Dr. Marlow looked at her for a moment, and then said; "That's something that Brian will have to tell you, if he decides to. I can't betray a confidence between doctor and patient. Just give him some time and be kind and gentle. He's having to deal with something pretty heavy."

"Were his injuries worse than we thought? Is there something really wrong with him that you're not telling me? Please, tell me if there is," she begged.

"You know I can't," he said. "Until Brian chooses to tell you, you'll just have to respect his wishes."

Not knowing what else to do at that point, she left and went to Mary's house. Knocking on the door, she waited impatiently for someone to answer. When Mary opened the door, she blurted out; "Mary, have you seen Brian today?"

"No. Come on in. I was just getting ready to go see him. Why do you ask? Is something wrong?"

Moving past her into the house, Miranda walked over to the window and stood with her back to the room. Taking a deep breath, she slowly turned to face Mary. After all Mary had been through, Miranda didn't want to upset her any more than she had to. Finally, she said tiredly, "I don't know. I went to see Brian as usual today and he practically threw me out of his room."

"What?" Mary asked, startled.

"It's true," Miranda said. "I don't understand it either. Maybe he's just been in the hospital so long he's totally fed up with it, but that doesn't explain his attitude. He was angry and belligerent, and yelled at me. I've never seen Brian like this in my life. I asked the doctor what was wrong but he won't tell me. There are laws about confidentially between doctor and patient he has to abide by. I just don't know what to do. Since he was mad at me, maybe you and Doug can find out what's wrong. He might tell you."

Mary sat down abruptly. "That's strange," she said. "Yesterday, he was just fine. I'll go and see him and let you know if I find out anything, OK?"

Nodding, Miranda left after giving Mary a hug and a kiss. "Please find out what's wrong," she whispered.

A couple of hours later the phone rang. Hoping it was Brian, Miranda picked it up eagerly. "Miranda, this is Mary."

Disappointed that it wasn't Brian, she asked anxiously, "Mary, what did you find out?"

"Nothing. He just clammed up when I asked him why he had been rude to you," she said. "I begged him to tell me what was wrong, but he just said it was something he had to work out on his own. I asked if he was keeping something from me about his health, but he said he was fine. In fact, he said the doctor would be releasing him soon. I don't know what to tell you, Miranda, except to keep trying and maybe he'll tell you sooner or later."

She did try, over and over again. Brian just would not tell her anything. Even though he wasn't always as angry with her as he was the first day, he was never kind. Sometimes he was hateful, other times just quietly rude, turning his back and refusing to talk to her. She had a deep sense of disquiet. She knew something had to be terribly wrong, and if he would just tell her what it was, they could work through it.

Although he hurt her terribly, she tried not to show it. She repaid his rudeness with love and kindness; reaching out to touch him, even though he sometimes shrank away from her. Once, it seemed as if he were about to say something; his fingers clinging to hers a moment before jerking away. As she glanced up at him, she saw horrible suffering in his face; his eyes black with pain, before he quickly turned away.

Finally, even her patience wore thin, and one day she said angrily; "Brian, you have to tell me what's wrong. If you don't, I'm going to talk to your doctor and he will have to tell me something!"

Stubbornly, he just stared back at her, saying nothing. She left, almost slamming the door. What was she going to do? She had tried everything and nothing seemed to work. She had to give it one more try with his doctor, but this time she didn't get any further than the last time.

"I've told you, I just can't give you any information about Brian. I have to respect his wishes. It would be a breach of medical ethics if I were to tell you anything," Dr. Marlow stated firmly.

"But you don't understand! He's so angry all the time. He won't talk to anyone, not even his parents. Surely his well-being is more important than any medical ethics. Can't you please tell me something; anything that we can use to get him to talk?"

"I'm sorry, my dear. I wish I could. I've asked Brian to talk to his family about this, but he refuses. He told me that under no circumstances was I to tell you anything. So you can see my hands are tied."

Desperately she begged; "We were just hours away from getting married! Don't I have a right to know what's wrong with my fiancé?"

"But you're not his wife yet, and even if you were, Brian still has a right to his privacy," Dr. Marlow replied.

Despondently, she walked away; not knowing what else to do. There was no way to find out what was wrong with Brian unless he chose to tell her; and unless circumstances changed, she didn't see him doing that. Why? What was so wrong that he couldn't tell anyone? Her heart sat like a rock in her chest. She was so frightened that Brian was going to die, and she wouldn't be able to be there to comfort him; to say goodbye. Her heart ached to take him in her arms and ease the pain of what he was going through. As it stood, there was nothing she could do, because he wouldn't let her.

After getting nowhere with his doctor and not wanting to subject herself to any more pain, she didn't go back to see him while he was in the hospital. She just couldn't take any more of his silences and cruelty. The only way she knew when he was out of the hospital was because Mary called and told her he had been released. When Miranda asked how he was, Mary started to cry.

"I'm scared, Miranda. There's something dreadfully wrong with my son, but he won't tell me or his father. If he would even tell Nathan, it would be better than keeping it bottled up inside, but he won't. He just keeps saying he has to work it out. When I ask him about you, he just gets angry and storms out."

Miranda called his home, but he just hung up on her. Going over to his house one night, his housekeeper said he didn't want to see her. Walking away, unhappily, she knew there was nothing more she could do unless he chose to confide in her.

Chapter Forty-Six

Nathan and Grace had long since gone home, leaving Doug and Mary terribly unhappy. Something very wrong was happening to their beloved son and there wasn't anything they could do to help him. They were scared and upset; even thinking that he may be dying. Maybe something terrible had happened during the accident and it was incurable or inoperable.

Miranda voiced all their fears by saying to Mary, "Brian must know how scared we all are, but for some reason, he just won't tell us what's wrong."

"I find it hard to believe my son is that selfish, so it must be something he's unable to face, much less tell us," Mary said sadly.

Brian returned to work but didn't let Miranda know. Karen came to her office shortly after his return.

"Miranda, Brian is in his office. Do you want to come in and say hello? He may need you in a little while to go over some urgent matters that need to be addressed quickly."

Miranda suddenly realized that Karen didn't know anything about what she and Brian's parents were dealing with. "What am I going to say to her," she whispered. She didn't want to hurt Karen or make things difficult for her with Brian by saying too much.

"I'll go see him when he rings," she finally said. "Karen, Brian has changed quite a bit since the accident and you may be shocked by his behavior. If you have any questions, just speak to Brian."

"I don't understand," Karen said.

"Neither do I," Miranda said. "But, hopefully, Brian will be OK soon and explain what's going on with him. In the meantime, I'm just going to do my job and hope he gets back to his old self. Just don't be surprised when you have to work with him."

Karen shook her head as she left Miranda's office. She had known Brian for years and had no idea what Miranda was trying to tell her. She soon found out! Brian certainly was different. He didn't treat her as an old friend; instead he was curt and almost rude when he gave her instructions.

"Brian, why are you acting this way?" she questioned.

"What way is that?" Brian asked sharply.

"Rude," Karen said quietly. "Brian, what's going on with you? We all missed you and are happy you are back. But, you seem so different, and you've never been rude to me or anyone else in your life."

"You wouldn't understand, Karen. So just leave me alone and get the work done. I need to get caught up," Brian said turning his back on her.

Karen left his office in tears, not able to understand anything that was happening. A few days after Brian returned, several employees asked her why Brian was so different. She didn't have an answer for them.

He very seldom called Miranda into his office and did so only if absolutely necessary. In which case, he was very brief and to the point, with no unnecessary conversation.

Miranda couldn't forgive him for his cruelty toward his parents. His bruises and injuries were healing nicely, and he seemed normal on the outside. But, on the inside, everything was different.

He seemed angry all the time and Mary sobbed as she told Miranda that she had noticed signs of him drinking. "He's never had a drinking problem in his life, so whatever is going on with him has to be horrible."

A couple of weeks after his release from the hospital, Brian disappeared. No one knew where he had gone. Mary and Doug were frantic when they called Miranda to ask if she had seen him. They called everyone they could think of, but nobody had any idea where he was. Nobody had seen or heard from him. Miranda frantically tried to find him too, but she didn't have any luck either.

When he disappeared without a word, she didn't know what to do. She talked to the Board of Directors and they advised her to just keep doing what she had been doing until Brian could be found. They suggested that she put any big projects on hold as long as she could. They also recommended that she talk to the manager of the Tulsa office. He had taken over for Brian a few times in the past when Brian needed to get away. His name was Eric Monrovia.

She lost no time in calling Eric and he flew to Medford the next day. Between the two of them they managed to sort out some of the stickier problems. Miranda liked working with Eric. He was very precise and organized and could get right to the root of a problem. He was very likeable. He seemed like a tough, vigorous man, and would be a good person to have in a tight situation. Miranda found she was very thankful for his presence and help over the next few days. She knew she could never have handled things without his help.

Eric was tall, thin, and blond. He wore glasses and his hair was almost Ivy League short. He wasn't exactly handsome in the traditional sense, but he was friendly and nice. He believed in working hard and wasn't afraid of tackling a tough project.

Chapter Forty-Seven

Andre stopped in to see Miranda several times, just to see how she was doing. He didn't know the complete story, but enough to know that she was in a lot of pain. It reminded him so much of what she had been like when he first met her. Over the last few months he watched her grow out of that pain and become a cheerful, happy woman. It hurt him so much to see what was happening to her all over again...and would have given anything to take away her suffering.

Even though it was something he had fought long and hard, Andre loved Miranda. He knew how much she cared for Brian, even though he had never heard her say that she loved him. Andre had often watched her face and witnessed the glow in her eyes whenever she was with Brian. Knowing that a life with her was out of the question, Andre never intended to let Miranda know how he felt. It was enough that he could be here now to comfort her.

One afternoon, Andre walked into Miranda's office and stopped just inside the door. "Miranda, there's a question I have about the Zegimal drug trials. Do you have a minute?" She was standing with her back to the room, so he was surprised when she didn't answer right away. When she finally turned around he realized she had been crying. Tears were visible on her cheeks and she was holding a tissue to her eyes.

"I'm sorry to let you see me this way, Andre."

"I'm pretty sure I know what it's all about," Andre said quietly as he walked to where she was standing. "There have been a lot of rumors about Brian's behavior which I know can't be easy for you, and now I understand he's not coming to work. What can I do to help?"

"You don't know the half of it," Miranda said as tears trailed down her cheeks. "I assume you don't know Brian has disappeared and none of us know where he is or even if he's OK?"

"Disappeared?"

"Yes, he just left town. His Mom and Dad are worried sick and so are the rest of us. I'm sure you know how strangely he's been acting at work. He won't tell any of us what's wrong so we can help."

"I've heard rumors," Andre said. "But, I don't know what is true or just gossip. You haven't heard from him either? You are supposed to be getting married...unless that has changed."

"We're still engaged, but the way things are going, I'm sure that will change," Miranda said sadly.

"Miranda, come with me. I think you need someone to talk to and work can wait. Let's go to the lake where we can have some privacy."

"That sounds good," Miranda said tiredly. "We'll stop by and let Karen know we'll be gone for a while."

At the lake, they found a secluded bench and Miranda confided in him about Brian's behavior change while he was still in the hospital.

"You're saying that one day you went to see him and he just threw you out without an explanation?!" Andre asked.

"Yes," Miranda said as a sob escaped. "Andre, I don't know what to do."

Andre held Miranda in his arms while she cried desperately. He felt helpless and he was angry at Brian for what he was doing to her. If confronting Brian was what she needed, he had no problem with doing so, even if it cost him his job.

"Can I talk to Brian for you, when he returns? He needs to know what his horrible treatment is doing to you," Andre said angrily.

"No... Andre no... I won't let you jeopardize your career for me. No way," she said vehemently.

Miranda hadn't meant to break down, but the agony she was feeling and Andre's sympathy was more than she could bear. "Andre," she sobbed, "I'm watching a good man slowly destroy himself and I don't know what to do about it. He won't let me in! If he would only talk to someone...but he won't! His parents have no idea what's wrong and now he's disappeared and no one knows where he's gone. He could be hurt; and we wouldn't know about it. His parents and I are getting frantic. I have no idea what to do!" Miranda said desperately.

"I wish I knew what to tell you. As far as I know, no one has any idea where he's gone, and why. Management is starting to get very concerned. The rumors about his behavior are all over the building. I don't know what will happen when he comes back to work."

"Andre, what if he doesn't come back? What is going to happen then?"

"I guess the company will have to hire someone to replace him sooner or later. Things can't keep on the way they are now. I'm starting to hear rumors from the main office in Oakland that they may start looking for a replacement before long."

"Oh no," she gasped. "They can't do that, can they?"

"Of course they can. It will have to go through the Board of Directors and may take some time, but it will happen if he doesn't show up shortly; and take command again."

"I'm so scared for him, Andre," she said tearfully.

"So am I, sweetheart. I just can't imagine what's wrong with him. He's certainly not the same man I've known all these years. I hope that whatever's wrong, he'll get some professional help. He can't go on hurting himself, you, and everyone else this way. Sooner or later, something will snap."

"I know. I've done all I can to help him, but he just pushes me away. He even refuses to confide in his family. That, I find hard to understand! I can't even imagine what could be so bad that he can't even talk to them about it. They've always been a very close family."

Chapter Forty-Eight

It was such a shock when, a few weeks later, out of the blue, Brian walked into Miranda's office. Jumping to her feet, she ran to him, almost flinging her arms around him.

"Brian! Brian, where have you been? Your parents and I have been worried half out of our minds! Why didn't you call someone? Have you been to see your parents to let them know that you are all right? Please tell me where you have been?" she almost begged.

Instead of answering, he examined her face for a moment as if memorizing it. Then, pushing her arms away, he turned his back on her and walked over to the window, staring sightlessly out at the park. So low she had to strain to hear him, he said; "I'm sorry you were worried. I just had to get away for a while to think things through."

Afraid to move or say anything that might upset him, she waited for him to go on. When he didn't say anything else, she finally asked him again; "Brian, where did you go?"

Still speaking quietly, he asked; "What business is that of yours where I went?"

Suddenly, it was as if a dam had broken and she found herself almost screaming at him; "What do you mean; 'What business is it of mine'?! You've been gone for weeks, and your family has been going crazy wondering where you were! I've been trying desperately to keep this company afloat, and you have the nerve to ask me that?! I don't understand you at all! As far as I know, we are still engaged, so why shouldn't I ask you where you've been? You disappear for weeks and expect me to accept it without question?!" She stormed around the room, getting angrier by the moment.

Angry himself now, he shouted back; "Well, we can remedy that right now!   As of this moment, we are no longer engaged. Got that?" Stalking to the door, he wrenched it open.

Hurting, she sank onto the edge of her desk, which was the nearest thing to her. Otherwise, she probably would have fallen to the floor. Her breathing was rapid and it was all she could do to keep from crying out like a wounded animal. "Oh Brian," she whimpered.

At the door, Brian turned to look back at her. A dreadful look of suffering crossed his face, and he reached out as if he might touch her. Instead, he hesitated a moment, and then turned and left her office.

After that, his anger seemed to be directed toward everyone. The atmosphere around the office was unhappy, to say the least. The entire staff began keeping out of Brian's way because they never knew what he was going to do next. If they crossed him in any way, they got browbeaten or yelled at. Miranda had never known Brian to use profanity, but sometimes she would hear him cursing at someone. A few months ago this company had run like a well-oiled machine.

Now, everything was in chaos. The old Brian they once knew no longer existed. Several employees' submitted resignations and others asked for a transfer to a different branch of the company. Without much hope and realizing things might never get better, Miranda thought about her own career and knew she needed to take steps to secure her own future. She just wasn't ready yet to give up on Brian.

Several co-workers asked Miranda what was wrong with Brian. They didn't understand why he had changed so much, and what had caused it.

"I don't know," she replied sorrowfully. "I wish I did! I'm watching a good man being tortured inside and I don't know what to do to help."

As the weeks went by, Miranda noticed that even though Brian was able to handle the business end of things, he seemed to be drinking a lot more. At first he had been careful not to drink at the office, but now she noticed he seemed under the influence more and more.

Miranda quit calling Mary because there didn't seem to be anything for either one to say anymore. She missed talking to her, but lately whenever she called, Mary was too upset to say very much.

Chapter Forty-Nine

The last time Miranda saw Sharon, Brian's friend, was at the hospital when Brian was getting better. At the time Brian disappeared, Miranda called Sharon's house and Allen answered. He told Miranda that he hadn't seen nor heard from Brian since he left the hospital. So, it was a complete surprise when she ran into Sharon outside of a store one day.

Before she could say anything, Sharon said; "Miranda, it's so good to see you. Do you have time for a cup of coffee? I know a nice restaurant just down the street that serves a good cup of coffee."

"Sure. That would be nice." As they walked a few doors down to the restaurant, Miranda said; "I've been wondering how you guys are. How's Ryan? I bet he's really getting big."

"That's one of the reasons I'm in town. He's been growing out of all of his clothes and I stopped in to pick him up a couple of things."

"And the new store in Klamath?" Miranda asked. "Do you have it open yet?"

"It's being renovated," Sharon answered. "We hope to open next month, if things go as planned. How have you been doing?"

Just then, the waitress interrupted them to ask what they would like to order. After getting their order, she left, leaving Miranda to answer Sharon's question. Reluctantly she said; "I'm not doing well. I assume you have heard about Brian's behavior lately? Have you seen him?"

"I almost wish I could say no, for your sake," Sharon answered. She waited for a moment while the waitress set their coffee down, then went on. "Allen and I were hearing rumors about him from everywhere and neither one of us wanted to believe them. After all, we've known Brian for years. The things we were hearing made no sense and didn't sound at all like the Brian we know. So, we decided to go visit him."

"What happened?" Miranda broke in anxiously.

"When Brian answered the door, he had a bottle of beer in his hand and looked so rumpled and unkempt that I had a hard time believing it was him."

"'Well, come on in. Don't just stand there,' he said so rudely that we almost turned around and left."

"But you didn't?"

"No, but I wish we had. As we walked through the house I could hardly believe my eyes. Do you remember the beautiful, immaculate house you saw the night you came to Brian's?" she asked Miranda.

"Sure I do. It was gorgeous and, as you said, immaculate, like it always is. Why, what was wrong?"

"I don't know if you'll believe me when I tell you," she said soberly. "It wasn't filthy, but Brian certainly hadn't done any cleaning for a while. There were magazines, newspapers, and beer bottles lying around; and it looked cluttered and dusty. After we followed him in, he just slouched down on the couch, drinking his beer. When Allen tried to talk to him, he had nothing to say. You know how fond of Ryan he's always been? He didn't even ask about him. His eyes were glassy and I'm not even sure he was fully aware that we were there. I decided to make him some coffee, but that was a mistake."

"Why?"

"The kitchen was really messy. There were a lot of dirty dishes and the counters hadn't been cleaned for a while. I couldn't believe I was in Brian's house. He loves that house, and for him to be so uncaring doesn't make any sense. It made me so sad," Sharon said, wiping tears from her eyes.

Shocked, Miranda murmured, "I wonder what happened to his housekeeper? It's hard to believe he's living in such a mess."

"I asked him about that, and he said he let her go," Sharon said. "Miranda, please tell me what is wrong with Brian?" Sharon implored. "I love him so much and Allen has always respected him more than any man he's ever known. I know it sounds crazy, but we both went home that night and cried. It almost killed us to see him this way."

As Sharon looked up at Miranda, she caught the haunted look in Miranda's eyes, and tears shimmering near the surface.

"Oh, Miranda. I'm sorry. I didn't mean to make you cry too!"

Wiping her eyes with a tissue, Miranda mumbled, "It's OK. I wasn't sure if I could cry anymore. To answer your questions, I'm just as much in the dark as you are. One day we were just fine and the next..." A sob escaped before she could go on. "The next day, everything just fell apart. Sharon, he won't even let me talk to him. I tried going to his house, only to be turned away. At the office, if we have to work together, he only talks about business. I don't dare bring up anything personal any more. We just end up yelling at each other. I avoid him as much as possible. Everyone else at work does too. He's become unbearable to work for."

"If he's that bad at work, how's the company doing?"

"Well if it weren't for Eric..."

"Eric. Who's Eric, may I ask?"

Miranda was surprised at Sharon's tone, and wondered why she had spoken so sharply.

"Forgive me," Sharon said a moment later. "I'm sorry, but I guess I was jealous for Brian. Isn't that crazy?"

"No. It actually makes sense under the circumstances. Sometimes I feel like the whole world has turned upside down, and I'm the only sane one left. Eric is a company executive out of the Tulsa office. He's been helping me keep things afloat until Brian gets better, or they replace him."

"Is that possible?"

"At this point, anything is possible. There have been rumors about him being replaced."

Getting to her feet reluctantly, Sharon said she had to go. As Miranda walked out with her, she didn't know what to say. Sharon turned on the sidewalk and gave her a warm hug. "You hang in there. I don't know how, but I just know Brian is going to get through this. Do you have any idea at all about what caused him to act so strangely?"

"I talked to his doctor several times and all he would say is that Brian has to tell me," Miranda replied. "Brian won't even talk to Mary and Doug about what's wrong. The doctor simply told me that Brian had to deal with something pretty heavy. Sharon, I'm terrified that he might be dying!"

"What makes you say that? It didn't occur to either Allen or me that he might have been hurt so badly that he won't recover. Surely, he would tell someone if that were the case."

"Well, what else could cause him to act so strangely? Sharon, it's been months now, and no one, not even his brother, can get close to him."

"I would give anything if someone knew the answers," Sharon said. "Miranda, please don't give up on him. If you love him enough, surely that will make a difference somehow."

"I do love him...desperately." –It felt strange saying those words out loud to someone for the first time– "But I just don't know what else I can do. Sharon, will you call me? I need to talk to someone once in a while, or I may go insane."

Holding her hand tightly, Sharon nodded and then quickly left; but not before Miranda saw the tears in her eyes.

Chapter Fifty

As the days went by and nothing changed in Brian's behavior, Miranda noticed a couple of women going into his office. They were strangers to her and she knew they didn't work for the Medford branch. When she asked Karen about them, Karen just said they were former friends of Brian's. Even though she asked, she couldn't get anything else out of Karen.

In the past, it had been Brian's policy to keep personal business strictly to non-office hours; but recently, it was not unusual for her to see a woman she didn't know enter or leave his office. The strange thing about it was that no one ever saw the same woman twice.

When Miranda started work in the Medford office, a couple of her co-workers made it their business to tell her about some of the women in Brian's life. After getting to know Brian, Miranda wasn't surprised. Of course, women would be a part of Brian's life. He was handsome, rich, and probably one of the most sought-after bachelors in Oregon. Now, the company was rife with rumors that some of his old flames were back in his life.

What stunned and hurt Miranda the most was that Brian seemed to enjoy flaunting them in her face. As she passed his office one day, the door opened and he came out, his arm around the waist of a very beautiful blond. Although aware of Miranda standing there or maybe because of it, he pulled the girl against him. As she watched in stunned disbelief, he gave her a passionate kiss while his hands moved sensuously over her body. Tormented, Miranda crept back into her office and closed the door; unable to even cry anymore.

Watching him torment Miranda was almost the last straw for Karen. She came out of Brian's office one day so mad she told Miranda she was thinking of quitting.

"Please don't do that, Karen. I don't know what I would do without you. When everything seems to be going insane, I can always count on you to give me some perspective. Have you tried asking Brian what's wrong?"

"Yes. Several times."

Miranda asked eagerly, "Well, what does he say?"

"Nothing. He just says it's something he has to deal with, and he doesn't want to talk about it. I even got mad and yelled at him, telling him that it was affecting everyone, but it didn't do any good. Today, I asked if he enjoyed hurting you. That's the one time that I felt as if I might be getting through to him."

"Why? What happened?"

"I saw horrible suffering in his face and tears shimmering in his eyes. For a moment, I thought he was going to break down and cry, but then he turned away and gruffly told me to leave. When I started to go over to him, he just yelled at me to get out. I love him Miranda, but he's not the same man I used to know." Holding out her arms, Miranda hugged her tight for a few moments.

* * *

A few days after Miranda saw Sharon, she decided to give Jennifer a call, hoping that she might have talked to Brian. They had seemed to be very close, and Miranda was getting desperate for some answers. Jennifer wasn't home so she left a message on her answering machine. A couple of days later, Jennifer returned her call, asking if Miranda would like to have dinner with her. At the restaurant, they talked casually about Jennifer's job, and then Jennifer asked, "What on earth is going on with Brian? I presume you still work for him?"

"Yes. What have you heard from Brian? Have you talked to him lately?" Miranda asked anxiously.

Jennifer seemed reluctant to answer for a moment and Miranda wondered why.

Finally, Miranda said, "I know you and Brian have been good friends for a while and I'm sure you have heard some of the rumors about how he's been acting. I was hoping that you have talked to him. I thought maybe you were the one person he might confide in. He certainly won't talk to me, but from your question, it sounds like you're as much in the dark as the rest of us."

"Let's put it this way... I hope it's a long time before I see him again," Jennifer answered reluctantly.

"What on earth do you mean? What's happened?"

"I knew about Brian's accident, of course, but I was out of the country when it happened. That's why I wasn't at the wedding. As soon as I came back from France, I went to see him in the hospital and he seemed to be doing fine. He was in good spirits, and I assumed you two would set another wedding date soon. I got pretty busy and didn't call him, but a few days ago I started hearing rumors he was drinking pretty heavily. Later that day, one of my friends saw him at a bar with some woman, and he seemed to be draped all over her."

A gasp from Miranda made Jennifer reach across the table and take her hand. "I won't say any more if it's going to upset you so much," she said with compassion.

After a moment, Miranda motioned for her to go on. "I don't want to hear this, but I have to," she said apprehensively. "Maybe something you say will help me to understand what is going on." Their food had arrived, but neither was able to eat much. Miranda sat picking at her food as Jennifer continued.

"I decided to call Michael and I asked him if he knew anything. He didn't, but he was having a few friends in, so he said he would call Brian and ask if he would like to come. I arrived a little late, but Brian looked all right, and seemed to be having a good time, although I noticed he had a drink in his hand. Did you notice when you came to his house, that first time, he never drank anything except at dinner?" Jennifer asked.

"I didn't really pay attention to what he was drinking... Why?"

Jennifer answered, "Brian's never been much of a drinker. I just saw him drink a beer or a glass of wine once in a while. The other night, I noticed as the evening wore on, he always seemed to have a drink in his hand. He also seemed to be slurring his words a little. I still didn't think too much of it, and when he asked me to dance, I said OK. Boy, was that a major mistake!"

"What do you mean?"

"You know Brian. Have you ever known him to be out of line with women; pushy or inappropriate?"

"No, of course I haven't." Then she paused and said, "Until lately, that is. I've never known him to be anything but considerate and polite, until after his accident," Miranda answered.

313

"Well, he certainly wasn't that night.   Miranda, are you sure you want to hear the rest of this? You really don't need to."

Numbly, Miranda nodded, and Jennifer explained; "Well, in the nicest terms I can put it, he wouldn't keep his hands where they belonged and I ended up having to slap him."

Horrified, Miranda just stared at her. Unable to find her voice, she whispered; "What else happened?"

"To make the story short, Michael took exception to his behavior and they almost ended up in a fistfight. Instead, Michael was able to get him calmed down enough to put him in a cab and send him home. Neither one of us have heard a word from him since."

When Miranda was able to think straight, she asked, "You said this was a few days ago?"

"Yes, why do you ask?"

"No reason in particular. I've just noticed a couple of women in Brian's office lately. He seems to enjoy flaunting them in my face for some reason," Miranda said sadly.

"Are you two still engaged?" Jennifer asked. "I guess that's a stupid question to ask, isn't it? I'm sure you wouldn't stay engaged to a man who was acting the way Brian seems to be. Do you have any idea why he's acting this way?"

Getting to her feet, Miranda said tiredly; "Jennifer, I'm going to go now. Thank you for talking to me, but the last few weeks have been a nightmare and I don't feel up to staying any longer. To answer your question, Brian ended our engagement, and as hard as everyone's tried, we can't get any answers out of him."

"Of course," Jennifer said, jumping to her feet. "I'll pay the bill. You go on home. I wish I was able to give you some answers. Please take care of yourself and if you ever feel like talking, call me."

Chapter Fifty-One

Miranda was miserable. Her whole world was falling apart around her. She cried so easily these days. Her nights began to remind her of what she went through with Roger, only worse. She wasn't sleeping or eating and was losing weight again. Nothing had much meaning anymore. She often thought of quitting her job and moving somewhere else. She even wrote a letter of resignation, but couldn't bring herself to give it to Brian. Even though it tore her up inside to see him this way; not seeing him at all seemed even worse.

Her one solace and tie to reality became Eric, and she turned to him more and more. He called often and flew in to see her regularly; even though Brian was back at the office.

One day, Eric called and when Miranda answered the phone, he said; "I just wanted to check on you and see if the office is running smoothly."

"Not exactly," Miranda said. "I'm Brian's assistant, but you wouldn't know it these days. He's been using some of the secretaries to do some of the work I should be doing. I just don't know what I'm doing here anymore."

"I'm so sorry things are so bad. I will never understand this new version of Brian. He's always been so stable and in control. He just seems like a different person to me."

"Oh, he definitely is."

"Can you have dinner with me tomorrow night? I'll fly in to see you if you aren't busy. Maybe I can help sort out some problems you are having at work."

"Are you sure, Eric? I know it's not easy to fly in just to see me and you must be busy with your own work."

"Not too busy to come and see you," Eric said softly.

Holding back a sob, Miranda said, "It would really be nice to see you, then. Thanks, Eric."

When he arrived, Eric presented her with a beautiful bouquet of flowers. During dinner, Eric questioned her about Brian and how things were at the office. Reluctantly, she told him about some problems she was trying to figure out; so the next morning he went to the office with her to help sort them out. She hated to say goodbye when he left because it felt so good to talk to someone who understood how hard things were.

A couple of weeks later, he flew out and took her to an *Always Patsy Cline* concert. She was surprised to learn they both loved Patsy Cline and had all of her albums. During the concert he took her hand, interlacing his fingers with hers. Even though his touch was warm and comforting, Miranda didn't feel physically drawn to him. She liked and admired Eric because he was smart and very dedicated to his job, but beyond that, she didn't feel anything other than friendship. He was not Brian!

After a dinner date, when she realized he was going to kiss her, she turned slightly and he kissed her cheek. He laughed it off as if it wasn't important, but Miranda was afraid she was hurting him. She thought he was starting to care for her, but couldn't bring herself to give up the solidarity he brought her. She needed something right now to keep her rational and Eric was a comfort to be with. She thought often about telling him that she would never love anyone but Brian, but couldn't quite bring herself to do so. For one thing, it would be embarrassing if she was misreading Eric's interest in her.

Miranda was mentally and physically exhausted trying to keep the company going smoothly. As a result, she didn't have the energy to focus on anything else. She didn't trust her own instincts when it came to Eric. She didn't know if she was misunderstanding his interest or intentions; and it felt like she was stumbling around in the dark.

She couldn't help remembering her friendship with Shawn, and now Andre. Both of them were hurt because she wasn't able to return their feelings and she was afraid the same thing might happen with Eric.

Days seemed to blend into each other with Miranda struggling to sort out complicated problems, figure out her role in the company, and decide what her future held. One particular day had been an extremely hard one for Miranda, and she was feeling overwhelmed. Several of the employees came to her about problems she didn't know how to solve. Brian was nowhere around, but Eric happened to be in town. She called him several times to go and see if he knew how to solve their issues. There was more and more unease at the office because of Brian's lack of leadership, and she kept thinking about a call the night before from Cindy which had really upset her.

"Miranda, since things are such a mess with Brian, why don't you come back home? You've told me about how Brian's treating you and everyone at the office, so just hand in your resignation."

"Cindy, I'm not ready to give up on him yet. I just know something bad happened to him and he'll tell me sometime."

"You're living in a fool's paradise if you think that's going to happen after all this time, sis. I know you're not that naïve, Miranda. Come on!" Cindy said sharply.

Total silence met her comment. Miranda was too hurt to respond.

"I'm so sorry, Miranda. I didn't mean to say that. I'm just so concerned about you."

Miranda still didn't reply, and Cindy could hear her crying softly. "Randi, honey, I'm so sorry. Please forgive me. Please?"

Finally a quiet, "I forgive you. Goodnight, Cindy."

"I love you, sis," Cindy said, before she realized she was listening to a dial tone.

Miranda was still upset about everything, especially the call from Cindy when Eric came back into the office. She quickly tried to wipe tears from her eyes so he wouldn't see them, but wasn't quick enough.

"Miranda, what's wrong? Has something happened?" Eric asked as he walked over to her and put his arm around her. "Is there something I can do?"

Miranda turned and looked up at him. "It's just been a bad day, Eric."

He reached up and brushed a strand of hair back as he gazed at her. Slowly, he brushed his lips against her cheek. "I'm sorry," Eric murmured as he slowly pulled her against him and she buried her face in his shoulder.

A strangulating sound made Miranda break away from Eric. Brian stood in the doorway. She hoped she would never see such naked hurt and anger in anyone's eyes again. But, even with the rage, she sensed hopelessness about him. Oh God, if only she knew what was wrong! If only she knew what was wrong she could help him.

After Brian left, Miranda was shaking so badly that she felt sick to her stomach. Why had he looked at her that way? Did he hate her? Nothing Eric could say or do would comfort her.

"Miranda, what can I do? I hate to see you so upset. Can I talk to Brian? Tell him how much he's hurting you?" Eric asked.

"No...No, Eric," Miranda said frantically. "It will only make it worse. Please, I'd like to be alone."

Eric touched her shoulder before leaving, and she was thankful for his comfort. It was all too much, and she knew she had to give up her job. She could no longer work in this intolerable atmosphere. She loved Brian desperately, but the anger she had seen in his eyes frightened her. She wasn't afraid of what he might do to her physically, but she was frightened that he might completely destroy her.

She took her letter of resignation and went into Brian's office later that day, but stopped in her tracks after opening the door. She was disgusted by what she saw, but she was also overwhelmingly sad; sad for the destruction of a wonderful man.

He was slumped over his desk, a nearly empty whisky bottle nearby. His hair was uncombed, his clothes wrinkled and stained. The once immaculately-dressed man looked like a drunk.

Sidling over to where he lay, she pushed at his shoulder.

"Huh?" he mumbled. Raising bleary eyes he stared at her. "You!" he exclaimed. "What do you want?"

"I want to talk to you but can you please go wash your face and try to sober up a little?" With a little persuasion, he stumbled off to the bathroom. When he came back he looked a little more presentable.

Sadly, she looked at him before she asked, "Brian, what has happened to you? You're destroying yourself and I want to know why. I deserve that much from you. I am leaving the company and you won't see me again, so please tell me what has happened to make you this way."

Suddenly, blindingly angry, she started pounding on him with her fists. "Tell me what happened to you! The wonderful, brilliant man I once knew, isn't anything but a stupid drunk!"

Towering over her in a blind rage, Brian grabbed her flailing arms.

"You want to know what's wrong with me?" he laughed drunkenly. "Ha! Ha! That's funny," he laughed mirthlessly. Turning his back on her, he staggered away and crouched down as if in agony.

Going to him, she reached out to touch his shoulder.

"Don't touch me!" he growled.

"Please, let me help you. Whatever it is, it can't be so bad that we can't work it out. Please, tell me what's gone so wrong! Please, Brian."

Finally looking up at her, Brian asked; "If I tell you, will you go?"

"Yes," she whispered, tears shinning in her eyes.

"I'm no longer a man," he said.

"What do you mean you're no longer a man?" Miranda asked puzzled. "I don't understand."

Turning to her he shouted; "I look like a man. See? Two arms, two legs, face, hands..." —spreading his hands so she could see. "I look the same on the surface, don't I? But, I'm half a man. I can eat, talk, walk, and breathe, everything just like any other man..." But suddenly, almost incoherent; "I can't make love to you. I'm dead inside. I'm a freak! I have no feelings for a woman. Do you understand? Now get out!"

Sliding to the floor, Miranda sat with her back to the wall; too stunned to move. If what he said was true, she couldn't leave him. What demons he must be living with! She remembered the once vibrant man who had held her in his arms at the beach. The man she almost made love to. She couldn't believe she would never feel that way again with him...never again... Tears running down her face, she buried her face in her hands.

"Oh Brian," she sobbed, "I'm so sorry. Why, oh why, didn't you tell me? I wouldn't have left you. I would have helped you. Why didn't you at least tell your parents?"

Roughly, he pulled her to her feet. "Do you think I want your pity? You promised to go, so please get out!"

"No Brian," she said stubbornly. "This time I'm not leaving. Do you think crawling into a bottle is the answer? Are you sure there is no hope for you?" She looked up at Brian with tear-filled eyes.

He walked over to his desk and slumped into his chair, bowing his head in his hands. Going over to him timidly, she reached out her hand to touch his shoulder. She had been mistreated by him so many times that she was afraid of what he might do. "Brian, what did the doctors say? How did this happen? Did you get a second opinion? Are you sure there's nothing they can do?"

Tiredly, sadly, he shook his head. "When I hit the telephone pole, I injured my abdomen and groin area. The doctors think my injuries were severe enough to make my condition permanent. Some say there may be a slight chance everything will become normal, but most don't hold out much hope. I've been on medication, and a few weeks ago they started some kind of injections, but they all say it's probably permanent," he said speaking so low she could hardly hear him.

Moving closer, she put her arms around his shoulders and dropped her head onto his. "Brian, Brian," was all she could say.

Her sympathy became too much for him and he began to weep. Cuddling him in her arms, she cried with him. She cried for all the loss. He cried out all the pain and anguish he had been feeling, all the longings he felt for what was gone. He still remembered what it was like.

With his arms stealing around her waist, he buried his face in her breasts. She stroked his hair lovingly, and feelings welled up in her that almost overwhelmed her. She loved him, that's all that mattered. If they were never to make love or have children, she would be content. She would rather be with him the way he was than with any other man.

Lifting his head with her hands, she kissed his lips gently. "Are you sure, Brian, that there is something the doctors didn't tell you? We'll go see other doctors."

He flung away from her and paced the room. "Don't you think I've tried? Remember all the women you've seen me with?" He laughed, mockingly. "Each failure was worse than the last and more humiliating. That's why I turned to the bottle more and more. I finally realized it was useless and I was just torturing myself for nothing. This is the way it is, and the way it's going to stay."

Turning back to her, he gave her a bleak smile. He had been so heartless to everyone he loved; Miranda, his parents, siblings, friends. He had no right to be forgiven by her or anyone else. He didn't deserve to be loved by her. He had forfeited her love, hadn't he? He was so horrible to her for such a long time, pushing her away, hurting her unbearably, and here she was being so kind to him.

"Miranda, please forgive me for being so cruel to you. Just forget about me and go on with your life," he said turning away desolately. "I'm no good to anyone. I have to make a life for myself but it can't include you. Do you understand?"

"No," she said, going to him again and putting her arms around him. "Making love isn't everything."

"Maybe not to you," he snarled, "But I might as well be dead."

"Don't say that. Please, Brian." Miranda begged. "Please don't!" Tugging at his arm, she pulled him around. Putting her arms around his neck, she held him tightly. "I'm not going to let you get rid of me that easily! I can still be what you wanted when you first asked me to marry you; a good host, friend and companion. None of that has to change." She knew Brian still believed that she loved Roger and she was willing to leave it that way for now. Letting Brian think she didn't care about the physical part of their relationship might make him willing to marry her. They could sort out the future together. She wanted that more than anything she had ever wanted.

She hated to lie to him, but for his own sake and sanity, she felt that this was the best possible way to handle it. She was afraid that if she threw caution to the wind and told him that she loved him, she would never see him again. She just couldn't take that chance.

Running her hands along his back and shoulders for comfort, she laid her head on his chest. Taking his hand, she pressed a kiss into his palm. He suddenly tensed, then froze.

Wondering what was wrong, she gazed up at him. He pushed her away slightly, staring at her. "Miranda, would you kiss me?" he asked huskily. Complying, she touched her lips softly to his. At first he didn't respond, and then his lips came alive on hers. Tasting, touching, he couldn't seem to get enough. His hands roamed her body at will. He crushed her to him and then picked her up in his arms. He twirled her madly around the room, laughing crazily.

Thinking he had lost his mind, Miranda struggled to get down. He continued to laugh and cry at the same time, raining kisses on her face. Pushing against him, she finally started to pound at him with her fists.

"Let me down! Brian, have you gone crazy?"

"Crazy!" he shouted. "Yes, I guess maybe I have." He pulled her fully against him, and murmured; "Miranda, I want you so badly it hurts. Somehow a miracle has taken place and my life has just been given back to me."

"Oh, Miranda," he breathed, "It wasn't my problem with the other women. You must be the only woman that can turn me on." Shyly, she pressed her face into his chest, so thankful that she didn't know what to say.

"You've taken away the hell that I've been living in since the doctors told me about my condition, Miranda, dearest. How can I ever repay you for sticking by me and not leaving when I told you to

325

go? I have been so brutal to you these last months. I can't understand why you didn't leave long ago. Why did you stay?"

"Because there was nowhere else for me to go, and I guess I never gave up hoping that somehow, someone could bring you back to me. Thank God it happened before you completely destroyed yourself," she said softly, hugging him to her.

Lifting her face, he said, "Marry me, please, Miranda." Joyously, she nodded. A miracle had taken place, and even though he didn't say he loved her, he needed her. She had been the one to save him from the black despair he was living in. They would have a good life together, she just knew it.

Leaving the office, he and Miranda went immediately to see his parents. When she opened the door, Mary was grabbed and swirled around the room.

"Brian, put me down," she said. Looking at their faces, she knew everything was finally all right.

"Doug!" she called, "Come here quickly, there's something you have to see."

When he arrived in the living room, it was to see Mary hugging Miranda and Brian, laughing and crying at the same time.

"What's happened?" he asked.

"Our son has come back to us," she said flinging her arms around her husband. "Doug, our son has come back to us!"

After a long conversation and some embarrassment, Brian's parents knew what he had been afraid to tell them. Pulling Miranda into his arms, he gave her a hard kiss. "If it hadn't been for Miranda, I don't think that I would have ever gotten any better," he said.

His parents made a quick call to Nathan and Grace to tell them that Brian was now OK. They said it was too complicated to explain over the phone, but that they would write. Nathan and Grace both wanted to talk to Brian himself, just to hear his voice. It had been over six months since everything started to go badly; and they had been so worried, so far away. After connecting with a conference call to both of them, Brian said a subdued, "Hello."

"Brian," Nathan and Grace spoke at once.

"Is that really you?" Grace asked Brian and he could hear tears in her voice. "Are you really OK? We've been so worried about you, and Mom and Dad as well."

"Brian, how could you do what you did to all of us?" Nathan asked angrily. "We've been out of our minds wondering if you were going to die or something. I just don't understand, bro. How about explaining yourself?!"

"Nate," Grace said quietly. "Let's hear what he has to say first. We don't know what he's been going through."

Grudgingly, Nathan agreed to listen.

"Nathan, Grace, I am so sorry. I've been unfair to you, Mom and Dad, and especially to Miranda. I want to give you the details of what happened to me in person if that's OK; but right now I will just say, I received some devastating news from the doctor after my accident. It's very personal, and needless to say, I went over to the dark side for a while. Please forgive me, and give me a chance to explain when I see you. Miranda has forgiven me and agreed to marry me, which is very humbling to me, and Mom and Dad are saints!"

"We'll wait for an explanation," Grace said. "Won't we Nathan? I am just so happy you are back with us. It was awful wondering what was happening to you. Please don't ever do anything like that again, OK?"

"Of course I forgive you, as long as everything is going to be all right," Nathan said. "It will, won't it, Brian?"

"I promise. Mom wants to speak to you. Thank you both for listening to me. I think you will understand after I explain everything. I love you both. Hug the kids for me and tell them I love them."

Brian heard a sigh as he asked hesitantly, "Will you both come to the wedding?"

"Of course," he heard Nathan say.

"If you're sure you will show up this time, I'll be glad to come," Grace said.

Brian could hear the smile in her voice, and he chuckled. "Thanks, both of you. Miranda and I can't wait to see you guys soon."

The next day, at the office, Brian held a meeting for the entire staff. He apologized for the awful way he had been acting. He explained that the accident caused a temporary medical problem and his medications along with alcohol caused a lot of problems. He didn't pull any punches or justify his actions. Miranda was very proud of him.

"Although I am not using the medications as an excuse for my actions," Brian told the assembled group, "I take full-responsibility for my actions, and hope you all will forgive me for my unprofessional behavior."

Someone asked if his medical problems were still an issue.

"No, I am thankful to say. Everything is OK and I hope all of you will accept my apology for the terrible way I've been treating everyone. Please feel free to come and see me so I can apologize personally."

After Brian went back to his office, Miranda was overwhelmed when so many stopped by her desk to let her know how happy they were.

Brian was working at his desk when someone knocked on his door.

"Come in," he called. He paled as he looked up to see Andre standing in the doorway.

"Andre," he said. "Please come in." He motioned to a chair but Andre remained standing. "I know you must have a lot of questions since I know how much you care for Miranda. I'll be honest and try to answer any questions you have."

Eyes dark with anger, Andre asked; "Brian, do you have any idea what you've put Miranda through? Miranda just told me you two are still getting married. I don't understand. How could you be so cruel to her and just walk back into her life as if nothing has happened? How heartless can you be? I've held her in my arms while she cried. I've seen her pain and uncertainty. I've watched her turn to Eric and hoped he might be able to make her happy, but here you are; back in her life ready to hurt her again. It's unforgiveable!"

"Andre, please sit down and I'll try to explain. I know how much I hurt Miranda and she's forgiven me. I don't deserve her forgiveness and will work every day for the rest of my life to make it up to her. I won't tell you all the details, but I was told by my doctor that I would be impotent for the rest of my life. He prescribed several medications which had some terrible side effects; and that, along with my drinking, created someone I didn't even recognize. As a young man, I hope you can at least understand how utterly devastating this information was to me. I wanted to marry Miranda and spend the rest of my life with her and suddenly it seemed impossible. Andre, I'm not making excuses. I allowed myself to drink and I let my anger at fate rule my actions."

Andre's face paled as he listened to Brian. When Brian stopped talking, Andre sat quietly without speaking.

"Brian, I'm sorry I was so rude. I love Miranda and I couldn't stand seeing the hurt and pain in her eyes, especially since she was so happy with you before the accident. I just couldn't understand, but now I do. I hope you will make her happy and realize what an exceptional woman she is."

At the door, Brian spoke quietly. "Miranda is the most important thing in the world to me, Andre. I will spend the rest of my life showing her that. Thank you for being there for her. I know you helped her get through this whole mess." Without a word, Andre reached for Brian's hand and silently shook it before leaving and quietly shutting the door.

Brian sat for a while staring sightlessly out the window after Andre left. He knew he didn't deserve a future with Miranda and the wonderful life he enjoyed, but he was thankful for everything.

Brian confided in Miranda later that night about how grateful he felt. "I feel so humbled to have so many people come by and see me. I don't deserve it; after the way I've acted and treated them. I saw tears in more than one person's eyes as they accepted my apology. I never thought about asking the doctor if my medications were causing some of my erratic behavior, but I'm thankful we got in to see him this morning. It made me realize what a fool I was to start drinking. I haven't felt sane for a long time. Miranda, when I look back, I can't believe I treated you so horribly. Please, please forgive me," Brian begged.

"Of course I forgive you. I can't begin to imagine the torment you were going through. I know one person who is beyond happy you're back to normal," Miranda said.

"I know," Brian said. "Karen? She cried quietly when I told her everything was going to be OK. I felt so horrible afterward. I can't imagine what I've put everyone through, and I am beyond blessed you still want to marry me. I still don't understand why you're willing to forgive me..."

"Because, deep down, I knew that man was not you. I held out hope for so long that you would return to all of us, and help us understand what happened. And, you did."

"Not before almost losing you and having my parents disown me," Brian finally smiled. "I talked to Mom and Dad a long time last night. They still don't understand why I didn't tell them what was wrong, and I really don't understand it myself. I was in a fog and couldn't see beyond the pain. Drinking was the last straw, and I knew deep down that it was wrong, but couldn't seem to stop. Your anger was what finally broke me. I guess I thought if I treated you badly enough, you would leave. It was agony seeing you every day while knowing I would never make love to you. You know how much I want you, don't you?"

"Absolutely," Miranda said as she touched her lips to his.

Chapter Fifty-Two

This wedding day, so unlike the other one, was warm and golden. Everything in nature seemed to be rejoicing with them. The birds sang more sweetly and the flowers seemed to be brighter. The air smelled fresh and sweet.

To Brian, watching as she walked slowly toward him, she was absolutely breathtaking. He found it impossible to look away. She left her hair long and flowing, enhanced by a beautiful veil. Her eyes gazed steadily into his as she moved unwaveringly toward the altar.

As she repeated her vows in a quiet, steady voice, Brian was captivated by her beauty and grace. He loved this woman. Together they could create a family and future of their own; strong enough to blot out the sadness of the past.

Although it was a small wedding, Miranda was so glad she decided to get married in a traditional wedding gown. Brian did not realize she loved him, but she did. In the meantime, she was so thankful she was marrying the man she loved with her whole heart. As she looked down at the beautiful ring Brian placed on her finger, she knew she was not making a mistake. Miranda admired the beautiful intertwined white gold wedding and engagement ring Brian slipped onto her finger. Her rings and the one she slipped onto Brian's finger were symbols of her love. In her heart she knew her love would be enough to bring joy into their lives, and someday he would love her as much as she loved him.

Walking down the aisle, her hand held firmly in Brian's, Miranda felt so blessed. It was so wonderful to see Cindy and Roger again when everything was so perfect. For the first time, Miranda could watch them together and not be envious of their happiness. That was a glorious feeling!

Later, as she mingled with the wedding guests, she glanced over at Roger and realized just how much her life had changed. Her heart didn't even change its beat when she looked at him. She just felt warm and tender toward him, and now to her, he was her beloved brother-in-law.

Brian was tied up for a few moments with some of his friends, so Miranda made her way over to where Cindy and Roger were talking to Nathan. She slid her arm around Cindy and listened quietly to the conversation. When Roger realized she was there, he moved to her side.

Watching her face, Roger now knew she had found what he and Cindy had. "Can we talk for a minute?" he asked.

"Of course," Miranda said as she stepped away from Cindy.

"You are happy now, aren't you, Miranda? You love Brian, don't you?"

"Oh yes," she breathed softly. "So very much."

Holding her close for a moment, he said, "I'm so happy for you. Will it be all right now to tell Cindy? She realizes something was wrong, but when I wouldn't tell her, she didn't pry."

Hugging him tightly, she nodded. "Yes, tell her, but make sure she knows how much I love Brian. Then it will be all right."

Now, she knew what it was to truly love someone. She turned, feeling Brian watching her. As she made her way to his side, she gave him a radiant smile, tenderness in her eyes as she reached for his hand.

He looked down at her wonderingly. "What had happened to her? She didn't seem to be upset at all over seeing Roger. She almost appeared relieved. Could it be that she didn't love Roger anymore?" Brian thought. Did he dare hope?

It seemed as if he had loved Miranda from the first moment he saw her. He felt as if she were the very air he needed to breathe. He had taken a tremendous gamble in asking her to marry him. Could she possibly have some feelings for him? He didn't begrudge any memories she had, but she belonged to him now, and he wanted to be the only man in her heart. If only it was possible that his dream of being the father of her children could someday come true.

He looked down at his radiant bride. Dare he tell her he loved her? Would she reject his love? He had promised her that he wouldn't take advantage of her again, and he would keep that promise, no matter how hard it was to do so. If he were to make a mistake now, it could destroy any fragile beginnings of love she may feel for him. He just couldn't take that chance. He would have to take it a day at a time, praying that she would come to love him as he loved her.

Their honeymoon trip was to be a surprise for Miranda. Brian only told her to pack what she would need for a couple of days and he would buy her anything she needed when they arrived. He refused to even give her a hint—even though Miranda teased him unmercifully.

"You won't be disappointed," he laughed. "Just plan on being surprised and thrilled," Brian said as he wrapped his arms around her. Her arms crept up around his neck as she leaned in and kissed him softly. He returned her kiss and then leaned back and looked at her. "Hey, Mrs. Chandler."

"Hey, yourself, Mr. Chandler," Miranda laughed. "Mrs. Chandler. I love it." She smiled up at him and wrapped her arms around him, marveling at how wonderful it felt.

"I don't want to let you out of my arms," Brian murmured as his lips softly caressed her cheek and then her lips; "But we're going to miss our flight if we don't get going. I think I heard the limo drive up a moment ago."

Miranda kissed him tenderly and then slipped out of his arms. They grabbed their suitcases and Brian locked the door as they left. When they arrived at the airport, Miranda was thrilled to find out they were headed for Bali, Indonesia.

"Brian, you remembered," she whispered. "Thank you."

"I remembered," Brian said softly. Then he chuckled as he teased, "I promise you that you won't be shivering in a shower this time."

"Oh Brian," Miranda lightly punched him on the arm. "You would have to remind me of that. No fair!"

Brian smiled at her shining eyes. They sparkled with unshed tears as she reached for his hand. "Since the best time to go is after February, I wanted to make one of your wishes come true," Brian said.

"I still can't believe you remembered what I said," Miranda murmured. "That was a long time ago."

"I remember a lot of things, and what's important to you is hard to forget," Brian teased. Miranda smiled back as he continued to give her information about Indonesia. "No other island brings together sunshine, beautiful beaches, lush green forests, and an incredibly unique charm and spiritual air the way this island does. This makes it one of the best honeymoon destinations in the world. We are staying at an all-inclusive resort, The Patra Anvaya Beach Resort, directly on the Indian Ocean and only a few minutes from the airport."

Miranda held his hand as the plane reached elevation. "Brian, you are such a wonderful man. I have to pinch myself to realize I'm now Mrs. Brian Chandler," she said as she lifted the arm rest and snuggled against him.

Chapter Fifty-Three

It was so beautiful when they arrived in Indonesia. There was a slight breeze, the ocean sparkling in the sun as it was sinking into the horizon; the sky was bold, brilliant and rich with colors of yellow, orange, and blues, and the clouds were edged with reds mingling with the grey clouds. Miranda and Brian watched enthralled as the sun sank slowly into the ocean, bathing the waves and wispy clouds in a burning glow of colors until it disappeared, leaving a peaceful silence.

After checking in, they walked out onto their own private terrace overlooking the Indian Ocean, marveling at the lights of the city in the distance. Traffic sounds were muted, leaving only the sounds of nature; crickets chirping, frogs croaking, seabirds, and the sound of the ocean softly lapping against the rocks.

"I made reservations for dinner at 8, so would you like to freshen up before we go?" Brian asked as he reluctantly turned away from the lovely scene.

"Sure, I wouldn't mind a shower. It won't take me long," Miranda said as she walked over to her suitcase. "At least this time I'm not freezing," she teased as she glanced back at him.

"And you can take your shower without your clothes on this time," Brian teased back.

Giggling, Miranda asked, "Do I have time to unpack, or should I wait until we get back? I know it's evening here, but I haven't even figured out what day it is," Miranda laughed as she looked at Brian.

"While I take a shower, maybe you can figure it out, unless you already know," she teased.

"We have time to unpack if you want to, and yes, we're 14 hours ahead of Oregon. We are now into Tuesday. I'm afraid we'll find ourselves suffering jetlag for a couple of days."

Brian watched as Miranda moved to where their suitcases were sitting. She was so very lovely, and it was hard to believe she was now his wife. She seemed happy, too. Her eyes were sparkling, and she hummed to herself as she quickly unpacked their suitcases. As she gathered her clothes and headed into the bathroom, Brian sank into a chair and put his head into his hands.

How was he going to get through this week without making love to his wife? The last thing he wanted to do was leave this room. His only desire was to take his new wife into his arms and tell her he loved her to distraction; while spending the rest of the night making love to her. He wanted her so badly it hurt. In anguish, he thought of lying beside her in this big bed, unable to make the first move. Just the thought of it made his body tremble and he felt the sting of tears against his eyelids. A tremendous shudder wracked his body while a groan escaped his lips; as if dragged from his very soul. He didn't hear her come into the room.

She came and knelt quietly by his chair. "What is it, Brian? What's wrong?" As she reached out to touch him, she felt his shoulders tremble. "Brian, what's wrong? Have I done something to hurt you?"

He shook his head numbly and tried to move away from her touch. A soft grasp came from her, as she tenderly turned his face and saw the tears on his cheeks. Gathering him into her arms, she murmured, "Oh, my poor love. My darling, what's wrong?"

There was a sudden stillness about him, and then his hands came up and gripped her shoulders.   "What did you call me?" he asked huskily.

"My darling," she repeated.

"What does that mean? Miranda, do you love me?"

"Yes," she said quietly, and shyly. Raising up onto her knees she kissed his tear-drenched eyes.

Dinner was forgotten! Brian gathered Miranda into his arms, his kisses soft and filled with wonder. His wife loved him! They made love gently but with a hunger long unrequited and longed for. Afterwards, Miranda snuggled in his arms and asked him how long he had known that he loved her. Her lips were bruised and her body felt so contented from his caresses. She had never known that making love could be this wonderful. She felt as if she were floating on air. She didn't think it was possible to be as happy as she was right now.

"You know," Brian said quietly, "Probably from the first moment I saw you, I knew something was dreadfully wrong, but I couldn't put my finger on it. Your sister was getting married, yet you seemed so unhappy. It wasn't until I saw how you turned your face so Roger had to kiss your lips that I started to understand what might be causing your pain. Later, I started to realize you must have made a sacrifice so Cindy could be happy. If she had known how you felt, she probably would never have dated Roger, much less married him. You gave up a lot, because you loved your sister, didn't you?"

"Yes, but because of it, I gained so much more than I ever dreamed possible," Miranda said softly, lovingly. A silence fell for a few moments as their lips met again. "I love you, Brian, never doubt that."

"I won't, my beautiful darling," he said between kisses. "Now, are you ever going to answer my question?"

"Sure, if you'll remind me what the question was!" she giggled. His hands had started to roam, trailing a sensual caress along the sensitive hollow of her spine, leaving her senses inflamed by his touch. "You're beginning to make me very forgetful."

She was running her hand lovingly over his chest, tangling her fingers in his silky hair, as she had so often longed to do. Huskily, he murmured, "Aw, now you're making me forget! I think it was something about what you gave up for your sister."

"Oh, that." Laughing and moving out of his reach for a moment, she said; "I met Roger first and fell in love with him right away. I felt he was my whole life. Now I know that what I felt for him was very tame, compared to what I feel for you." Sliding back over to him, she gave him a fierce hug and kissed him thoroughly before continuing. "From their first meeting, Roger and Cindy were attracted to each other, and I just couldn't stand in their way."

"Oh my darling, how you must have suffered!" Brian said softly. Kissing her tenderly, he went on; "I know the kind of pain you've been in because that's what I've been suffering. I felt as if my insides were being ripped apart and there was nothing I could do about it. I never dared hope that you would come to love me. How did it happen?" Brian asked.

"I'm not sure," Miranda answered. "It must have been a gradual process, because I started to feel happy. First, I enjoyed being with you and then I began to look forward to each day, knowing I would see you. I became puzzled about how I felt because I still missed Roger, but found I was thinking more about seeing you than I was about him. Your kisses surprised me; the way you made me feel. I was probably in love with you in Washington, but you became so distant after that dance. What happened? Why did you turn so cold all of a sudden?"

"I realized that I was pushing you into something you probably didn't want, and was afraid that if I moved too fast...I would lose you," Brian said. "I had already decided to ask you to marry me, and knew I had to gamble all my hopes on that. If you had said no to my proposal, then I would have staked everything on the cards and told you that I loved you. I would have had nothing else to lose."

"I wish you had," Miranda sighed. "It would have saved a lot of pain for both of us."

"Maybe," he said thoughtfully, "But it still wouldn't have changed anything that happened after my accident. Even if I'd known you loved me, I would have pushed you away."

"That's probably true, but neither one of us will ever know for sure, will we?"

"No, I guess not."

He turned her tenderly into his arms. His kisses were gentle and sweet at first, but soon became a raging fire. He loved the passionate way she came alive in his arms. There was no way he would ever let her go. He wanted to be the father of her children and he wanted most of all to grow old with her by his side.

"Miranda, do you remember anything about the night after Cindy's wedding?" he asked her later as they lay in each other's arms.

"Are you really going to tell me what happened that night?" she asked hopefully. "I knew something had. I kept having this memory of you being with me, but I didn't know if it was a dream or not."

After telling her what had taken place, Miranda kissed him tenderly. "My sweet love, you sure have been through a lot with me. It warms my heart that you were willing to put yourself through something so disturbing for someone you hardly knew." Softly she asked, "Why?"

"I knew my own heart," he replied. "I awoke with you in my arms that morning, and even though you thought I was Roger, I knew there was no point in kidding myself. I was already in love with you. I left, not knowing if I would ever see you again, but knowing that you would forever be in my heart."

Their lips met tenderly. Brian nuzzled her neck, feeling the strain of the last few months seep out of him. Pulling away from her slightly, his eyes were riveted to her lovely breasts, narrow waist, and long, slender legs. "You're so beautiful, Miranda, and I love you so."

"I love you. I need you," she said, responding fiercely.

His mouth possessed hers with a fierce passion. "Don't ever leave me, Miranda! You are the air I breathe, you are my very soul." His fingers trembled as he traced the curves of her face; and a sensuality entered his face. He threaded his fingers through the silken length of her hair.

"Oh, Brian! Brian, my love!" Miranda breathed ecstatically, not knowing that his name on her lips was the sweetest words he had ever heard.

Chapter Fifty-Four

In New York, a year later, they walked hand in hand along the beach in the moonlight. This beach was warm, calm, and almost placid; not wild, windy and rugged, like the Oregon coast. The weather was perfect; with a soft, tropical breeze moving gently through the air, rustling the leaves in the trees. This past year had brought joy beyond description.

A few days earlier Miranda walked into Brian's office after a long hard day at work. "Brian, can we get away somewhere for a few days? I would love to go to New York, do some shopping, and maybe see a play."

Brian pulled Miranda onto his lap, kissing her soundly before answering. "Sounds like fun. I think we can take a break by Wednesday. We don't have any major projects right now and everything else can wait."

"Really?" Miranda grinned. "I'm so tired Brian. I think we both need a little down time."

"How does a week in New York sound? See what plays are running and I'll get plane reservations for Wednesday."

After a week in New York, they flew back to Eugene because Miranda wanted a chance to talk to Cindy. Their radiant faces told Roger everything he needed to know. A momentary frown crossed Brian's face when Roger asked if he could speak to Miranda alone for a moment.

Then remembering the loving woman he had held in his arms the night before, he smiled and said; "Sure. Just don't keep her too long. I can't bear to be away from her for more than a few minutes at a time."

Blowing him a kiss, Miranda followed Roger out of the room.

"I haven't been able to find the words to tell Cindy yet. Maybe it would be better if you told her?"

Smiling, Miranda said, "I'll be glad to. Don't worry, Roger. I love Brian so much that she'll know everything's OK."

It wasn't quite as easy to tell Cindy as she had thought it would be. With Cindy facing her, she wasn't entirely sure where to start. Finally, she said; "Cindy, I love Brian more than life itself. I know I've found a part of myself that's been missing for a very long time. I wanted you to know this before I tell you something I've been unable to until now."

Quietly, Cindy said; "You loved Roger, didn't you?"

Her face now pale, Miranda asked gently, "Cindy, when on earth did you first suspect that?"

"I guess deep down, I've always known, but just didn't want to accept it. I loved Roger, the way you now love Brian, and I couldn't bear the thought of not being with him. I want you to know I would have given him up in a second, if I had known for sure. The problem was that you were so insistent that the two of you were just good friends, so I took the easy way out. Can you ever forgive me? I can't even imagine the suffering you must have gone through! I guess I really began to realize the truth after you came to see us and brought Brian with you. Roger knew, didn't he?"

"By that time he had guessed, yes. There is nothing to forgive. If it hadn't happened this way, you, Roger, and I would have all been miserable; and I never would have met Brian. I would go through it all over again if I knew Brian would be waiting at the other end. I love you so much and the only reason I'm talking to you about it is because I want to put it all behind us. You did nothing wrong. You loved Roger." Joyously, they hugged each other, too filled with happiness to let any sadness come between them.

* * *

Brian took Miranda back to Indonesia, where they first realized they loved each other; a time of wonder and discovery. Now, in this place of sand, surf, and magic, Miranda looked up at Brian in the moonlight, smiling into his beloved face. He stooped down and picked her up in his arms, his lips seeking hers. She responded passionately as always, her arms going up around his neck and her fingers threading through his hair. As they sank down onto the sand, she welcomed him joyfully, giving him all the love she was capable of.

"Brian," she murmured, "Is there anything that could make you happier than you are at this moment?"

"No, darling. You give me more joy than I ever imagined possible! You are all I'll ever need."

Tenderly taking his face between her hands, she asked teasingly; "Not even a baby?"

Stunned, he stared at her in disbelief. "Are you sure?" When she nodded, he said; "I guess I was wrong then. I am happier!" Kissing her softly, gently, he said, "I love you, Miranda, my beautiful wife; you... and our baby."

About the Author

At the age of 69, Shirley Hoisington finally realized a dream she had since childhood! She published her first book! She lived much of her life in the Pacific Northwest and many of the details in Beyond Despair comes from her own experiences. She was born in 1949 in Fairview, North Carolina as Shirley Whitaker. Her parents moved to Oregon in 1966 where she married Richard Nickels in 1972. They were living in Gillette, Wyoming when her husband, Richard, passed away in 2006 and Shirley moved back to Battle Ground, Washington. She worked many years as office manager for a non-profit organization until she retired in 2015. She met and married her husband, Robert, in 2015.

She and her previous husband, Richard, had three girls, and she now has six grandchildren! Her daughter, Amanda, asked Shirley to go with her to a creative writing class in the late 90's and thus Beyond Despair was born. The class stirred up a long-buried dream of wanting to be an author; and with the help of her daughter, Barbara, and the encouragement of family and friends, she has finally written and finished her first novel! She has also written a children's book (which she hopes to publish) and plans on continuing her dream of writing.